Readers love
Acsquidentally In Love
by K.L. Hiers

"This book has a bit of everything I love, a good mystery, magic, romance, humor, and action. K.L. Hiers has me hooked and I can't wait for more!"
—Bayou Book Junkie

"Hiers rolls worldbuilding mythology, delicious flirting, erotic scenes, and detective work into a breezy and sensual LGBTQ paranormal romance."
—Library Journal

"It's a great mystery and such a fun book. You guys will really be missing out if you don't read this story. I can't wait to see what comes next."
—Love Bytes Reviews

By K.L. Hiers

A SUCKER FOR LOVE
Acsquidentally In Love
Kraken My Heart
Head Over Tentacles

Published by Dreamspinner Press
www.dreamspinnerpress.com

HEAD OVER TENTACLES

K.L. HIERS

Published by

DREAMSPINNER PRESS

5032 Capital Circle SW, Suite 2, PMB# 279, Tallahassee, FL 32305-7886 USA
www.dreamspinnerpress.com

Head Over Tentacles
© 2021 K.L. Hiers

Cover Art
© 2021 Tiferet Design
http://www.tiferetdesign.com

Cover content is for illustrative purposes only and any person depicted on the cover is a model.

Trade Paperback ISBN: 978-1-64405-928-9
Digital ISBN: 978-1-64405-927-2
Trade Paperback published August 2021
First Edition
v. 1.0

Printed in the United States of America
∞
This paper meets the requirements of
ANSI/NISO Z39.48-1992 (Permanence of Paper).

CHAPTER 1.

"LOCH," SLOANE Beaumont began calmly, "you cannot threaten to turn the mailman inside out."

"But I can," Loch argued defiantly. "It's actually really easy once you know how. You just start at the feet and roll the skin upwards—"

"I'm not saying you can't do it, as in you're not physically capable of it," Sloane growled. "You're an ancient and very powerful god. I have no doubt that you could, but what I am trying to tell you is that you can't keep threatening him! We've been over this!"

"Ah!" Loch nodded in understanding. "What you mean is I should go ahead and do it because a clear example needs to be made!"

"No! Ugh!"

"You are so confusing, but you do look very pretty when you're mad." Loch batted his eyes, quickly changing gears. "Your eyebrows are so very luscious and thick, and you remind me so much of that nice human who plays Spork in the movie about trekking through the stars."

"Hey, focus!" Although Sloane did appreciate the flattering comparison, he was not letting Loch get off so easily. "We're talking about something important."

"Mmm, yes. You."

"Loch."

"Your eyes are like warm pools of dark chocolate, and your lips, oh, I could go on about your lips for eons!"

"Loch!" Sloane groaned again, sitting down beside him on the couch and taking his hands. "Remember how you can't reveal that you're a god because it would cause mass panic since most of the world is Lucian now and believes the old gods aren't real?"

"Yes!" Loch said cheerfully.

"Turning the mailman inside out? Good way to cause panic!"

"But he keeps wrinkling my catalogues." Loch huffed. "I like the catalogues. And I like them best when they are not wrinkled. There is a definite crease!"

"Azaethoth!" Sloane scolded, invoking Loch's true godly name with a growl.

Beneath his red curls and bright green eyes, there was a great dragon of legendary proportions hiding. Loch spent most of his time in his mortal vessel, but Sloane never forgot what he really was under that gorgeous facade. The novelty of scolding an ancient god like a stubborn child was not getting old anytime soon.

Loch pouted and crossed his arms. "Fine. I will fix the creases myself like some peasant."

"And?"

"And I will not turn the mailman inside out," Loch added sullenly.

"Thank you," Sloane breathed, rewarding Loch with a sweet kiss and savoring the minty taste of his lips.

Loch smiled and sent a grayish tentacle out from his sleeve to nuzzle against Sloane's cheek.

Sloane shuddered pleasurably. Any contact with Loch's godly flesh was utter bliss. It was still hard to believe sometimes that a giant tentacled dragon was crammed inside that human body.

"Mmm, let me take you to bed," Loch purred, more of his tentacles slithering out to pull Sloane into his lap. "I want to apologize for my awful behavior."

"We have a case." Sloane playfully swatted at him. "Remember? Jay Tintenfisch? Works with Milo? Mysterious disappearing roommate? Cat might be guilty?"

"Yes, I remember, but that can wait until I'm done apologizing."

"No. We did plenty of that last night and this morning!"

"So? It's tradition to celebrate an engagement with intense physical coupling—"

"Work first, playtime later." Sloane wiggled out of Loch's lap, grabbing his hands and pulling him to his feet. "Come on."

Loch let himself get dragged up from the couch, mumbling, "Fine. We'll go, but I'm going to complain the whole time."

"Big surprise." Sloane chuckled as he led Loch downstairs to his car.

"I liked the old car," Loch said, huffing as he got settled into the passenger seat. "The old car had personality. This car is shit."

"The old car got blown up by a very angry witch," Sloane reminded him.

"Yes, but we shared our first kiss in that car."

"You mean when you tricked me into kissing you."

"God of Tricksters," Loch said with an unapologetic smile.

Sloane rolled his eyes, frowning when his phone rang.

"Hey!" It was Milo Evans, Sloane's best friend and former coworker when he still worked for the Archersville Police Department as a detective.

"Hey! What's up, Milo?"

"You need to come by," Milo insisted. "Like, right now."

"Right now?" Sloane glanced at the time. "I'm supposed to be meeting with a new client."

"It's about the blue goo."

"Oh?"

"Look, it'll take, like, five minutes!" Milo sounded particularly excited. "It's super important! I have to tell you, in person, like right now."

Sloane flinched, and he glanced sideways at Loch. Milo was known to be passionate even about mundane things, but the blue goo in question was of particular concern. "Okay, we'll be there in five."

"Okay! Hurry!"

"What is it?" Loch asked, tilting his head. "Did Milo anger Lynnette again?"

Lynnette was Loch's little sister; well, technically, she was Lochlain's little sister—the hot guy whose murder had started it all. Because Loch was living in a copy of Lochlain's body, Sloane wasn't sure if the familial connection still counted or not.

Milo and Lynnette had moved in together a few weeks ago, and things had been a bit bumpy.

"No," Sloane replied, "it's about that goo."

"You're willing to risk tardiness to meet our new client over some magical slime, but not for hot, primal mating?" Loch wrinkled his nose.

"I promise, lots of mating later!" Sloane argued. "This could be important!"

Loch grumbled his protests the entire drive, and Sloane didn't even wait for him to get out of the car as he hurried to the front door of Lynnette's house.

Sloane blinked when Milo answered the door with his face covered in black ash, asking carefully, "Are you okay? Is your beard… burned?"

"Oh! I'm good!" Milo patted at his thick beard with a sheepish grin. He was big, broad, and always smiling. He bowed to Loch as he finally caught up. "Nice to see you, Your Most Holy Tentacle-ness!"

Milo was a recent convert to the Sagittarian faith. He was a bit exuberant, but Loch loved the attention.

"Greetings, furry mortal child," Loch said sweetly, wiggling his fingers in a friendly wave.

"You guys have got to see this!" Milo ushered them inside and led them into the kitchen, where he had set up a small laboratory.

There was still a faint smell of smoke, and judging by the broken glass underfoot, something had definitely exploded.

"What the hell?" Sloane gasped in horror. "Dude, Lynnette is gonna kill you if you don't clean this up—"

"Just listen," Milo whined, grabbing a dish towel to wipe off his face. "You first found the blue goo when Lochlain was murdered, right? After Loch took over his body and you guys went back to his apartment to look for clues?"

"Yeah. We also found it at Kunst's house."

"After he blew up the car," Loch helpfully chimed in.

"Right!" Milo confirmed. "All places Bad Robert had been, so we always assumed it was him. But you know where I didn't find any? In the yard after you went all Starkiller on his ass."

"So?"

"I found some definite worm slime, but it's not the same stuff as the goo. Follow me here for a second. I think the blue goo belongs to another god," Milo said slowly.

"Are you freakin' serious?" Sloane scoffed and exchanged a worried glance with Loch. The old gods were not known for their sanity, most of them having gone insane when they went into their deep slumber.

"Yeah," Milo replied with a grimace. "I've been blowing myself up all morning testing it again to be sure." He grabbed two plates from the counter, offering them for Sloane's inspection. "Look for yourself. Lefty is the original blue goo, all refined down. Right is the slime from Bad Robert."

Sloane held up his hands to form a triangle for a perception spell. He recognized the blue residue immediately, the holographic aura familiar and equally uncomfortable. The worm slime had a similar shine, but Milo was right.

They weren't the same.

"It's definitely godly. Like, for sure. We know it's not Loch, and if it's not Bad Robert… well." Milo eyed Loch. "Any idea who might have been awake running around with your brother trying to end the world?"

"How much time do we have?" Loch retorted dryly. "It's a long list."

"Seriously." Sloane squeezed Loch's arm. "Can't you, like, go back to Zebulon and do, like, a head count or something? I mean, shouldn't we be worried?"

"I'll reach out to my sister," Loch soothed, pulling Sloane into a tentacle-filled embrace. "She still wakes often. Maybe she'll know who Toll was hanging out with."

"Toll?" Milo put the plates away.

"Tollmathan," Sloane replied. "God of music, poetry, and plagues. Aka Bad Robert?"

"Right! Sorry!" Milo grinned sheepishly. "Still trying to learn them all."

"The most important one to remember is Azaethoth the Lesser," Loch said. "Me."

"How soon can you talk to your sister?" Sloane asked, trying to get the conversation back on track.

Loch closed his eyes and clicked his tongue. "Done! Mm, I hate to wake her up so early, but I suppose we do need to start discussing wedding plans, after all."

"Wedding plans? What?" Milo squeaked, grinning at them and clapping. "You mean, wait, did you, you two…?"

"Loch asked me to marry him last night at Lochlain and Robert's wedding," Sloane confirmed. "We didn't want to announce it then and steal any of their thunder—"

"I wanted to," Loch said with a soft huff. "Sloane wouldn't let me."

"Ahhh! Congrats!" Milo gushed. "That's so awesome!"

"Don't say anything yet! We want to make an official announcement later!" Sloane pleaded. "And maybe keep this new god business hush-hush. I don't want anyone freaking out if it turns out to be nothing."

"Okay! Can do!" Milo looked around at the huge mess he'd made. "Little help, my super awesome starlit friend? Lynnette might come home for lunch, and well…."

"I got you." Sloane wiggled away from Loch's many arms so he could clap his hands together. All the broken glass was immediately made whole again and the smoke cleared, all evidence of the disaster magically gone.

"Phew!" Milo sighed in relief. "You're a lifesaver!"

"You guys doing okay?" Sloane asked sympathetically.

"Yeah. She's been super moody lately and I think she wants to kill me? But then she's super happy and doesn't want to kill me."

"You should mate with her more often," Loch advised. "Mating is a wonderful way to declare your love, and it solves almost every problem—"

"No, it does not," Sloane scolded. "You should try talking to her first. Don't listen to him, Milo."

"Hmmmph," Loch fussed. "Right, don't listen to the all-powerful immortal being who has lived for thousands of years and gives really great advice."

"Your advice is terrible."

"No, it's not."

"When that little girl at the wedding was being picked on, you told her to summon a swarm of bees."

"Do unto others as they've done to you."

"Thanks, guys," Milo said with a chuckle, "but I think we're gonna be okay. Moving in together can be way stressful, you know?"

"Let me know if we can help. I'll call you later if we hear anything," Sloane said to Milo with a warm smile. He gave his friend a big hug. "Gotta run! Gonna go see your buddy Jay!"

"Oh good, so he called you?"

"Yeah, he called me yesterday at the wedding. He's my new client."

"I told him to set something up with you. I knew you'd try to help him. Everybody else kinda thinks he's going crazy."

"Said you guys worked together down at the department, right?"

"Yeah, he's over in IT, and his office is down the hall from the forensics lab. They put him where the old janitor's closet used to be." Milo grimaced. "Hope you can help him out! He's a nice dude!"

"Thanks for the referral, by the way! We'll talk soon!"

"Take care, mortal child," Loch said, waving a tentacle as he followed Sloane back out to the car. "Mmm, my sister is on her way. It may take her some time to find a willing vessel."

"You guys can just… talk to each other? Just like that?"

"Mm-hm. As long as she's not dreaming too deeply, my sister always hears me."

"Well, hopefully she can help us." Sloane started driving them toward his office. "It makes me nervous as hell thinking that Bad Robert wasn't working alone."

"I can think of many others that it could have been," Loch said with a shrug. "Top of the list is Gronoch. He would have been next in line to rule after Tollmathan. Perhaps it was him? Although, he's a very heavy sleeper…."

"It wouldn't have been your sister, right?" Sloane hated to ask. "Galgareth?"

"No," Loch said with a firm shake of his head. "She wouldn't do anything to hurt mortals or endanger this world. That much I'm sure of."

"All right," Sloane said, drumming his fingers on the steering wheel. He frowned when his phone rang again.

It was Robert Edwards, the good one.

"Hey!" Sloane answered cheerfully. "Thought you guys were leaving for your honeymoon?"

"Almost!" Robert laughed, sounding a little nervous. "Look, uhm, could I speak to Azaethoth? Or maybe just put me on speaker? It's sort of, uhm, personal, but…."

"Oh sure! One second!" Sloane passed the phone to Loch. "Put it on speaker."

"Azaethoth the Lesser here," Loch announced. "God of Tricksters, Thieves, and Divine Retribution."

"Hello, Azaethoth!" Robert gushed, sounding even more nervous now. "I know this is very last minute, but we're getting ready to leave for the airport, and I'm terrified of flying." He took a deep breath. "Would you be willing to give me and Lochlain a blessing of protection for our trip?"

Sloane glanced at the time worriedly. They were so going to be late, but he nodded at Loch with a strained smile.

"Of course, my dear child," Loch said happily. "We'll be right over."

"You can just meet us at the hotel!" Robert exclaimed. "Wynne Hotel, right downtown! Thank you so much!"

Sloane groaned as he took his phone back, making a quick right turn to get them redirected to the hotel. "I don't normally ask you to use your godly powers, but if you could make every light green? That would be great."

"I am yours to command, my sweet Starkiller," Loch declared, always eager to show off his abilities.

They whizzed through the busy streets, and Sloane pulled up to the front of the hotel in mere minutes. He spotted Robert and Lochlain waiting for them by the door, and he put the car in park before waving them over.

Robert was a handsome young blond, and Lochlain was the mirror image of Loch. They were absolutely identical, right down to their gorgeous smiles, but the similarities ended with their physical appearance.

While Lochlain reminded Sloane of a fluffy kitten playing with a bit of string, Loch was a full-grown tiger on the prowl and definitely never up to any good.

The newlywed couple hurried over to the passenger side, and they both bowed their heads respectfully in greeting.

Loch rolled down the window with a very pleased smile. "Hello, my faithful ones."

"Hi!" Robert waved, kneeling down beside the car and trying to appear inconspicuous. "I hate to rush, but we need to leave soon—"

Loch reached out his hand, one of his tentacles slithering out from his sleeve and poking Robert in the middle of his forehead. "Great Azaethoth will be with you on your journey. His whispers will guide you and his starlight will guard you."

Eyes fluttering from the rush of divine contact, Robert sighed in relief. "Thank you… thank you so much."

Loch smirked at his twin, asking, "And what about you, my most devoted follower? Would you like a blessing?"

"I already have all the blessings I need." Lochlain smiled adoringly at his groom. He grinned as he added, "Although I did hear about another shiny exhibit coming to town…."

"Ohhh, do tell," Loch pressed eagerly.

Lochlain had become the trickster god's most beloved follower by being a bit of a trickster himself. Lochlain was a very talented thief and had earned Loch's respect with his profitable and clever heists.

The pair were capable of great mischief when they were together, and Sloane was quick to protest, "No felonies until after the honeymoon is over, and we really have to go!"

"We do too!" Robert grabbed Lochlain's hand, laughing at how he and Loch both pouted. "You can play with your patron god when we come home!"

"Take care, guys!" Sloane hurriedly drove away, tires squealing. He hadn't meant to take off like that, but they were dangerously close to being late to meet with their new client.

When his phone rang again, he wanted to throw it.

"What now?"

Loch picked it up to investigate, saying, "Ah, it's Fred!"

"Don't answer—"

"Hello, Fred!" Loch said cheerfully. "How are you doing, dear child? Any new bits or pieces rotting off?"

Fred Wilder was Lochlain's best friend, a Sage, and a ghoul. His body had been destroyed by a fire and through forbidden sorcery, Lynnette created him a new one. Ghoul bodies were essentially husks, shells that would hold a resurrected soul.

Loch's body was technically a ghoul since it was a copy of Lochlain's, but he could maintain its integrity through his divine essence. Ghouls like Fred, on the other hand, required special magic to keep their bodies from rotting.

"Nah." Fred's gruff voice rumbled through the phone. "All of that is fine, but I appreciate it."

"It's my pleasure," Loch said with a warm smile. "Let me know if there's anything else I can do for you."

"There is something," Fred said, pausing uncomfortably. "Things have been going really well with my ghoul doctor friend, but I need to talk to you about somethin' personal."

"Ah, your penis," Loch said without missing a beat. "You're worried about copulation. Sloane and I are on our way to an appointment, but afterwards—"

"Not exactly," Fred grunted.

"—I will happily examine your penis."

Fred grumbled and hung up.

Sloane scrubbed a hand over his face. "Smooth. Very smooth."

"What?"

"Don't worry about it." Sloane laughed, still blushing from secondhand embarrassment.

"Mortals are so uptight," Loch snorted, crossing his arms as he pouted.

Sloane parked outside his office, quickly unbuckling his seat belt. "Okay, come on. We're finally here."

Loch reached over to slide his hand up Sloane's thigh. "Mmm, you're so tense, my sweet Starkiller.... You need to relax."

Trying to ignore how his cock stirred at Loch's touch, Sloane argued, "I'm tense because we're gonna be late. We literally have four minutes—"

"I can make you come in two," Loch promised, pushing closer.

"Loch," Sloane protested, but his voice didn't sound so strong. Loch already had his pants unbuttoned, one of his larger tentacles snaking its way down into his underwear and making him squirm. "Shit, shit, shit.... You'd better be quick."

"I'll be so very quick," Loch purred, kissing Sloane as his tentacle swallowed down his cock and sucked hard.

Sloane bucked up into the wet heat, gasping against Loch's lips. Any physical contact with Loch's godly self was incredible, and Sloane's entire body was at once flooded with a spectacular heat that made his heart ache.

Making love with Loch wasn't just amazing, it was absolutely otherworldly, and oh, those tentacles, the things they could do.

Most of them were merely prehensile, but there were three that were especially unique. Two of them were equipped with small mouths that had several delicious talents, including sucking with mind-numbing pressure and dispensing thick loads of divine seed.

But the third one….

The *tentacock*.

That thing was a god in its own right.

Sloane clung to Loch's shoulders, and he groaned when another tentacle slipped between his legs and petted around his hole. It didn't penetrate, only teased and nudged as the other continued to suck away.

"Come on, my love," Loch urged, kissing along his ear and nipping. "I'm so hungry for a taste of you…."

Sloane whimpered brokenly, the ache in his balls making him tremble. He prayed that no one could see what was happening in the front seat of his car; they were in a public place, right in the middle of the day.

Shit!

The thought of someone watching them made this insanely hotter, and he came immediately with a loud cry. He fucked up into the tentacle's willing mouth, gasping and twitching. "Loch! Oh fuck, oh yesss!"

Smiling smugly, Loch stroked him through it and slowly withdrew when Sloane swatted at him. "There. Don't you feel better?"

Sloane melted into the seat, flushed and satisfied, grinning. "Yes, I feel much better…." Then he looked at the clock. "Fuck! Two minutes my ass! We're freakin' late!"

Loch was all smiles as he followed Sloane frantically racing into the office. There was a young man with glasses waiting at his door with a large pet carrier in his arms. He didn't seem too upset by their tardiness, but Sloane was already saying, "Hi! Mr. Tintenfisch? I am sorry that I'm late. It was utterly unavoidable."

Loch snickered. Had he been close enough, Sloane would have elbowed him.

"Hi!" the young man said. "It's okay! You can just call me Jay." He smiled down at the carrier. "This is Mr. Twigs!"

"Please, come in," Sloane said, trying to fix his hair as he opened the office door. He ushered Jay in, saying politely, "So, your roommate is missing?"

"Yes," Jay said, setting the carrier on Sloane's desk and opening it up. "Everyone at the department thinks I'm going nuts, and Milo said you would be able to help me."

"I'll definitely do my best!"

"My roommate has been missing for almost two days now, and this is not like him at all. He hasn't been to work, he hasn't been home, but his car is still in the parking lot. The detectives wanted me to wait before filing a missing persons report, and nobody is listening to me."

"And you think that Mr. Twigs here might be responsible?"

"I'm Silenced, so you know, no magic for me, but I know the sound portals make. I've heard it on a ton of documentaries. I know I heard one right before he vanished, and no one else was home except Mr. Twigs."

The cat slinked out of the carrier and perched right on the corner of Sloane's desk, its tail swishing. It was fluffy, black, and it was wearing small round sunglasses.

Loch kneeled down, eyeing the cat suspiciously. They were nearly nose to nose, locked in an intense stare.

"Huh," Sloane said, blinking slowly. "The cat... wears sunglasses?"

"Oh!" Jay blushed. "I know it sounds crazy, but his eyes are really sensitive to light. So yeah. I tried to take them off and he got really upset."

"Wait, you didn't buy them?"

"Oh no!" Jay laughed. "He had them on when I found him. He's a rescue, and he's, like, literally the sweetest—"

"He is a foul and wretched creature!" Loch suddenly shouted, spinning wildly and promptly smacking the cat across the room. "Go back to the depths of Xenon, you disgusting fiend!"

"Mr. Twigs!" Jay screamed in horror.

"Azaethoth!" Sloane roared, shocked and furious. "How could you? It's just a cat!"

"That is not a cat!" Loch argued, his tentacles beginning to unfurl. "It's a monstrous fiend that just looks like a cat!"

"Owww," a new voice complained, the fluffy black cat picking himself up from the floor and yowling in complaint. He hopped back up on the desk, his tail lashing as he hissed, "That was super rude!"

"Mr. Twigs…?" Jay stared in awe. He started to reach for the cat but drew back. "You're… you're talking?"

"Duh," the cat replied sweetly. "Now, Jay, why don't you forget all about this and go to sleep?"

Jay's eyes rolled back, and he immediately dropped on the carpet face-first.

"What the fuck are you?" Sloane demanded, his hands moving to summon a shield of bright starlight. Loch stood in front of him protectively, his thick tentacles writhing around him and poised to strike at any second.

The cat laughed, transforming into a very thin and very naked young man. He tilted his sunglasses down, grinning slyly to reveal a mouthful of pointed teeth as he teased, "Meow, motherfuckers. Name's Asta. I'm here to save the world."

CHAPTER 2.

"SAVE THE world?" Sloane brought his fingers together for a perception spell while maintaining his shield of starlight.

Whatever Asta was, he definitely wasn't human. The glimmer of his aura reminded Sloane of Loch's, a bright array of colors that was almost prismatic. It wasn't as bright, but still eerily beautiful.

"Yes." Asta sat on Sloane's desk and made himself comfortable. "Can humans hear well? I'm here to save the world. Get it that time? Ahem. I'm heeere tooo saaave—"

"Lies," Loch growled, pointing his finger right in Asta's face. "You will leave this world at once, you disgusting little Asran fiend!"

"Asran," Sloane repeated dumbly, his shield faltering for a moment. "He's an Asra?"

The Asra were powerful feline changelings that were known for being quite mischievous. They had been created by the gods as servants, but they refused to obey their godly masters and rebelled.

According to Sagittarian lore, Great Azaethoth gave the Asra the world of Xenon to end the war. It was a plane of existence that bridged the home of the gods to the mortal realm. Those left behind were said to have fallen into the dreaming with the gods.

"Yes!" Asta made a face. "Is there an echo in here? Weird. I was personally sent by our prince, His Most Royal Highness Elysian, to guard little Jay here."

"Why?" Sloane demanded.

"To save the world."

"But how?"

"By protecting him."

Sloane threw his hands up in frustration, snapping, "You're no freakin' help! You're not answering the questions!"

"But I am!" Asta argued. "You're just not asking the right questions!"

"He's an Asra," Loch sneered. "They only speak in riddles, and they cannot be trusted. I'll open a portal and take him back to Xenon at once."

"Nice meat suit," Asta commented, peering over Loch curiously. "Azaethoth? Is that you in there?"

"You can see him?" Sloane frowned.

"No, but I can smell him, and the wiggly tentacles were kind of a clue," Asta drawled with a roll of his eyes. He smirked at Sloane. "Guess that makes you Starkiller, eh?"

"You know who I am?" Sloane couldn't hide his surprise, and his stomach clenched at the memory of how he'd earned that nickname.

"When a god's soul comes zooming through Xenon, people tend to notice," Asta whispered loudly.

"Okay, fine, got it," Sloane said firmly, determined to get back on track. "Now, please tell me. Why does Jay need to be protected?"

"Well, look at him," Asta scoffed, waving at Jay, still sleeping down on the floor. "He's Silenced! He's in constant danger, and he has no way to defend himself."

"Is that why you made his roommate disappear?" Sloane pressed. "Was Jay in danger from him?"

"No, I just didn't like that prick. He kept kicking me when Jay wasn't looking."

"You've been just… what, been pretending to be his cat?" Sloane looked up to the ceiling, trying to ignore Asta's nudity as he uncrossed his legs.

He couldn't be sure, but it looked like Asta had two….

No, he was probably seeing things.

"Yup," Asta replied, thankfully crossing them back together.

"Can I take him back to Xenon now?" Loch growled. "Please?"

"Hang on," Sloane pleaded, trying to make eye contact with Asta without glancing below his waist. The sunglasses made it difficult, his voice strained as he said, "Okay, you were sent here to protect Jay because he's Silenced. Which means the threat is something magical?"

"Ding-ding!" Asta clapped excitedly. "Huh! You really are a good detective."

"So what's the threat?"

"Something bad."

"Is the threat a person?"

"No."

"Another Asra? Wait. No…." Sloane thought back to Milo's analysis of the blue goo. "Is it a god?"

"Yes!" Asta clapped again.

"Which god?"

"Oh, how should I know?"

"You knew who Azaethoth was!" Sloane argued.

"Uh, yeah, duh," Asta griped, peering at Sloane over his sunglasses. "You two are like the new Brad Pitt and Angelina Jolie of celestial beings. Come on, now. Everyone knows who you are."

"As they should," Loch said with a snort. He beamed proudly. "I told you we would be legendary."

"While that's very sweet and also weird, can we please get back to why Jay needs to be protected?" Sloane asked.

"I'm here to keep that squishy meat bag safe," Asta replied. "If he gets nabbed, the world ends. Do you get it? Do I need to use smaller words?"

"Very helpful, thank you so much," Loch said quickly, looking to Sloane with a hopeful pout. "Now can I send him back?"

"No!" Sloane wanted to tear his hair out. He took a deep breath. "The Asra stays!" He whirled back on Asta. "And you! I need some real answers."

"Ask real questions!" Asta snorted.

"Okay." Sloane paused to think. "Jay is Silenced, but there must be something very special about him. Yes?"

"Maaaybe," Asta cooed coyly.

"What makes him special?"

"He's Silenced."

"Oh, for the love of Great Azaethoth... okay, how about why would a god want someone who was Silenced?"

"To make them into a weapon," Asta replied gleefully, obviously enjoying this game.

"A weapon?" Sloane stared, and then he looked worriedly over at Loch. That didn't sound good at all. "Asta. Please. If you know something, you need to tell us."

"Tell you what?" Asta prompted.

"Enough!" Loch snapped, his tentacles unfurling and whipping around Asta, dragging him into a crushing hold. "Speak! Now!"

"Mmm...!" Asta cried out in surprise, and he struggled to get free as his face turned bright red. One of Loch's tentacles curled around his neck, squeezing tight.

Sloane felt bad for the writhing Asra, watching him gasp and moan desperately. He hated it, but they needed answers, and this interrogation was going nowhere.

"Tell us the truth, you wretched waste of furred flesh!" Loch snarled, his godly fury so unbridled that Sloane half expected to see a dragon appear right there in his office.

"Mmm, harder...." Asta groaned, his eyes fluttering as a crooked smile curled his lips. "Harder, Azaethoth, please...."

"Oh!" Sloane blushed as he suddenly realized Asta's cries were far from sounds of distress.

Loch dropped Asta immediately and sneered in disgust. "You are foul."

Asta laughed breathlessly, sitting up and rubbing his throat. "Ha! Wow, Azzy. That was nice," he teased. "Thanks."

"Talk. Now." Loch narrowed his eyes. "Or I promise you won't find what I do next very nice at all."

"Uggghhh, fine." Asta pulled himself back up on Sloane's desk. "I came here because Jay is the next target. This god, whoever he or she is, has been snatching up little Silenced mortals for months now. Like, by the hundreds."

"But there's been nothing on the news," Sloane protested. "If someone was really out there kidnapping that many Silenced people, the police would have noticed by now! They would be looking into it!"

"I bet you believe what you read on the internet too. Widen your scope a bit, my starlit friend. This is happening all over the world. People go missing all the time, okay?"

"How did the Asra figure it out, then?"

"Because us Asra are smart," Asta replied smugly. "King Grell and Prince Elysian magically deduced who the next victim is gonna be and sent me here to protect him."

"And how exactly does a god make a Silenced person into a weapon?" Sloane sat down at his desk, eyeing Asta warily.

"How should I know?" Asta whined. "I don't know how it's being done. I just know that it's happening and it's really not good, okay?"

"We shouldn't trust anything he says," Loch said, moving to stand beside Sloane. "It could be a trick."

"But what if he's right?" Sloane frowned worriedly. "You remember what Milo told us. There was another god walking the earth. And now this? It has to be connected."

"It doesn't have to be, does it?"

"What are the freakin' chances of multiple gods running around trying to end the world?"

"Very unlikely," Asta chimed in. "Heavy sleepers, you know."

"Fine, what do we do now?" Loch glared at Asta hatefully.

"Well, there's no case here." Sloane gestured to Jay. "We know what happened to his roommate—wait, Asta, where did you send him?"

"To Xenon," Asta scoffed. "Duh!"

"Bring him back!" Sloane groaned in frustration. "Gods, poor guy is probably scared out of his mind! And hey! Jay is already really worried, okay? He's been talking to the police!"

"Fiiiine," Asta fussed, sticking out his long tongue at Sloane. "I'll be back in a minute, party poopers. Keep an eye on Jay!"

"We will. Thank you."

A luminous portal opened up in the floor, and Asta dove right in. The portal vanished as quickly as it appeared with a distinct pop.

"Well," Sloane said with a click of his tongue, "this has been an interesting morning."

"Interesting, hmm?" Loch leaned close, his tentacles rubbing over Sloane's shoulders.

"A god running around kidnapping Silenced people to make them into weapons that are going to somehow end the world?" Sloane didn't realize how tense he was until Loch's massage deepened, melting beneath his divine touch. "Mmm... this is beyond interesting. It's insane."

"We'll find the immortal who's causing all this mischief and retrieve the missing humans," Loch soothed. "Don't worry so, my sweet Starkiller."

"Mmmph, how can you be so sure?"

"Because together you and I can do anything," Loch said with a warm smile, curling one of his tentacles against Sloane's cheek.

"I love you." Sloane smiled and reached up to cradle the slick coil.

"And I love you," Loch said adoringly. "All will be well."

"Mr. Tintenfisch is still passed out," Sloane observed. "Maybe we should try to wake him up?"

"Perhaps we should wait until the Asra returns," Loch said with a thoughtful hum. "This all might be a bit much to explain without the safe return of his mate to comfort him."

"Roommate, not his mate."

"What's the difference?" Loch wrinkled his nose.

"Roommates are just people who live together," Sloane explained. "Even though they're sharing a home, they might not be romantically involved."

"Why not?"

"Because they might be living together for financial reasons, or maybe they're just friends."

"But not actively exploring each other's bodies for carnal pleasure?"

"No."

"Huh." Loch thought it over for a long moment, pursing his lips. "That's ridiculous."

"No, that's just what some people do." Sloane laughed. "Finding out the Asra are real? Now that's ridiculous. I can't believe it. I know how crazy that sounds, considering I'm engaged to a god, but it's still pretty amazing."

"They're not that impressive," Loch sniffed, his tentacles extending and wrapping around Sloane possessively. "They change into cats, and they're exceptionally annoying. I can turn into a dragon, and I'm absolutely wonderful."

"And humble too," Sloane teased.

"Hmmph. Why do you care so much about the pesky Asra?"

"I guess I just never thought about it," Sloane said, hugging Loch, "but if you and all the old gods are real, then logically so are all the other races from Sagittarian lore, right? The Asra, the Vulgora, the Eldress?"

"Yes, but…." Loch looked troubled, his tentacles recoiling slowly.

"But what? What's wrong?"

Before Loch could answer him, there was a frantic knock at the door. Jay was still motionless on the floor, and Sloane jerked away from Loch in a panic. He did not want to try to explain to anyone why there was an unconscious man in his office.

"Oh shit! Shit, shit, shit!" Sloane hurried over to kneel beside Jay, giving him a frantic shake. "Come on, wake up!"

Jay was sound asleep, his eyes closed and appearing most peaceful. He didn't stir.

"What's wrong, my love?" Loch followed after Sloane and appeared confused as to why he was so upset.

"Anybody could be behind that door!" Sloane shook Jay harder and still with no response. "What am I supposed to tell them?"

"That a troublesome Asra put him to sleep and... ahhh, so." Loch nodded in understanding. "Mass public panic because no one believes any of us are real."

"Help me get him up," Sloane pleaded, grabbing one of Jay's arms. With Loch's tentacled assistance, they hurriedly scooped him into the nearest chair.

Loch tried to keep Jay's head up, but it kept flopping limply against his chest. Loch tilted it back and Jay's mouth hung open. Satisfied with that, Loch said, "Well, he's breathing. That's good! Mortals take naps, right? We will just say that he's napping."

The urgent knocking came again, and Sloane called out, "Just one moment, please!" He groaned, asking Loch anxiously, "What did Asta do to him? Why isn't he waking up?"

"How should I know?"

"Because you're an all-powerful ancient god! Could you at least try to wake him up?"

"Jay Tintenfisch! I am Azaethoth the Lesser, brother of Tollmathan, Gronoch, Xhorlas, and Galgareth. I am the son of Salgumel, he who was spawned by Baub, the child of Zunnerath and Halandrach, they who were born of Etheril and Xarapharos, descended directly from Great Azaethoth himself, and I command you to awaken!" Loch demanded in a booming tone, smacking Jay with a tentacle on top of his head.

Jay remained sound asleep.

"Huh." Loch scratched his head. "Sort of thought that would work."

"Azaethoth?" a small voice called out from the door. "Hello? Is that you?"

"Who is it?" Loch called back in a singsong tone.

"Galgareth," the voice declared triumphantly, "sister of Tollmathan, Gronoch, Xhorlas, and Azaethoth the Lesser. I am the daughter of Salgumel, he who was spawned by Baub, the child of Zunnerath and Halandrach, they who were born of Etheril and Xarapharos, descended directly from Great Azaethoth himself!"

"Sister!" Loch exclaimed, leaping to the door to open it.

On the other side was a young teenage boy with bright purple hair and several lip rings. The boy squealed with excitement, jumping into Loch's arms and hugging him tight. "Brother!"

"Wait, so, do all gods introduce themselves like that or...?" Sloane trailed off, unable to resist a grin at how happy Loch was embracing his sister.

"It has been far too long." Loch was smiling from ear to ear. He sounded positively giddy, and he could barely contain his tentacles. "I've missed you."

"And I've missed you!" Galgareth exclaimed. "I came as quickly as I could! It's not as easy as it used to be to find a willing vessel."

"Who are you wearing?" Loch snorted.

"This is Toby." She gestured at her young body. "Most of my worshippers these days are children trying to dabble in ancient magic behind their Lucian parents' backs! I take what I can get!"

Sloane waited patiently while the two siblings chatted, a little unsure if he should interrupt. After all, this wasn't an ordinary reunion.

"Bah! You look fine," Loch promised. "No one will notice!"

"Hey, I've got him at least until the end of summer!" Galgareth said with a quick laugh. "His parents think he's gone to camp."

"But it's not even spring yet!"

"Toby says they're not very attentive. They'll not even notice that he's gone." She narrowed her eyes thoughtfully. "Definitely gonna have to do something about that later."

"I'll be more than happy to help!"

"Hmmm, and by 'help' you just mean that you want to stir up some trouble." Galgareth smiled fondly.

"Oh, sister, you know me too well. I've missed you. I'm so glad you could come." Loch looked back at Sloane with a big smile. "I want you to meet my mate, Sloane Beaumont."

"Hi," Sloane said, waving hesitantly. He didn't know what was the polite thing to do when greeting an ancient goddess.

Shake hands? Bow? Offer a goat?

Hugging was apparently the proper move, as Galgareth stood on her toes to hug Sloane around his neck. "Ah! Sloane! It's so lovely to meet you!"

"Wow! Yes! You too!" Sloane laughed, hugging back firmly. "It's an honor, truly! To meet the Goddess of Night and Serendipity? This is awesome!"

Galgareth beamed up at Sloane, her blue eyes turning into black voids filled with stars. Sloane had seen Loch's eyes do the same before, and it was just as breathtaking to see a glimpse of the immortal hiding in that small human body.

"The honor is mine, Sloane," she said. "Thank you for making my brother so happy."

"He's amazing," Sloane confirmed, reaching for Loch's hand. "I really can't wait to be part of your family… which… uh… by the way…." He suddenly felt awkward, but there was a definite elephant in the room that needed to be addressed. "About your brother… your, uh, other brother?"

Gal held up her hand, reassuring him, "If you're worried about Tollmathan, please don't be. What's done is done, all right?"

"That's really incredibly nice of you, since I killed him," Sloane mumbled.

"He tried to kill you," Loch snarled.

"Well, he's still your brother!"

"Our brother was an arrogant fool." Galgareth smiled sadly. "You did what had to be done and did so with Great Azaethoth's blessing. I will miss him, but Toll didn't understand that the world will never be the way it was before.

"Humans decided they didn't need us and made their choice to create new gods of their own. That's the way things are now, and it makes the few worshippers we still have all that much more precious to me.

"If Toll had succeeded and actually woken up Salgumel, even those few faithful would have turned against us when they saw their world being destroyed. We must respect the whims of mankind and care for the flock we still have as best as we can."

"That's why you still walk the earth every winter solstice?" Sloane asked with a bittersweet smile. "To remind people you're still here?"

"Yes," Galgareth said sweetly. "It's not much, but I still wake from the dreaming every year to bless all the solstice candles that are lit for me. There's one family that still burns a whole tree for the sacred fire, and I always visit them first."

"That's really beautiful." Sloane could still remember lighting solstice candles with his parents, and it warmed his heart to think Galgareth had actually been there to visit them year after year.

"What about me?" Loch huffed. "I wake up too!"

"You woke up to help Lochlain steal things," Sloane retorted.

"Which was beautiful!" Loch protested.

"Yes, I'm sure all your felonious assistance was just lovely," Sloane soothed sarcastically, patting Loch's arm.

"Thank you," Loch preened and leaned into Sloane's touch. He hugged him against his chest, beaming at his sister as he purred, "Isn't my mate incredible?"

"I'm so pleased you were able to find someone to put up with you." Galgareth giggled, winking at Sloane. "Mother is going to love him."

"She's coming?" Loch immediately perked up.

"Urilith?" Sloane stared in amazement. "Goddess of Fertility and Children? That Urilith?"

"Yes!" Galgareth laughed. "I woke her before I left. I told her all about the wedding, and she's so excited! She fell back asleep a few times, but she's definitely coming."

"Wow." Sloane looked up at Loch with a bright grin. "I guess we'd better get started on planning our wedding, huh?"

"Yes," Loch replied, "and after seeing a mortal wedding, there is so much room for improvement. There needs to be a fire."

"We can do that."

"Better presents."

"We can have a registry."

"Hmm, an orgy would be nice, but participation wouldn't be mandatory for guests—"

"No," Sloane said flatly.

"You're no fun."

"So," Galgareth cut in, "not that I'm not enjoying the wedding chat, but who's the sleeping human?" She nodded at Jay, whose head had fallen forward, and he was drooling on himself.

"An Asra's little pet," Loch said as he made a face. "I'll explain it all on the way to our home. You will love it! It's very small, and Sloane's furniture is all, oh, what do they call it? Secondhand, yes!"

"Wait! What are we gonna do with him?" Sloane demanded. "Asta still isn't back! We can't just leave him here in my office!"

"Take him with us, obviously," Loch replied without hesitation. "He needs to be protected, yes? What better protection than two old gods and a starlit witch!"

"Of course!" Sloane threw up his hands. "Me and two ancient gods, one of whom looks like he's freakin' twelve, dragging around an unconscious man! What could possibly go wrong?"

CHAPTER 3.

LOCH CARRIED Jay outside to the car while Sloane and Galgareth opened all the doors and kept a lookout. The last thing they needed was someone seeing them and calling the police for what probably looked like a very strange kidnapping.

"So," Galgareth mused, "there was someone else helping Tollmathan, and you think it's the same god kidnapping Silenced mortals now?"

"That's about the size of it," Loch confirmed. "I was hoping you might have some ideas of who it is."

"Well, huh, let's see… most of our cousins are definitely sleeping, so are most of our uncles and aunts…. Uncle Babbeth is definitely asleep, but I don't know about maybe Merikath or Bestrath."

Sloane jogged ahead to get his car unlocked, Galgareth trailing behind as she listed off more names. He'd just opened the door and hit the unlock button when a strange shiver ran up his spine, as if someone had brushed the back of his neck. He jerked his head up, looking all around until he saw the source of the odd feeling.

There was a young man standing in the middle of the street staring right at him. He didn't look much older than Galgareth's current vessel. His hair was stark white, and his eyes were dark red, burning holes into Sloane's as he demanded in a startlingly deep voice, "Give me that human. Right now."

"I'm sorry, but he's not available at the moment," Sloane said hastily, glancing back at Loch. "Little help here?"

"Who is that?" Loch scoffed, scowling at the young man.

"I don't know, but he wants Jay."

"Well, hmmph." Loch hugged Jay against his chest like a prized stuffed animal. "He can't have him. I did not carry his unconscious body all this way just to give him away to some child."

"Give me the human," the young man repeated, crossing his arms over his chest. "I don't want to tell you again."

Sloane flexed his fingers together for a perception spell, and his heart skipped a beat when he saw an empty, white aura. "Loch," he said, his voice tense, "he's Silenced."

"Oh, pfffft." Loch eased Jay into the back seat with Galgareth's assistance and shut the door. "What's the problem, then?"

"Remember what the Asra said," Sloane mumbled, itching to put up a shield. The boy didn't appear armed with any weapons, and there was no danger of any magic being used against them.

Even so, Sloane's stomach was churning with worry. Something felt wrong about all this.

"Last time." The young man's lip curled in an annoyed sneer. "Give me the human… or else."

"Or else what?" Loch taunted, strolling from the car and into the road. "I don't particularly like threats."

"It's not a threat," the young man warned. "It's a promise."

"Ohhh, my precious little mortal." Loch cackled in delight. "You have no idea the agony I'm about to bring down upon you…."

"No agony!" Sloane warned.

"Fine," Loch groaned, rolling his head back like a stubborn child on the verge of a tantrum. "Very mild discomfort so my mate doesn't get mad at me. He'll withhold physical pleasure from me if I don't behave myself, and I really—"

Something struck Loch in his chest, invisible but massive, and the force sent him flying through the air and crashing into the bushes outside the office door.

"Loch!" Sloane shouted frantically.

"Azaethoth!" cried Galgareth.

Sloane ducked behind the open car door, his thoughts turning into a turbulent blur as he threw up a shield of starlight around himself and Galgareth. He hadn't seen the boy move, nor had he heard a single chant of a spell spoken.

Magic required an object to conjure it. That object could be a wand, the words of a spell, or a simple gesture, depending on the skills of the witch. The only person Sloane knew who could work magic with only a thought was Loch....

But he was a god.

"Loch!" Sloane called out again. "Are you okay?"

"I'm about to do something mass-panic causing!" Loch growled as he dragged himself to his feet. He picked leaves out of his hair, swearing, "Ohhhh, so *very* mass-panic causing, indeed!"

"Just wait! Let me think!" Sloane pleaded. Before he could decide what to do, the car door he'd been hiding behind was ripped clean off. It flew away and landed in the street with a loud crash. He stumbled back, wide eyes fixed on the young man.

He still hadn't moved a muscle, and yet Sloane's new car was now short a door.

"My fucking car?" Sloane hated how he snapped, angrily whirling on the young man and throwing his hands up in disgust. "Come on! What the hell!"

The young man calmly walked toward him, seemingly without a care in the world. He might as well have been strolling through a park.

"Get away from us!" Galgareth warned. "If you force my hand, I swear that I will leave this vessel and I will tear you into little pieces!"

"Gal, you stay there with Sloane," Loch snarled. "I'll handle this!" He raised his head high and stomped forward to cut the young man off before he could get too close to the car. His tentacles were rising from his arms, and the pavement was cracking beneath his feet. "And you! Nasty little child! Stay away from my mate!"

The young man snorted, staring Loch down fearlessly as *something* came out of him.

Sloane could see it now as a wave of clear energy through his perception spell, and he struggled to identify it. There was no defined aura—no fire or water, no hint of what kind of magic this was. He watched Loch struggle to fend it off, and he was struck with a stab of crippling fear.

What kind of mortal being could fight a god so effortlessly? Was this the weapon the Asra had warned them about?

Sloane threw out a spell meant to silence all magic in hopes of helping Loch fight back. He gasped when Galgareth's hand dropped on his shoulder, her divine energy flowing through him to fuel the spell. He closed his eyes, using her power to seal it, and waited anxiously.

Another wave burst forth from the young man's chest and struck Loch so hard that his body went tumbling across the street.

"Loch!" Sloane cried frantically. "I can't silence him!"

"It's not working!" Galgareth shrieked, staring down at her own hands in horror. "Azaethoth, I tried—"

"Stay away, both of you!" Loch was hit again as soon as he stood up, his feet skidding as he came to a stop several yards away. Black fluid was leaking from his mouth and running down his chin, and he glared furiously at the young man. "Ohhh, you foul little thing. Now I'm really getting annoyed."

Sloane couldn't stand by and watch Loch get hurt. "Protect Jay!" he shouted to Galgareth and took off from behind the car, lunging forward with a shield to block the next attack.

It was hard trying to aim while looking through the scope of his perception spell, but he put everything he had into his shield as he leaped in front of Loch. "Get away from him!"

The shield cracked as the young man's energy struck, but it didn't break. The shield held.

Sloane continued to pour his magic into the spell, pressing forward and driving the young man back several paces. He was overjoyed that it seemed to be working, but his hopes sunk as the man slowly lifted his hand.

The energy was now moving through his fingers, channeled by a twist of his wrist, and the cracks in Sloane's shield grew. He didn't know what else to do, grabbing hold of his shield and hurling it at the young man as hard as he could.

It was raw starlight, powerful and unstable, slamming right into the young man's head.

The young man stumbled when it hit him, groaning in pain, and Loch came strutting around Sloane to take the opening for a counterattack. Brilliant light spun from his hands, and it tore at the young man's body.

The young man threw his arms up to block the magic, but the intense energy was already eating away at the sleeves of his jacket. The fabric simply peeled away, and his skin was starting to sizzle. There was something on his arms, some sort of symbol, but Sloane was too caught up watching Loch to get a good look.

He rarely saw Loch use his true power, fully expecting the young man attacking them to surrender at any second. Inside Loch's mortal frame was an ancient god, and his magic was endless. There was no way that any normal human being could withstand it, not without burning into ash.

But it didn't happen. The young man suddenly pushed back against Loch's energy with a furious scream, the resulting explosion of power violently hitting Sloane and Loch like a tsunami. The street ruptured, asphalt shattering down the block and all the streetlamps popping, raining glass everywhere.

Sloane landed over by his car, the air knocked from his lungs, and he didn't see Loch right away. He tried to move and found that he couldn't, his chest aching as he tried to breathe in. The side of his head was on fire, and something wet was dripping down his neck. "Oh gods…. Loch…? Loch!"

"Sloane!" Galgareth cried, hurrying over to his side and trying to help him up. "You're bleeding!"

"What the hell is he?" Sloane saw that Galgareth looked just as worried as he felt. "Where's that… little fucking… prick…!"

"I don't know," Galgareth whispered urgently, "but we need to get out of here."

"Ugh, wait! I've gotta help Loch!" Sloane staggered up on unsteady legs. "Whatever happens, you have to protect Jay! Please!"

Loch was suddenly there next to him, tentacles and arms wrapped all around him and holding him close. "Sloane, you're hurt—"

"Loch! Watch out!" Sloane sensed that shiver again and jerked defensively as he struggled to put together another shield.

The young man was coming at them again, his ruined jacket discarded as he raised his arms to summon an enormous wave of energy. Sloane could see the symbols on his forearms more clearly now, at least a dozen of them, and they were all small circles with arrows running through them.

The symbols were glowing with a hint of blue, something familiar that Sloane couldn't immediately place. He didn't have time to identify them or give any thought as to their purpose, groaning in pain as Loch laid him in Galgareth's arms.

"Take care of him," Loch commanded. "I'll be right back."

"Loch, no…." Sloane groaned, gasping and wincing in pain. He watched helplessly as Loch started back to the street to fight.

"Enough of this!" Loch's eyes turned black and flooded with stars. Sloane could see the godly dragon inside of him struggling to escape as Loch charged head-on at the young man.

They clashed, and the collision was deafening, a flash of light blinding them all with the powerful aftershocks shaking the car next to them. Sloane and Galgareth clung to each other for dear life, and then Sloane heard a name:

Alexander!

It wasn't Loch or the young man who had spoken, and the voice sounded strangely far away, even though Sloane had been able to understand it clearly. He looked all around, trying to identify the source, but he couldn't see anything. As the intense light faded away, only Loch remained.

The young man was gone.

"What… what happened?" Sloane called out weakly, his heart up in his throat hugging his tonsils. "Loch? Hey! Are you okay?"

"I'm fine." Loch returned to Sloane and embraced him. He kissed him, deep and passionate, murmuring, "I'm fine, Sloane. I'm here. I'm yours."

"What happened?" Sloane demanded, clinging to his lover and patting him all over to make sure he was really unharmed. "Where did he go? And what was that voice?"

"I have no idea." Loch rested his hand on Sloane's chest. "And I don't care right now. You're hurt, my love. I need to heal you."

"We should really go." Galgareth jerked her head to the car.

People from the office building were peeking out from the doorway, and traffic had completely stopped at the corner from the destruction of the road.

"Shit," Sloane mumbled.

"The police will certainly have been notified after that spectacle," Galgareth said more urgently. "We need to be anywhere else but here."

"Home. Let's go home."

Against his better judgment, Sloane let Galgareth drive. She insisted she had experience, and Sloane didn't want to argue. Someone who appeared so young behind the wheel was a risk, but it was a better option than letting Loch, who had only ever driven in Mario Kart, do it.

Galgareth swung around in the street to retrieve Sloane's car door, reattaching it with a snap of her fingers. It was a little crooked, but it would hold for now and hopefully not draw any more unwanted attention.

Sloane sat in the back seat with Jay, who was still blissfully asleep, while Loch's tentacles reached back from the front seat to tend to his wounds. He closed his eyes, letting Loch's divine touch ease the burn of what was probably several broken ribs and a deep cut on the side of his head. The pain faded, leaving only the uneasy twist of his stomach to deal with.

"I've never seen anything like that," Sloane said quietly, voicing his troubled thoughts. "He was Silenced. Totally Silenced… but he was using, well, he was using something against us!"

"It couldn't have been magic," Galgareth chimed in. "Our silencing spells would have stopped it!" She frowned, her borrowed fingers fidgeting against the steering wheel. "Unless...."

"Unless what?"

"Unless he wasn't using mortal magic," Loch supplied, one of his tentacles taking Sloane's hand and giving it a squeeze.

"Like an Asra?" Sloane glanced between the two gods in the front seat. "Is that what you mean?"

"No," Galgareth said with a quick shake of her head. "It's definitely godly. He must have a totem or some other kind of artifact imbued with a god's essence or something blessed by one of us. It's the only explanation."

"Because even those who are Silenced can still use magical objects," Sloane said thoughtfully. "So, find the object, destroy it, take out his power?"

"In theory."

"What happened back there?" Sloane tugged at Loch's tentacle. "Did he really just disappear?"

"I don't know," Loch replied, his brow furrowing with an unusual amount of unease. "One moment I had him in my grasp, and then the next... he was gone. Like passing through a portal."

"So? What if he did?"

"Any form of teleportation requires extremely powerful magic," Galgareth said forlornly. "It's very difficult for those not born with it to learn, and I don't know of any magical object that can give that much power to a mortal, much less a Silenced one."

"Maybe it was just an illusion?" Sloane suggested. "Maybe he cloaked himself with invisibility or something?"

"Maybe." She looked back to the road. She didn't sound very certain.

"What about the Faedra?" Sloane sat up straight in his seat. "They're everlasting creatures who can manipulate time and space, right? Could this guy be one of them? Maybe an Asra? They can teleport. I mean, he didn't have the pointy teeth, but there's a chance, right?"

Galgareth glanced sideways at Loch, asking him bluntly, "He doesn't know?"

Loch sank down in his seat. "It hadn't exactly come up."

"What?" Sloane pressed. "What hadn't come up?"

"The other beings," Loch said with a sad sigh. "The Faedra, the Asra, the Vulgora… the many things that end in 'a' that are everlasting. They once all walked the earth as we did, worshipped us like humans… but then the dreaming came, and not all of them followed us to Zebulon."

Sloane didn't like where this was going. "What happened to them?"

"They died," Loch said flatly, his tentacles slowly drawing back, as he was clearly uncomfortable with this conversation. "Those that stayed here, anyway. They were hunted down by humans, either slain for their precious parts like the Eldress for their horns or the Vulgora for their scales, or they were murdered outright for being abominations in the eyes of the Lucian god."

"That's horrible!" Sloane's heart wrenched at the thought. It was a bit awkward mourning creatures he didn't know fully existed until today, but he felt sick all the same.

"Our greatest failure as gods," Loch said with a bitter sigh, "was not being able to save them."

"But they're not all gone, right?" Sloane offered a hopeful smile, and he reached over to squeeze Loch's shoulder. "The Asra we met today, what about him?"

"He comes from Xenon," Galgareth explained, pulling into the apartment parking lot. "The Asra who rebelled against us founded a new world there, a little kingdom of their own. If any of the other everlasting peoples live? That's where they would be."

"Maybe someone there knows about this Silenced problem?" Sloane frowned down at Jay. "The Asra is the one who warned us about it. Someone there has to know something more about what is going on."

"We can't." Galgareth frowned. "Gods are forbidden from entering Xenon because of the peace treaty the Asra made with Great Azaethoth. Trying to go could start a war."

"Besides," Loch said grumpily, "their kind shouldn't be trusted. They would have never risked leaving unless they had something to gain from it. That little fiend is not telling us all that he knows."

"He's also still not back yet," Sloane mumbled, unbuckling his seat belt and sighing wearily. "Guess it's time for another fun round of carrying the unconscious man around in broad daylight?"

"Oh, I can't wait," Loch drawled miserably.

They worked quickly to get Jay inside without anyone seeing, Loch depositing him on Sloane's couch with a huff. He looked to Galgareth, asking, "Can you try to wake him up? I'm getting tired of dragging him around."

"You're a god with limitless strength and stamina," Sloane chided.

"It's beneath me."

"I'll try, but I don't think I'll have any luck." Galgareth kneeled beside the bed. "An Asra's word is as good as a curse."

Sloane wandered into the kitchen as he tried to get a handle on the last few hours. His body was still tingly from the rush of adrenaline and fear that had squeezed his heart so terribly.

Loch followed him, his arms curling around Sloane's waist and holding him against his chest. "Oh, my sweet Starkiller. I was so worried."

"Me too," Sloane confessed, wrapping his arms around Loch's neck and kissing him firmly. "I've never seen anything like that before."

"He wasn't that powerful," Loch protested. "If I had shed my mortal body, I would have simply eaten him and it would have been over with."

"Are you sure about that?"

Loch was offended, pouting. "Very certain, thank you. Hmmph. You doubt me?"

"He almost broke my shield." Sloane kissed Loch's cheek to soothe his wounded pride. "I've never felt power like that before… except…." His skin shivered again. "Except when I held the sword made of starlight from Great Azaethoth and killed Tollmathan."

"So," Loch mused, "the source of the boy's power is godly without a doubt."

"Yeah, I think so. And the name—did you hear the name?"

"What name?"

"Alexander. Right when you two smashed into each other, I heard a voice calling out."

"I didn't hear anything." Loch frowned, turning to ask his sister, "Gal? Did you hear anything when I bravely defeated our adversary? A name, perhaps?"

"No." Galgareth left Jay's side, walking over to join them in the kitchen. "I didn't hear anything."

"Weird." Sloane scratched his neck. Maybe he had been hearing things. "I guess Jay is still out?"

"I can't wake him up without the Asra who put him to sleep," Galgareth said. "The spell won't let him die of starvation or dehydration at least, but he could stay like this forever."

"Great!" Sloane groaned. "My client is under a sleeping curse. That's wonderful."

"Is he really still a client?" Loch wondered out loud. "I already solved his case."

"Wait! You?"

"The Asra did it. Case closed."

Sloane let Loch have his moment, reaching for a magnetic notepad that hung on the fridge. He grabbed a pen and drew a rough sketch of the symbol he'd seen on the young man's arms.

"What are you doing?" Loch poked Sloane in the side with a tentacle.

"This is what I saw on that guy's arms," Sloane said, adding the last arrow. "It's Sagittarian, I think. See, we have a new case now."

"We do?"

"All the Silenced people who are missing plus figuring out who is after Jay and why," Sloane replied patiently. "The Asra probably isn't telling us everything, but that guy coming after us is proof that something hinky is going on."

"And the doodle?"

"I just told you. It's what I saw on the guy's arm. He had a bunch of them. I could see some sort of blue stuff…." He paused, looking at Loch's hands. "You said you grabbed him, right?"

"Yes?" Loch held out his hands expectantly. "I had a hold of him, and then he vanished away."

Sloane held his fingers out for a perception spell, and he gasped when he saw the glimmering blue residue on Loch's hands. "Loch, it's the goo! The blue godly goo!"

"Huh, look at that," Loch said, cocking his head and wiggling his fingers. "Perhaps my mysterious brethren helped place those odd symbols on him."

"Oh! I know what that is!" Galgareth said excitedly, tracing the shape on the paper. "It's a binding symbol! For binding spirits in necromancy."

"Like with ghouls?" Sloane asked. "Where a person's soul gets bound to the ghoul body?"

"Indeed. A ghoul body is no different than any other inanimate object you'd bind a spirit to. But you say you saw this on the young man?"

"Yes," Sloane confirmed. "They were all over his arms, but I saw his aura. He's not a ghoul."

"That is troubling," Galgareth murmured. "The boy is very much alive, and this means that something's been bound to him."

"That shouldn't be possible," Sloane scoffed. All magic dealing with soul binding and ghouls was highly illegal, and he admittedly didn't know much other than the basics. "You can't bind two living souls together… right?"

"It shouldn't be possible, no. Oh, how I wish Babbeth was awake," Galgareth fussed.

"God of Death and Lost Children?"

"Yes, he'd know what this all means." She pulled absently on one of her lip rings. "Souls are his expertise, obviously, and he could tell us what's bound to that boy and how to break it. What we really need is a necromancer! Ulgh, but I haven't seen one in centuries."

"Really?" Sloane glanced at Loch, and he grinned. "Centuries, huh?"

"What?" Galgareth glanced between them quizzically. "Do you know a necromancer?"

"Well, as a matter of fact, I do."

CHAPTER 4.

"HER NAME is Lynnette Fields," Sloane explained as he got behind the wheel of his car. He went to shut the door, and he frowned as it promptly fell off again. He silently prayed that it wouldn't rain any time soon. "She's Lochlain's sister."

"Lochlain?" Galgareth asked from the back, getting settled with Jay's sleeping body next to her. "And he's the one whose body Azaethoth has?"

"This is a ghoul copy made by Miss Fields." Loch slid into the passenger seat and clapped his hands. The car door magically reattached itself, though it was still at an odd angle. "She's a very talented witch, and yes, she's my sister in a sense."

"Aww! That's so nice!" Galgareth gushed. "You finally have another sister!"

"One who knows all about necromancy," Sloane said. "She's raised at least one ghoul I know of, a friend named Fred. Hopefully we'll catch her at home."

A quick text to Milo confirmed that Lynnette was home on her lunch break. Sloane pulled up to her house with a cringe when he saw some neighbors working out in the yard. Their heads turned when they saw the state of Sloane's car.

"Stay here with Jay for a second," Sloane said firmly, jogging up to the front door and knocking. While he waited for Lynnette or Milo to answer, he glanced back at the car.

The door had fallen back off, and both Loch and Galgareth were gone.

He turned back to find them standing beside him, cursing, "Shit! I told you guys to stay in the car!"

"Why?" Galgareth blinked. "I want to meet the necromancer!"

"Waiting in the car is boring!" Loch complained.

"Jay! Because Jay is still in the car!" Sloane almost shouted, and he groaned in frustration.

"Uh, hello?" Lynnette opened the door, still in her waitress uniform from the restaurant she worked at and very confused. She was an attractive ginger like her brother, and her long curly hair was currently tied up in a tidy bun. "Hey, Sloane! Loch! Uh. What's going on? Oh, by the gods! What happened to your car?"

"We need some help," Sloane said.

"Hi there," Galgareth said cheerfully. "My name is Galgareth, sister of Tollmathan, Gronoch, Xhorlas, and Azaethoth the Lesser. I am the daughter of Salgumel, he who—"

"Galgareth?" Lynnette squealed, her eyes wide and totally in awe. As a devout Sage, she knew exactly who she was talking to. "Oh, my stars. Galgareth, your goddessness, I'm so honored!"

"We need your assistance identifying a strange symbol, dear mortal child," Galgareth said. "I've been told you're a great necromancer?" She glanced at the uniform. "Strange robes... huh. Everything's changed so much!"

"Wow! Yes! Sort of!" Lynnette took out her scrunchie and frantically ran her fingers through her hair. "I'm Lynnette. Lynnette Fields. I'm more of an amateur necromancer.... Eh...." She tilted her head at Sloane's car. "Is there someone else in there?"

"He's my client, Jay Tintenfisch," Sloane replied, worriedly looking over at the curious neighbors. "He's been put to sleep by an Asra and—"

"An Asra?"

"Look, he's fine," Sloane insisted. "But we need to move him inside without hopefully drawing any more attention. He's in serious danger."

"Okay. Wait a second." Lynnette dipped into the house and returned with a pair of bright purple sunglasses. "Come on, I got this."

Sloane followed Lynnette back to the car, watching her take off Jay's glasses and slide on the shades. They pulled him out of the car as Lynnette shouted dramatically, "Wow! How much have you had to drink, buddy! Whew, smells like a brewery in here!"

"Is this really gonna work?" Sloane mumbled, grateful for Loch joining them to help lift Jay up. They slung his arms over their shoulders and walked with him to the house.

Jay's head wagged like a bobblehead doll, but the sunglasses stayed on.

"It'll work, shush." Lynnette raised her voice again, exclaiming, "And in the middle of the day? Who gets so drunk on their lunch break!"

Sloane stole a glance over to the neighbors, who were definitely watching but weren't rushing for their phones to call the authorities. Once they had crowded into the house, they moved to the couch to safely deposit Jay.

"What the crap?" Milo popped up from the kitchen. "Babe, I heard you yelling and…. Uh… hey… everybody. Hello, your godliness!"

"Hello, dear mortal child," Loch said sweetly. "Good to see you again."

"Okay!" Lynnette planted her hands on her hips. "So, what's going on here exactly?"

"Sorry, babe," Milo said with a cringe, cutting a sharp glare to Sloane. "Dude, when you texted me, I didn't think it was gonna be a damn party!"

"Language!" Lynnette smacked Milo's arm. "We're in the presence of gods!"

"Huh? Who? I know Loch is a god, but wait, you mean the kid?" Milo stared at Galgareth awkwardly. "He's… he's a god?"

"She is the Goddess of Night, come on! Pay attention!"

Milo looked utterly helpless, and Sloane swept in to assist, quickly saying, "Listen, this is Galgareth, Azaethoth's sister. She came to help with the wedding and—"

"Wedding?" Lynnette squeaked, holding her hands over her mouth. "Wait, wait, who's getting married?"

"I am making an honest man out of Sloane," Loch said proudly. "After all of these months of raw, undiluted, primal passion, we are going to formally commit to one another."

"Yes, but—" Sloane tried to interrupt.

"When did this happen?" Lynnette rushed to embrace them both. "This is so amazing! I'm so happy for you guys! Congratulations!"

Sloane hugged Lynnette politely, trying again to explain, "Listen, please. This has to do with Milo's big discovery. The blue goo he's been testing?"

"Testing?" Lynnette arched her brows, and she eyed Milo suspiciously. "Testing where exactly?"

"He's discovered it belongs to another god who was down here with Tollmathan," Sloane said, trying to keep the conversation on track. "And now I think I know what that god was doing. Sort of. Maybe."

"Well, what is it? I'm guessing this has something to do with the passed-out guy on my couch?"

"Isn't that Jay?" Milo frowned. "I knew you were going to talk to him about that weirdness with his roommate, but what the hell?"

"Cat made the roommate disappear. I'll explain later—"

"What!"

"Look, Jay is Silenced," Sloane said firmly. "The Asra who put him to sleep has been watching over him because a god is out there kidnapping Silenced people and turning them into weapons. He said he had to protect Jay to save the world."

Lynnette clicked her tongue, slowly taking all of this new information in. "Right. Okay, and how is this god making Silenced people into weapons?"

"That's why we're here." Sloane reached into his pocket and brought out the piece of paper with his doodle on it. "We were attacked by a young kid who is Silenced and had these all over his arms with traces of that godly blue goo."

Lynnette took the paper and stared for a moment before her eyes flicked up at Sloane. "And you're sure he was Silenced?"

"Yes. I even tried to silence him with Galgareth's help, and it did nothing. He was still able to use some sort of…." He struggled to describe it. "Like an energy attack against us?"

"It was definitely godly power," Galgareth added gravely. "There is no mortal or everlasting creature that can cast like that."

"At first we suspected he was using some sort of magical totem," Sloane continued, "but that's a binding symbol, right? For souls?"

"It is," Lynnette said, clicking her tongue again. She was thinking hard, her lip curled up tight. A tense silence began, and everyone was watching her expectantly.

"What's an Asra?" Milo asked in a hushed whisper.

There was a collective groan from the rest of the room, and Sloane forced a smile. He patted Milo's shoulder. "They were the first race of beings that Great Azaethoth created who now guard Xenon, the bridge to Zebulon."

"They're very annoying cat people," added Loch with a sneer. "Highly overrated."

"Wait," Milo gasped. "Does this mean unicorns are real?"

"Eh, sort of?" Sloane grinned. "But we call them the Eldress, and not all of them had one horn. Some of them had dozens, and they didn't have fur. They had no skin, and they had teeth like needles, and uh, Lynnette, where are you going?"

Lynnette had suddenly left the room, and she called over her shoulder, "I'll be right back! Hang on!"

Galgareth sat on the end of the couch by Jay's feet, calmly announcing, "I've warded the house and set some traps to protect us in case the Silenced one returns. Huh. Seems that Azaethoth has done it here before."

"That's not the only thing I've done here before," Loch purred, and he leaned in to nip at Sloane's neck.

Sloane smothered a groan into his palm, unable to resist a bashful smile. He peeked through his fingers at Milo. "Sorry, Milo."

"It's cool! It's cool!" Milo grinned. "I guess I should be honored that a god wanted to get down in these humble digs, right?"

"Definitely," Loch said with a wink.

"Okay!" Lynnette shouted. "Gods and mortals, come to the kitchen!"

Sloane led the way, and he saw Lynnette had brought out a collection of old books and tattered scrolls. They were stretched out across the counter and smelled distinctly of must. He could feel the magic seeping right off the paper. "What are those?"

"Collectively, they're the grimoire of the Fields family," Lynnette said with a proud smile. "Forbidden magic passed down generation after generation. The magic enforcement police would seriously torch this stuff in a second if they found it. Everything I learned about necromancy is in here."

"Is there a CliffsNotes version?" Milo peered over the ancient papers.

Rolling her eyes, Lynnette said, "Look, the binding symbol you saw? It's used for soul binding when you're creating a ghoul. When someone first passes, you have to bind their soul to something to keep them from moving on too quickly. When Fred died, I bound his soul to a spoon.

"Once it's ready, you use the same symbol on the ghoul body to transfer the soul over and ta-dah! You've created your very own ghoul. But this isn't a true resurrection." She glanced at Loch. "When Great Azaethoth brought Lochlain back, that was the real deal.

"Raising a ghoul is a cheap imitation. Being able to bring a soul back from Zebulon and put them into their original body and restore their natural vitality takes power that no human has held in hundreds of years. We've been getting by with ghoul magic because it's all we have, and even that can fail if the binding doesn't hold.

"Now, some of those old resurrection spells are here, but they're written in godstongue, and I can't translate them."

"Godstongue is the language of the Sagittarian gods," Sloane said before Milo could ask. "Some dialects were unique to specific gods. Others were a bit more broad. Most spells are cast using some form of godstongue. Lucians claim that their God of Light invented it, but the language is totally Sagittarian."

"There are even some versions of the language that only the god that it was intended for can read." Galgareth reverently touched the old scrolls. "These look like Babbeth's. Maybe his consort, Rordanus."

"I believe they're from Rordanus," Lynnette said, a twinge of excitement in her voice. "I've been comparing these with some works down at the museum and… anyway! The point is that soul binding is not really true necromancy. You're kind of just moving a soul around. Now, what you're describing, a living being with a soul bound to him? That's a problem."

"Because two souls can't share the same body?" Milo looked quite proud of himself for contributing to the discussion.

"Exactly," Lynnette confirmed. "Gods can visit a mortal vessel for a time if the vessel is willing." She gestured at Galgareth. "Or if the vessel is empty." A nod to Loch. "But knowing all those binding symbols are on this mystery guy, well, I think I know why they're so keen on using Silenced people."

"Oh?" Sloane watched Lynnette flip through one of the books.

"Silenced people are totally cut off from magic," Lynnette went on, turning to a page that showed a bridge made of bright stars. "Even in death, they're forced to walk the bridge in Xenon to pass on into Zebulon. No magic, no free pass over the bridge.

"And the reason why you can't bind a living soul to another is because the magic of two souls would be too much for one body. It would destroy them both. But a Silenced vessel…?"

"A soul who has no magic?" Sloane's heart sunk down into his gut.

"With enough of those binding symbols," Lynnette concluded hesitantly, "anything could be possible. There could actually be another soul bound to him."

"So we have a Silenced person who's been bound with another kind of soul," Sloane said, hating how insane it sounded to say out loud, "and he's able to use that soul's magic?"

"Would explain why the silencing spells you tried didn't work," Lynnette pointed out. "The guy is already Silenced. What's giving him power is the soul that's attached to him, and I don't know if your magic will affect it. Souls are already sort of halfway into Xenon once they separate from their body. They don't fully exist in this plane."

"Great. So what can we do?"

"The only thing you can do." Lynnette flipped to another page. "You go after the bound object, which in this case is the guy. Break the binding symbols and it will free the soul that's bound to him."

"Break them?" Sloane stared. "They're, like, freakin' tattooed into his skin."

"Then you'll have to cut them," Lynnette said grimly. "Enough to break the outer circle, but maybe not all of them. You might just need to cut through a few of them to get the soul enough wiggle room to escape and break the rest on its own."

"Whatever's bound to him probably wants its freedom." Milo frowned. "Poor ghost dude. It's like a ghost slave, just stuck to this random guy."

"Maybe not so random. If I had to guess, finding a fitting Silenced vessel for this isn't easy," Lynnette continued, tapping her nails against the counter. "To actually pull off this kind of soul bonding and have it work is like one in a million. I guarantee Jay was the next prime pick, and that's why they want him so badly."

"Based on what criteria?" Sloane asked. "Star sign? Age? Weight?"

"Who knows!" Lynnette threw up her hands. "It could be completely random."

"There's gotta be more to this. Maybe if we figure out what's unique about Jay, we can find a pattern that will lead us to the god responsible for this."

"What we should go find is that pesky little Asra and wring his neck until he tells us what he knows," Loch declared.

"We're still very much forbidden from entering Xenon," Galgareth scolded. "The Asran King will start a war if a god sets foot there! You know this, brother!"

"Fine! We will seek out this Silenced mortal and wring *his* neck until he tells us what he knows."

"He kinda kicked our asses," Sloane reminded him glumly.

"That is a vicious lie!" Loch gasped. "He retreated before I could claim my victory!"

"Look, unless you're planning on going full tentacle dragon in the middle of downtown, we can't fight him anywhere in the city." Sloane reached to take Loch's hand. "We need to be careful."

"I think I might be able to translate some of these scrolls," Galgareth said, her eyes fixed on the old papers. "I'm not fluent in Rordanus, but I understand a few words. With Lynnette's assistance, we might be able to find something here that can help us."

"I'm going to see what I can dig up on all the Silenced disappearances," Sloane said. "See if I can figure out something that the police have missed. Might give us a clue as to how these people are being chosen, maybe keep any potential future victims safe."

"Why aren't we going after the Silenced mortal again?" Loch pouted.

"Because of the ass kicking, and we don't have enough information to make a smart move," Sloane replied wearily. "We need a plan. Come on, you like plans."

"I like plans for stealing things." Loch continued to pout.

"How about you guys go hit the books and let Jay stay here for a while?" Lynnette suggested. "He'll be safe with us. The warding spells are super powerful, and if anything comes up, we'll call."

"Okay," Sloane agreed, though a bit hesitantly.

"I promise the mortal will be safe," Galgareth soothed, a lavender tentacle moving out of her sleeve to stroke Sloane's chin. "Fear not."

"My sister is a goddess of her word." Loch's tentacles reached over to hug Sloane's waist. "All will be well, my sweet Starkiller."

Shivering from all the divine contact, Sloane found himself smiling. He took a deep breath. "Right. You're right. We'll figure this out."

"What can I do?" Milo asked. "I mean, I can't speak godstongue, but there's gotta be something I can do to help."

"Hey, what about that one guy, Ollie Logue?" Sloane snapped his fingers. "He's a linguist, right? Does some translation work for the Archersville PD?"

"Yeah, but he's out of town or something," Milo replied. "I don't know if he can translate godstongue, but he speaks freakin' everything else."

"Still might be worth trying to get in touch with him."

"He even speaks Klingon, dude."

"Well, in the meantime, do you have any more of the blue goo left to test?" Sloane asked, waiting for Milo to nod. "Maybe Galgareth can help you, see if there's any other way to identify who it came from."

"I'll be happy to assist however I can," Galgareth chirped. "Urilith, our mother, is still coming to visit, and I'm sure she'd love to help as well."

Lynnette's eyes widened. "Urilith...?"

"Goddess of Fertility!" Milo exclaimed, pumping his fist. "Ha, I knew that one!"

"We do still have a wedding to plan," Loch said brightly, nuzzling against Sloane's cheek. "Oh, I can't wait for you to meet my mother. She will adore you."

"I'm excited too." Sloane blushed as one of Loch's tentacles wandered over his ass. He tried to subtly swat him away, clearing his throat loudly. "But research comes first! We need to find out what god is behind this and—"

"Yes, yes," Loch groaned. "Do boring research, solve the case, save the world, and *then* plan the wedding. I understand, my love."

"Let's get going." Sloane chuckled, unable to resist a smile when Loch pouted at him. "I promise you can watch *Hell's Kitchen* while I read all the boring stuff, okay?"

"Ah, this is exactly why I'm marrying you." Loch's forlorn expression faded away instantly. "You know me so well."

They bid farewell, everyone promising to make contact if anyone made headway. Sloane plopped down into the driver's seat and closed his eyes, focusing his magic and clapping to reunite the fallen door with the rest of the car. He snorted back laughter as Loch slid in next to him wearing the purple sunglasses last seen on Jay.

Loch playfully tipped them down to bat his eyes at Sloane. "You know I look fantastic."

"Gorgeous," Sloane agreed, still laughing as he cranked up the car. He was quiet on the drive home, lost in thought. Loch's tentacles in his lap were comforting, but he couldn't stop worrying.

They were working blindly, and the Silenced young man who had attacked them could be anywhere by now, readying to strike again.

"You're thinking," Loch declared once they were back in Sloane's apartment, studying him skeptically.

"Technically, I'm always thinking."

"Mmm, no. This is different. Your face gets these cute little creases in it when you're thinking especially hard."

"I'm…." Sloane searched for the right words. "I'm worried, Loch."

"About?" Loch asked calmly, bringing Sloane in for a hug.

"Everything?" Sloane laid his head against Loch's chest. "There are literally hundreds of gods. It could be almost anyone doing this, and that guy, that kid? He's out there too."

"You're worried that you're in danger?" Loch kissed Sloane's hair. "I'll protect you, my love."

"I'm worried about everyone," Sloane whispered. "The whole world is in danger. This is the second time a god has tried to destroy it! First it was your crazy brother trying to wake up your even more crazy father! And now we don't know what this one is trying to do, and, and, and—"

"He or she is kidnapping innocent Silenced people to make terrifying magic-defying weapons?" Loch helpfully supplied.

"Yes!" Sloane scowled. "Why… why aren't you upset? How can you be so freakin' calm about this?"

"Because I am certain of our victory. Just as I am certain that I love you and that you love me, I know we will not fail."

His anger deflating, Sloane gazed helplessly up at Loch. "I want… I want to believe that."

"Believe it," Loch urged. "Believe in our love. Even after all the stars fall down from the sky, our love is eternal." He pressed his lips against Sloane's neck, his teeth teasing beneath his jaw. "They'll tell stories about us, about our love and how we saved the world. Not once, but twice!"

"Mmm…. Loch…." Sloane gave himself over, his eyes closing as Loch expertly pulled his clothes away. A surge of heat was bubbling up fast between his legs in anticipation of what was to come. "But the energy…. Galgareth said it was godly…."

"You're still so tense," Loch chastised gently, kissing down Sloane's bare shoulder. "You need to relax."

"If the energy was godly and the source of the guy's power is the soul bound to him… oh fuck!" Sloane groaned as his ass got wet, Loch sliding a tentacle down his pants to tease between his cheeks.

"Let me take care of you, my sweet Starkiller." Loch pushed the tip of his tentacle inside his hole and fucked into him slowly.

"We have research… so much research to do!" Sloane's voice didn't sound very strong, even to his own ears, and he couldn't help a small moan that escaped when Loch licked his ear. "Fuck! Focus, Loch!"

"I am very focused!" Loch insisted, thrusting in deeper. "I have a particular interest that I'm very eager to research."

"Mmmph, in what?" Sloane gasped.

"So glad you asked," Loch chirped. "You see, it's in human anatomy, and I just know you'll be able to help me."

CHAPTER 5.

LOCH CARRIED Sloane right to bed, his probing tentacle still inside of him as he laid him out across it. Making their clothing vanish was definitely within Loch's power, but sometimes he seemed to enjoy divesting Sloane the old-fashioned way. He tugged at Sloane's pants and underwear, deftly pulling them down in one motion and sliding his hands up his long legs.

"Mmm, Loch," Sloane panted, groaning when the tentacle in his ass pushed deeper. The stretch was incredible, but there wasn't any pain. All he experienced was intense pressure and pleasure, the tentacle swelling inside his slick hole and making him gasp.

Loch didn't have the patience to take off his own clothes, and they melted right off his body into nothing. His mortal frame was gorgeous and marvelously sculpted, with thick scars curling over his shoulders and down his arms. The scars were his tentacles, hidden on his body in plain view. As they lifted off his skin, they regained their natural hue and turned a bluish gray color.

As Loch crawled over Sloane, his tentacles curled around him, and he pressed their lips together in a fierce kiss. "Mmm, my love…. You always feel so good, so hot, so perfect for me…."

"Loch!" Sloane tried to spread his legs to help open himself up and relieve some of the pressure, clinging to Loch's neck as they kissed. The kiss was sweet, wet, and he sucked on Loch's tongue as his tentacle started to pound into him.

Nothing could compare to making love with a god. The slick slide of Loch's tentacles holding him down and pushing his thighs even farther apart felt fantastic, and Sloane gave himself over to it completely. Just one of Loch's tentacles was better than any cock he'd ever had, and he knew Loch wouldn't stop there.

Loch was already reaching down with his other slitted tentacle, the tip gently probing around Sloane's hole. He nuzzled against Sloane's cheek, pleading, "May I, my love? May I fill you?"

"Fuck, yes!" Sloane answered immediately, grunting as Loch pushed his legs back. His knees were touching his chest and he was completely exposed, his face blazing red hot.

Loch was petting the undersides of his thighs, watching his tentacle moving in and out of Sloane with the utmost attention. The second tentacle pushed inside ever so slowly, and Loch's brow wrinkled in concentration. "Oh, there... there you go, my love."

Sloane's head fell back, his chest heaving as his body fought against the new intrusion. There was a brief lick of pain before Loch soothed it away with a thought, and he groaned as both tentacles began to fuck him. They moved as one monstrous cock, slamming into him deeper and deeper, pressing into his most intimate places that had Sloane's vision nearly whiting out.

He could feel his orgasm building up within his loins, hot and throbbing, and he greedily rocked his hips down to meet Loch's rough thrusts. He was so full, his body flooded with desire, and sweat was beading along his chest. He wrapped his hands around his knees, trying to pull his legs closer to himself and catch the perfect angle. "Fuck, Loch... mmm, come on, baby...!"

"Getting close?" Loch panted, both of his tentacles thickening in response. "Are you going to come for me, my sweet Starkiller?"

"Yes, yes, yes!" Sloane pleaded.

"Mmm, I'm close too," Loch warned, his breath picking up as the pace of his thrusting increased. "Oh, my love... you feel too good... I'm going to release soon!"

"Oh yes! Come on!" Sloane groaned eagerly. It was almost too much, on the border of pain and ecstasy, and the pressure was about to burst inside of him. He pulled Loch close, their chests flush against each other. He dragged his fingers through Loch's thick hair as he gasped, "Please! Make me come!"

"With pleasure," Loch breathed softly, sealing their lips together as his tentacles twitched and pumped their hot loads deep inside of Sloane's tight ass.

Sloane shouted, breaking the kiss and writhing as his insides swelled, so full that he ached. Loch's tentacles were still fucking him, the sounds slick and wet now with his copious come splashing out with every thrust. That extra heat was enough to bring Sloane to climax, his whole body going rigid for one perfect moment of heaven before melting into shuddering bliss as his cock shot off between them.

Loch's tentacles didn't stop, still pumping and twisting inside Sloane's body to drag his pleasure on. Even as Sloane's cock gave the last drop of come that it had to give, he was still riding the crest of a beautiful orgasm. Slowly, he began to come down, clinging to Loch's shoulders and sobbing, "Oh Gods… oh my God…. Loch… baby…."

Peppering Sloane's damp skin with little kisses, Loch soothed, "You do wonderfully, my love… you always take me so well."

Sloane made a low and happy sound in reply, his body thrumming blissfully from head to toe.

"Mmm, feeling better now?"

"Yes." Sloane leisurely stretched his back and his arms up above his head. He flopped limp against the sheets with a happy groan. "I really needed that."

"I know," Loch said smugly, his tentacles gently pulling out. He kept Sloane's legs pushed up, squeezing his cheeks and spreading them wide as he pushed his thumbs down into his gaping hole. "Mmmm, look at what a mess I made of you."

"Loch!" Sloane gasped as a fresh wave of heat lit up his face. Loch's thumbs were slipping inside of him, gently stretching his hole wide open. He could feel Loch's come leaking out of him and down the cleft of his ass.

"You're so beautiful when you're full of my seed, my love," Loch soothed. "I love watching it gush out of you…."

"Fuck, Loch," Sloane hissed, his core clenching from hearing such lewd talk. Even though he had just come, he could feel his cock flexing with new interest. "You're so freakin' nasty!"

"You love it," Loch taunted, withdrawing his thumbs and eagerly slinking back up for a kiss.

"Mmm, I do." Sloane let their lips press softly together, unhurried and sweet. "I love it… it just… mmm." Loch's tongue had slid into his mouth and silenced any possible complaints. "Mmmph…."

Loch gently unfolded Sloane's legs, and he guided them around his waist. They held each other tenderly, the promise of another round lingering, but neither was in any hurry.

Sloane relished the skin-on-skin contact and how every one of Loch's kisses made him feel absolutely adored. He had never loved anyone like this, and being loved so deeply in return was a gift he would cherish for the rest of his life.

It was Loch whose patience ran out first, grinding his hips forward with a needy whine. His giant tentacock was tucked between his legs, the massive head rubbing against Sloane's slick hole.

"Mmm, just can't get enough of me?" Sloane mumbled, drowsy from their first tryst and smiling dopily.

"Never," Loch swore passionately. He tilted his head. "Well, at least not for the first thousand years. After that? Meh."

Sloane lightly smacked Loch's arm as he laughed. "Oh, you jerk! You don't mean that!"

Loch snickered, his eyes holding nothing but adoration as he looked over Sloane beneath him. "No, I don't mean that, my love. Have I offended you?"

"Eh, tiny bit?" Sloane ran his tongue over his lips when the head of the tentacock breached him. It was even bigger than both of Loch's slitted cocks combined, ribbed down its shaft, with a thick knot about ten inches down from the silky head.

"Allow me to make it up to you." Loch rocked his hips in short thrusts to work himself in.

Sloane whined, his body stretched out already, and yet there was still resistance. His nails dug trenches up Loch's back with every massive inch as it pushed into him. Even with all of Loch's magic, there was a burn, and Sloane tried bringing up one of his legs to find a way to relieve the discomfort.

"Here," Loch offered, one of his slitted tentacles ghosting on Sloane's lips. It was still wet from busting its load earlier, glistening in the light.

Sloane opened his mouth, and he eagerly took the thick length and sucked. He finally relaxed, tasting the sweetness of Loch's divine seed, and the tentacock eased its way in. He groaned, the tentacle in his mouth thrusting into the back of his throat as the tentacock moved in his hole.

He loved being stuffed from both ends like this, and his legs fell apart as Loch fucked him harder. He sucked on the tentacle pushing into his mouth, his eyes damp with tears, and he struggled to breathe through it.

Sloane could hear every deliciously moist squelch as Loch's tentacock pounded into him, and there was intense pressure winding up in his balls. He could feel his own cock getting hard again. Loch's mouth was hot against his throat, rolling their bodies together as he kissed and sucked at his pulse point.

Loch's other slitted cock was on the move, wiggling between their stomachs and swiftly sucking down Sloane's cock. He sighed, breathless and deep, praising, "Mmm, your taste is irresistible, my love... I could feast on you for eons...."

Sloane moaned, his eyes fluttering open and peering through his tears up at Loch. He cried desperately, lost in the starry black pools that Loch's eyes had become, endless galaxies gazing back at him with such love that it made him burn deep inside.

Here they were with Sloane's body being stretched beyond its mortal limits of pleasure, and Loch, the immortal, was providing this insane euphoria and looking at him as if Sloane was the amazing one.

Sloane came with one tentacle greedily sucking away his come as the other busted in his mouth. He gulped, his pelvis thrusting up from the bed as he rode out his climax, caught between the tentacle still slurping at his cock and the huge tentacock slamming into him.

"Mmm, yes," Loch growled, sliding his arms beneath Sloane's shoulders and embracing him. "My beautiful mate... I'm going to make you come again... and again...."

No mortal man could make such a promise, but Loch was no mere mortal.

He was a god.

A surge of warmth rushed through Sloane's body, tingling from behind his eyes down to the tip of his cock. Speared on Loch's magnificent tentacock, he could feel another orgasm creeping over him, and it was like being enveloped in warm silk. The warm feeling wrapped around him, the pressure growing until he couldn't take another second.

"Azaethoth!" Sloane screamed, his hips curling off the bed as he climaxed again, the knot of Loch's tentacock swelling up inside of him. His orgasm dipped and crested before he began to fall, only to be lifted back again as Loch's load filled him.

"Mm, Sloane." Loch kissed along Sloane's jaw as his giant tentacock continued to leisurely thrust. "You're so beautiful, my dear Starkiller... I love you...."

"Love you," Sloane managed to croak, and he gasped as another rush of hot fluid flowed inside him. He moaned, letting his arms fall back against the bed. His muscles were heavy and numb, and he grinned dopily. "Mmmm, baby.... Azaethoth... that was—"

There was an old black woman with a big gray afro standing in the bedroom doorway, sweetly beaming at the pair of them.

"What the fuck!" Sloane screeched, digging his feet down into the bed and pushing away from Loch. He groaned at the empty sensation he was left with, and he tried to ignore the come gushing between his legs as he put up a shield. "Who are you! What are you doing here?"

Loch turned to stare, his tentacles melding back into his skin as he gasped, "Mother?"

"Oh, my young one!" The woman rushed over to give Loch a big hug. She didn't seem to even notice that he was naked or sweating from recent coitus, or perhaps she just didn't care.

"Mother!" Loch hugged her back and grinned. "It's so good to see you."

Sloane scrambled to pull the sheets over him for some modesty, smoothing back his damp hair in the hopes that he might look somewhat presentable. He was beyond mortified, still very aware of Loch's fluids leaking out of him while attempting to appear as a respectable future son-in-law.

"I've missed you," she said, petting Loch's hair and kissing his cheeks. "You look wonderful."

"I've missed you too!" Loch smiled over at Sloane. "This is my intended, Mother. This is Sloane Beaumont. He is the most beautiful creature in all the universe."

"Hi," Sloane said anxiously, trying to keep a sheet wrapped around his waist as he rose to greet the goddess. "Urilith, it's truly an honor."

"Please," she insisted, reaching out for Sloane's hand, "call me Mother." She leaned in to kiss his cheeks. "I'm so very happy my young one has finally found his mate."

"I'm very happy that it's me!" Sloane laughed anxiously. "And uh, how long exactly were you watching us…?"

"Oh, just for a moment! I didn't want to interrupt you!" Urilith clasped her hands together. "It was just so beautiful! I do so miss the fertility celebrations our worshippers used to hold in my honor!"

"It's okay!" Sloane adjusted the sheet around himself. "I know it's not, uh, as weird for you as it is for me."

"Sloane's a bit shy." Loch playfully nudged Urilith, "But he is an exceptionally bright mortal. Kind, passionate, and he's simply stolen my heart."

"I'm sure he's wonderful," Urilith said sweetly. "Now! What about this wedding? Have you set a date?"

"Uh," Sloane stammered. "No? We hadn't really... I mean, he just asked me last night! Things have been... eh... complicated."

"Is this about Tollmathan?" Urilith's expression saddened.

"Kinda?" Sloane said weakly, guilt clawing at his insides. He felt exposed, even more so because he was still naked. "I mean... it's... I'm sorry...."

It had been awkward enough having this talk with Galgareth, but this was Urilith, Tollmathan's mother.

Urilith's hands cradled the sides of Sloane's face, and her eyes turned into dark oceans full of stars. "I lost my son long before you took his life, little one. The dreaming turned his heart to hate, and when you woke him up, that hate only grew.

"I mourn the soul that used to write poetry, who composed entire sonnets about the pale moonlight during the solstices, but that child died long ago. Fear not, little one. All is well."

"I... I... thank you," Sloane managed to say. He shivered from the touch of Urilith's hands. Even without being directly exposed to her divine skin, he was overwhelmed with a feeling of love and comfort.

"Now," Urilith said with a brighter smile, "we must plan this wedding! Perhaps at the spring equinox?"

"Well, if you don't mind, there's sort of another problem that's a little more pressing." Sloane cringed and glanced at Loch for assistance. With his help, Sloane began to explain everything that had happened.

As he spoke, Loch chimed in occasionally to fill in the gaps while Sloane quickly got dressed. Loch remained shamelessly naked.

Urilith listened intently, and her brow creased with worry when Sloane finally finished. "And you don't know which god is behind this dastardly caper?"

"No," Sloane replied. "We have some of the blue goo as evidence, but we don't know who it belongs to. Whoever it was, they were with Tollmathan before, and they put those binding symbols on the Silenced man."

"Toll was always closest with his brothers," Urilith said. "Gronoch and Xhorlas."

"You really think it could be one of them?" Loch scoffed, visibly uncomfortable.

"Who else would want to destroy the world?" Urilith held out her hands, and they dropped down by her sides. "Your father's kingdom was denied to them when we went into the dreaming. I could feel their rage even as we slept, and I can think of no one else who would want to do such a thing."

"But why go to all the trouble of making these Silenced weapons?" Sloane asked. "Why aren't they trying to wake up Salgumel again?"

"Oh, I'm sure they are, but they will need an army to fight the other gods," Urilith replied. "Should Salgumel ever wake again, there would certainly be a war. The other gods would wake and try to stop him."

"They want an army to fight the gods," Sloane realized out loud. "That's... that's insane!"

"Whatever this magic is that they're using to create these Silenced weapons is powerful and dangerous," Urilith said gravely. "I don't know what kind of soul they've bound to that boy, but...."

"But?" Loch frowned. "What is it, Mother? Why do you look so troubled?"

"I have my suspicions," Urilith said, letting Loch usher her out to sit down on the couch. "The power you're describing, the use of so many binding symbols, the residue...?"

"Yes?"

"Shit." Sloane flinched as his phone rang, quickly fumbling around to find his discarded pants and pull out his phone. "Sorry!"

"What an enchanting little device," Urilith chirped, staring curiously at the phone.

It was Milo calling. Sloane answered quickly. "Hey, what's up?"

"Look, Gal and Lynnette made a breakthrough," Milo said excitedly. "They found a spell, a chant that will break soul bindings! You'd have to keep chanting it over and over again 'cause it only breaks one at a time, but it could work!"

"That's incredible!" Sloane switched the phone to speaker so Urilith and Loch could hear. "This is something we could use against the Silenced kid, right?"

"Yes!" Milo sounded positively giddy. "You'll have to chant it once per binding, but if that freak pops up again, we got somethin' for 'em."

"Thanks, Milo. Hey, how's Jay doing? Any sign of the Asra?"

"Sleeping Beauty? Oh, he's fine. And no, no weird cat people or anything like that."

"That's good," Sloane said, running his fingers through his hair and trying to straighten himself up so he didn't look like he'd just had a god bang his brains out.

"Everything's cool," Milo promised. "How are things going with you?"

"Fine!" Sloane smiled at Urilith. "Loch's mother is here. She got herself a body, and well, uh, she's very excited about planning the wedding."

"Oh, so very excited." Urilith laughed and hugged Loch tightly. "I'm just so happy for you both!"

"Aww, she sounds awesome!" Milo cleared his throat. "Don't suppose she knows anything about the you-know-what doing whatever?"

"It's okay," Sloane said. "She already knows. And she thinks it might be one of Loch's brothers."

"Holy crap, that's not good."

"No, it's not." Sloane grabbed a pair of pants to give to Loch, and he paused when he heard the front door open. He tucked the phone against his chest, looking to Urilith and Loch. "The freakin' door's open?"

"Oh! That's my fault!" Urilith said. "I was just so excited to see my son, and I broke the seals when I came in! I must have left it—"

"Where is the mortal?" a familiar voice demanded, the white-haired visage of the Silenced boy slipping inside as the door slammed behind him. "Tell me now."

"I might need you to text me that spell," Sloane hissed. "Right now!"

"Oh, it's *him*," Loch growled, stalking toward the boy. "I owe you a beating of mass-panic-inducing levels, little one."

"Hey! What's wrong? Who is Loch threatening?" Milo cried.

"Our Silenced friend is here and he's—" Sloane gasped as Loch was suddenly thrown through the window, naked and clutching his pants as his body shattered the glass and vanished from sight. "Loch!"

Whirling around to face the Silenced boy, Sloane tried to put up a shield, but he was too slow. The same energy that pushed Loch out the window came back and struck Sloane right in his chest.

He could see flashes of light, white and sterile rooms, needles and pain, oh, the pain was beyond agony. He heard a voice, the echo of an urgent whisper:

Alexander… it's all right… I'm here….

It was all gone in a blink, and Sloane's stomach dropped as he realized he was falling out of the window and down onto the street. "Oh fu—!"

CHAPTER 6.

"—UUUCCCK!" SLOANE was falling, twisting his body around and trying to brace himself. The alley between his apartment building and the next held nothing but an old dumpster and certain death from being splattered on the pavement.

"Sloane!" Loch shouted, his tentacles shooting out and catching him. He cradled him close. "Are you okay?"

"Fine, oh, just fine!" Sloane clung to Loch's neck, still stupidly grasping his phone for dear life. "Oh shit! Loch! That guy is up there with—"

"Ah, ffffffuck!"

Jerking his head up, Sloane saw the Silenced boy come flying out the same window he and Loch had fallen through. He smacked against the adjacent building, but he didn't fall. He floated there, suspended in the air and glaring furiously.

A giant mass of yellow tentacles came thrusting out of the busted window, clawing and swiping at him.

"Mother!" Loch scolded. "You're not supposed to abandon your vessel here! Get back in that body right now!"

Urilith roared, an inhuman and terrifying sound, her tentacles writhing.

"I don't care!" Loch fussed. "If I can't abandon my vessel, then you can't either! I swear, who's the parent here?"

"Alexander!" Sloane called up, remembering the name from the vision. "Stop this!"

Alexander flinched, and his attention was now focused on Sloane and Loch.

"That's your name, right?"

As he descended slowly, Sloane got a glimpse of the strange energy pulsing around the young man. It was holding him, wrapped around his waist and lowering him down until his feet touched the pavement.

It almost looked like….

"My name is not important," Alexander spat. "All you need to know is that I will stop at nothing to get the mortal. Now, where is he?"

"How did you find us?" Sloane countered. "A watchman's spell? Did you tag Loch with one when he grabbed you before?"

"Mortal. Now." Alexander's voice carried a strict warning.

"No," Sloane snapped, wiggling out of Loch's arms. "Is it Xhorlas making you do this? Gronoch?"

"Last chance." Alexander strolled toward them.

"Milo," Sloane hissed into the phone, "what's the spell to break the bindings?"

"Confractus… uh, uh, uh…." Milo was flustered, stammering quickly, "Vinculo! Confractus vinculo!"

Sloane eyed Alexander, raising his hand and focusing on the edge of a binding symbol he could see peeking out from the edge of his sleeve. He closed his eyes, concentrating, speaking the words inside his mind:

Confractus vinculo!

Nothing happened.

"Milo!" Sloane barked. "It didn't work!"

There was a screech of metal as the dumpster lifted up from the ground and came hurtling right at them. Loch grabbed Sloane and threw him out of the way, but it put him right in the path of the dumpster. It crashed into Loch and he went flying down the alley.

"Loch!" Sloane stumbled against the wall, throwing up a perception spell to see if he could catch the next attack. He could see the waves of energy more clearly now as they writhed around Alexander's body.

Wriggling….

Curling….

They were tentacles!

"Holy shit," Sloane gasped. He quickly summoned a massive shield of starlight. He made it into a wall, blocking off the alley to protect himself and Loch, coming up behind him. He put all of his strength into it, shouting, "Alexander! Stop this now!"

The invisible tentacles pounded against the shield, ineffective at first, but cracks began to show when Alexander raised his hands to direct them.

"It's a god!" Sloane clenched his teeth together as he struggled to maintain the shield. "The soul that's bound to him—it's a god!"

"It can't be," Loch whispered in horror, quickly adding his power to keep the shield up. "How?"

"I don't know!" Sloane looked all around for his cellphone, spying it a few feet away from where he'd hit the wall. "Loch, can you reach my phone?"

"Yes!" Loch reached with one of his tentacles, swiping the phone and bringing it back. "Here!"

"Milo!" Sloane frantically shouted into the speaker. "Are you still there?"

"I'm here! I'm here, dude!" Milo cried. "What's wrong?"

"The spell didn't work!"

"Oh, shit! Shit, shit, shitty shit shit!" The line was muffled for a moment, and then Milo cursed, "For fuck's sake, it's not my fault your A looks like an O! Okay, Sloane! Listen! It's confractus vincula! Vin-cooool-ah!"

Sloane grunted, struggling to concentrate as he ran the spell through his mind once more.

Alexander was right at the wall, raising his hand and rapping against it. "Knock, knock…." he taunted. "Gonna let me in?"

Confractus vincula!

Alexander's arm snapped back, and he stared in faint surprise at a fresh stream of blood running down his hand.

It worked!

Sloane cast the spell again and again, closing his eyes as he concentrated on sensing the binding symbols. He didn't have to see them now; he could feel each one and focused on breaking them all.

Alexander screamed in pain, the ghostly tentacles waving around him frantically and pounding against the shield. He had to drop down to one knee, and he snarled from the agony of his skin being torn apart. "This won't... stop me!"

"Want some more?" Sloane taunted, flicking his hand to break another symbol.

"Fuck you!" Alexander seethed. He spat up a mouthful of blood and nearly fell flat on his face. "I can't... I can't give up...."

No more! an angry voice bellowed. *You're killing him!*

"Huh?" Sloane looked all around, but he couldn't find where it was coming from. "Who is that?"

"Sloane!" Loch growled. "What's wrong? Why did you stop?"

"You don't hear that?"

"Huh?" Loch strained to listen. "Sloane, I don't hear anything!"

Alexander, the voice soothed, *please... we have to go... come on.*

"No!" Alexander cried weakly, coughing up another splatter of blood. "We can't... he has to tell us...."

"That!" Sloane huffed.

I love you too much to watch you die, the voice snarled, and a bright light glowed around Alexander. *We must go!*

"Hey, wait!" Sloane shouted. "Alexander—"

In a flash, the light became totally blinding, and Sloane had to look away. A big rush of turbulent air nearly pushed him over, and Loch hugged him tight to keep him standing. When he looked back, his shield was in pieces and Alexander was gone.

"Well, fuck," Sloane snorted.

"Are you okay?" Loch asked, feeling over Sloane's body. "Everything's still in its proper place?"

"Yes," Sloane promised, and he kissed his cheek. "I'm okay, really. But what about you? You got thrown out a window, and then he hit you with a freakin' dumpster!"

"Hmmph! I'm fine! My magical vitality as a god keeps this body in tip-top shape."

"Then why does your arm look like it's popped out of place?"

"Oh. Hold on." Loch grabbed the affected arm and gave it a twist, forcing it back into the socket with a loud crunch. "See? Good as new!"

"And your pants?"

"Oh, hmm… seem to have lost those."

"Ulgh." Sloane scrubbed his hands through his hair. "You really didn't hear that other voice? Not Alexander, but the other one? The one who said he loved him too much?"

"No?" Loch cocked his head. "I could hear that the Silenced one was talking to someone, but I didn't hear anything else."

"Weird." Sloane tensed when he heard someone coming around the corner. He relaxed when he saw it was Urilith, back in her human form and rushing up to them.

"My child!" Urilith was crying. "I'm so sorry! I tried to help, but I was too big to get out of the apartment!"

"It's okay, Mother." Loch embraced her and patted her back. "We have to be careful in this new world. Not many mortals would appreciate our beauty now—"

"Enough about that! The boy!" Urilith said urgently. "The soul bound to him? I think it's a god!"

"So do I!" Sloane agreed. "I could see tentacles. Those waves of energy that he kept hitting us with? They're these ghost tentacle things!"

"Where is he now?" she asked worriedly. "What happened? I was trying to get down the stairs to come help you, and I couldn't even get through the blasted window!"

"Galgareth and Lynnette found a spell that breaks the soul bindings," Sloane replied, "but something's wrong. The god that's attached to Alexander? I don't know how to explain it… it's… I don't think the god is his slave."

"How do you mean?" Urilith gasped. "What god could want to spend eternity bound to some mortal?"

"I heard this voice, the same one I heard the first time we fought Alexander, and he was pleading for him to stop. Said that he loved him too much to watch him die." Sloane threw up his hands. "And that's when they disappeared!"

"You think the god did this ritual... willingly?" Loch frowned.

"I don't know, but it's obvious he cares about him. Maybe they're both slaves to the god who put all of this mess together to begin with."

"Perhaps we should retire somewhere safe?" Urilith glanced up at the broken window. It magically repaired itself as she suggested, "Somewhere that this Silenced boy won't be able to find us?"

"Which reminds me." Sloane held up his hands for a perception spell and scanned over Loch. "I thought maybe he'd put a tracking spell on you, like a watchman's spell, but there's... huh, there's nothing."

"How did he find us, then?" Loch grumbled.

"I don't know," Sloane said "but at least we know the binding spell works if he decides to surprise us again."

"Have you concluded your mating for the time being?" Urilith asked politely. "I know I interrupted your coitus earlier, but perhaps—"

"Oh, uh, no! We're fine! Mating was so good, and we are definitely done for now!" Sloane rambled. "Definitely, absolutely done."

"Really?" Loch asked thoughtfully. "Because I could be persuaded to go again...."

"No!" Sloane argued. "Just let me go upstairs and grab my laptop, and you're putting pants on. Then we're going over to Lynnette's house to regroup." He approached the bloody spots on the ground where Alexander had been wounded, passing his hands over the drying fluids.

A few bubbles floated upward, encasing themselves in a thin layer of starlight and dropping into Sloane's hand.

"Souvenir?" Loch snorted.

"More evidence." Sloane tucked them away into his pocket. "Might come in handy later."

Once Sloane retrieved his laptop and made Loch get dressed, they all hustled out to his car to drive back to Lynnette's. She was more than happy to receive the Goddess of Fertility into her home, and all the gods enjoyed a small family reunion in the living room where Jay was still snoozing.

"Ah! To have two of my children in my arms again!" Urilith cheered, dragging Loch and Galgareth into a crushing group hug. "I can hardly believe it!"

"We've missed you too!" Galgareth couldn't stop smiling. "We haven't all been together like this in ages!"

"Not since the last winter solstice feast," Loch remarked. "Hmm, maybe a thousand years ago?"

"Has it really been that long?" Urilith gasped.

Sloane left them to their reminiscing, stepping into the kitchen to set up his laptop. He found Lynnette in the midst of cooking a great feast. "I'm guessing you aren't going back to work?"

"Not when I have three gods to cook for!" Lynnette declared. "This is the chance of a lifetime! Oh, I bet Lochlain and Robert are gonna lose their crap when they hear about this!"

"They'll have their chance." Sloane chuckled, sitting down at the kitchen table and booting up his laptop. "Urilith and Galgareth will be around for the wedding we still have to plan… if we can get this case figured out first."

"Lemme guess," Lynnette teased, dropping some herbs into a bubbling pot and stirring the mixture. "Silenced guy kicked your ass again?"

"Something like that. Alexander is still set on getting Jay, but I'm starting to get the idea that he isn't doing this of his own free will."

"Alexander?"

"That's his name. I know it sounds nuts, but I hear things when I'm around him. It happened again when he hit me earlier. I saw, I don't know, I guess they were memories."

Pausing her stirring, Lynnette turned to eye Sloane curiously. "Memories?"

"Bad memories," Sloane said, trying to recall the frantic images. "He was in some room with white walls, looked like a hospital. And there were these needles, stabbing him constantly... it may be how they made the marks."

"Gross."

"Yeah. I want to try to reach out to him, but I don't even know where to start. The spell to break the bindings was working, maybe too well, but then he just disappeared again."

"Well, what are you gonna do now?" Lynnette nodded at the laptop.

"Still gonna try to find a pattern with all the missing Silenced people. If I can figure out how they're being chosen, maybe we can catch Alexander in the act."

"You don't think he's gonna keep coming after Jay?"

"Maybe. He might eventually give up and move on to an easier target. You know, one that isn't being guarded by a bunch of old gods."

"Unless there is just something super special about Jay that they want," Lynnette mused, licking her spoon.

"That's what I need to find out."

"Hey, guys!" Milo announced, bustling into the kitchen with his arms full of groceries. "Holy crap, our house is turning into a freakin' immortal convention!"

"Hey, babe!" Lynnette greeted. "Just drop those off on the table."

"I got everything you asked for," Milo said, obediently setting the bags down next to Sloane's laptop. "Even the goat cheese curd!" He paused, adding quietly, "But it's the store brand...."

There was a loud thwack as Lynnette smacked the counter with her spoon, her spine going rigid and her jaw clenching.

Milo's eyes went wide and the air tensed instantly.

"Store brand is fine," Lynnette said with a deep sigh, slowly relaxing and picking up her spoon again.

"I can totally go back," Milo offered, approaching her side now that the fear of being smacked with a spoon had passed.

"This is fine. Thank you, baby doll." Lynnette rewarded Milo with a kiss on his cheek before returning to the stove to check on the food.

"So! Any luck?" Milo asked.

"With?" Sloane said dryly.

"Well, anything!"

"I've just started." Sloane pulled up the city police department's website. "I'll let you know as soon as I do!"

"Good luck, dude!" Milo patted Sloane's shoulder. "If you need any help, just holler!"

Sloane found the missing persons section on the police department's webpage and began to compile a list of everyone missing who was also Silenced.

From there, he searched missing persons in the state and then all the neighboring states. The list was growing fast, and he still couldn't see a pattern emerging. He kept going, tuning out the noise of Lynnette's exuberant cooking and Milo nervously fussing over their godly guests.

He declined to join them when it was time to eat, far too focused on his research. There had to be a commonality between all the missing people, and Sloane was determined to find it.

By the time Lynnette was cleaning up the dining room from her grand feast, Sloane had completely lost track of how many hours had gone by.

"Still at it?" Loch asked, kneeling beside him with a fond smile.

"Yeah," Sloane said, finally taking a break and stretching his arms. It was dark outside, and he'd barely noticed. He was stiff from sitting in the same position for so long. "Crap, what time is it?"

"Time for you to pay attention to me." Loch took Sloane's hands and pulled him up to his feet. "You've been ignoring me for hours, and I simply won't have it."

"I've been working." Sloane lazily draped his arms around Loch's shoulders. He kissed Loch's pouting lips, teasing, "Aww, I'm so very sorry for offending the mighty god of thieves."

"As you should be," Loch fussed.

"I'm sure I can think of a way to make amends," Sloane offered, leaning in for another kiss.

"Mmm," Loch hummed pleasurably. "So can I. Several in fact, and none of them involve clothing."

"Oh? Tell me more."

"Me, you, a tub of ice cream, and a new episode of *Hell's Kitchen*," Loch replied with a salacious eyebrow waggle.

"That sounds amazing."

"The contestants have to taste test all different types of meat on this episode."

"All different types, huh?" Sloane grinned, loving how excited Loch was. "Mmm, that sounds really great. Probably make them try to identify alligator or ostrich or… huh." He stopped, the gears in his head slowly turning. "Types."

"Yes?" Loch cocked his head. "Different types. As in, not the same."

"Wait…. Holy crap! That's it!" Sloane exclaimed, jerking out of Loch's arms and scrambling for the laptop. "Loch, you're a genius!"

"Well, obviously." Loch paused for a moment. "And I'm a genius in this particular instance because…?"

"Type! Blood type!" Sloane typed as fast as he could, rapidly explaining, "All the Silenced people who were reported missing have the same blood type!"

Milo poked his head into the kitchen, calling out, "You guys okay?"

"I'm a genius!" Loch called back happily.

"The missing Silenced people all have the same kind of blood!" Sloane brought up the list of names he'd compiled and pointed. "They're all AB negative."

"No shit?" Milo came over to look and scratched his head. "Well, I'll be damned. What about Jay and our Silenced buddy?"

"According to his donor card from the Hazel Medical Research Institute, Jay is also AB negative," Loch said, holding up a card he'd just pulled out of a slim wallet. "Hmm, or it could be a plus sign. Whoever wrote this has atrocious penmanship."

"You stole his wallet?" Sloane snatched the wallet away.

"Yes, but it wasn't much fun."

"Yeah, stealing from a man who's been put to sleep by a crazy cat person isn't very sporting!" Sloane griped, looking over the donor card.

"Well, this pretty much confirms your theory, right?" Milo asked.

"I would need to test their blood to be sure." Sloane reached into his pocket to show Milo the samples he'd taken earlier. "This is Alexander's, and I can get some from Jay to confirm what his card says." He smiled innocently, saying, "Now, if only we knew someone who had access to laboratory equipment…."

"Sloane," Milo warned.

"It's just a little type-and-screen test," Sloane pleaded.

"Oh no!" Milo turned to flee the kitchen.

"Oh yes!" Sloane sprang up to his feet and followed him into the living room.

Urilith and Galgareth were sitting on the couch with Jay's unconscious body stretched out over their laps, Urilith mindlessly petting his hair. Lynnette was perched on a nearby armchair, all of them sipping wine and chatting.

The conversation came to a halt as Milo came running in with Sloane and Loch hot on his heels.

"Oh my stars!" Urilith blinked in surprise. "What is going on?"

"Come back here, Milo!" Sloane yelled, trying to corner him between the couch and the wall. "All the times I helped you out! Every time I saved your butt at work!"

"This is exactly what you got fired for, dude!" Milo ran around the other side, scrambling to stay out of Sloane's reach. "You can't be serious right now!"

They circled each other like wild animals, Sloane keeping Milo trapped behind the sofa with nowhere to go. Every time Milo tried to escape from one side or the other, Sloane was there to meet him.

"Look," Sloane pleaded, "I just need one little tiny test! Okay, maybe two to make sure Jay's blood type on his donor card is correct because we can't read it, but I swear that's it!"

"Dude!" Milo argued. "Not only could I lose my job, but did you forget that we got some crazy Alexander guy out there looking for Jay?"

"So?"

"How the hell do you think he's looking for him? There's no tracking spell on Jay, so he's probably trying to divine his location! Once we take his blood outside of these wards, it'll fuckin' ping! Blood that you want me to carry into the damn police station!"

"Come on!" Sloane argued. "Divining doesn't always work anyway, and the signal from a little tiny bit of blood will be really weak! Isn't Jay your friend?"

"We're not *that* friendly! I could get into so much trouble! And that's only if I survive!"

"Oh?" Loch asked excitedly as he hovered behind Sloane. "Is this illegal?"

"Definitely," Sloane replied with a grin. "Very illegal."

"That's it!" Loch confirmed. "We're doing it. I'm a trickster god, and it is my desire to partake in illegal mischief."

"Oh, come on!" Milo whined helplessly. "You can't play the god card on me!"

"What illegal shenanigans are you guys getting into?" Lynnette reached for the wine bottle to refill her glass.

Urilith shook her head, a yellow tentacle reaching out to still her hand.

"I need Milo to run one teeny, tiny little test on Alexander and Jay's blood to confirm my theory," Sloane explained. "There is a very small risk of Alexander coming after us, but we'll be in and out of the lab before anyone even notices!"

"This sounds like fun!" Urilith exclaimed, patting Lynnette's arm and turning her attention to Sloane. "May I accompany you?"

"Like, like for protection?" Milo perked up.

"Of course, Mother," Loch said sweetly. "It'll be a field trip! Mortals take those to places of education to stimulate their minds when they're young."

"Okay, it's not that I don't love the idea of having an epic godly entourage to protect my precious, vulnerable mortal body," Milo said, "but two gods? Really? You know you guys kinda... stand out."

"Come here, fuzzy one," Galgareth said, beckoning for Milo to lean over the couch. "If you're so worried...."

Milo tilted his head in, cautious but obedient.

One of Galgareth's tentacles unraveled from her arm, reaching out and bopping Milo right in the middle of his forehead.

"Ow!" Milo cringed. "What was that?"

"My blessing!" Galgareth said cheerfully. "I'm a goddess of serendipity! Happy accidents! Trust me, you'll all be fine!"

"Right!" Milo was miserable. "Your blessing is gonna help me sneak two gods and a formerly terminated employee into one of the most highly secured areas of the department while they try to protect me from a Silenced dude with the power of another god who might try to kill us, all while I'm carrying a sample of said Silenced dude's blood and the guy he's trying to kidnap to test. What could possibly go wrong?"

"Sweetie pie?" Lynnette cooed, her voice strained with obvious impatience.

"Yes?" Milo blinked owlishly.

"Trust in the gods."

CHAPTER 7.

TRYING TO coordinate sleeping arrangements with three old gods, three witches, and one sleeping Silenced mortal in a very small house was challenging, to say the least.

Lynnette and Milo tried to give Urilith their bedroom, but she declined the generous invitation. She opted to stay in the guest bedroom with Galgareth and share a small futon. After all, she said, neither of them really needed to sleep, and they were going to stay up talking.

That left Sloane, Loch, and Jay.

The couch pulled out into a full-size mattress, and Loch's offer for all of them to snuggle together wasn't sitting well with Sloane. The obvious awkwardness of Jay's unconscious body in the mix was just too damn weird.

"What if we made a little blanket nest for him?" Loch suggested, gesturing to the rug.

"It seems mean to just dump him on the floor." Sloane frowned. "I really want to sleep in our own bed, but I don't think it's safe to go home right now."

"Well, what if we take a little trip?" Loch left Jay on the couch and took Sloane's hand. "Somewhere… else? Somewhere special?"

"Where?" Sloane asked suspiciously.

"Do you trust me?"

"Eh. Most of the time."

"Close your eyes."

Sloane groaned dramatically but closed his eyes, a smile tugging at the corner of his mouth. He suddenly felt as if he was falling, squeezing Loch's hand and hanging on tight. The world spun, his head got light, and a faint breeze moved over his body.

The vertigo departed, and his feet were back on solid ground, his eyes quickly opening to find they were now standing in a lush garden. It was in full bloom, all the flowers colorful and fragrant, and the air was cool. Despite the late hour, there was a blueish glow that illuminated the sky and cast everything in a dreamlike hue.

"Where are we?" Sloane looked all around in awe. "Is this another one of your little god hideouts?"

"Mm-hm." Loch walked through the garden, leading Sloane alongside him. "There used to be hundreds of places like this, you know. Little bits of paradise hidden between our worlds for gods and mortals to play in."

"Like that waterfall made out of wine?" Sloane chuckled, recalling their adventures there quite fondly. Since the conclusion of their first case, Loch would often whisk Sloane away and show off these secret places. It was usually—no, always—to entice Sloane into having sex with him. "Oh! Or how about the old temple with all the erotic paintings? That place was fun."

"Exactly so." Loch laughed, parting some bushes and ushering Sloane forward.

Sloane stepped through, but he stopped short when he saw a large bed in the middle of a field of luminous flowers. It was surrounded by tall trees whose leaves formed a canopy above, the branches draped with strings of glowing blue orbs.

The flowers seemed to shift and light up at Sloane's presence, and he swore that the bed looked happy to see them.

"Loch," Sloane gasped. "It's… it's beautiful!"

"Do you really like it?" Loch asked eagerly, taking Sloane's hand and kissing his wrist. "I was going to give it to you as a surprise…."

"Give it to me?"

"As a wedding present." Loch smiled shyly. "Your very own little world. I can teach you a spell that'll bring you here whenever you'd like."

"Oh, Loch! I love it! Thank you!" Sloane hugged Loch's neck and kissed him sweetly. "Thank you so much. It's gorgeous. It's just... I don't even have the words."

Loch's eyes turned dark, sparkling with stars as he swung Sloane up into his arms. "Of course, my beautiful Starkiller. I would give you a thousand worlds just like this one to see you smile."

"Just one is more than enough!" Sloane promised.

The flowers turned and moved toward them as Loch carried him to the bed. The sheets were soft as silk, the pillow perfectly fluffed, and it was big enough to host at least a dozen sleepers.

Sloane stretched out across it, groaning happily. "Oh, this is the most comfortable bed ever! Mmm...." He suddenly lifted his head, narrowing his eyes and accusing, "Wait, did you guys have weird orgies here? Is that why the bed is so freakin' big?"

"Probably," Loch replied, lying down beside him and whisking their clothes away with a thought. "I can't say that I ever participated in any orgies here, but I did change the sheets." He winked. "Just for you, my love."

"You're so thoughtful." Sloane snuggled close and pressed their bare bodies together. He traced the line of Loch's tentacles as they unfurled from his arms to wrap around him. "Thank you. Really. This is amazing."

"I love you," Loch said, his eyes still dark and sparkling. His tentacles glided down Sloane's body, a slitted one rubbing between his cheeks. "Mm, now I have to think of something else to give you as a wedding present."

"No, you don't." Sloane's breath hitched as the tip of the thick tentacle pressed against his hole. His face was getting hot, and the warmth quickly traveled south, his cock growing hard between them. "Mmmph, I don't have anything for you yet, and I don't think I'm ever going to top a private little world as a gift."

"You've already given me everything I could possibly want," Loch promised, some of his smaller tentacles curling around Sloane's thighs.

"There has to be something." Sloane gasped as Loch rolled him onto his back. He could feel himself getting wet, and his pulse climbed as the tentacle at his ass pushed inside of him.

"Only you," Loch said, bowing his head down for a soft kiss. "All I want is you."

Sloane moaned, the kiss lingering as the tentacle slowly thrusted. It was so impossibly thick, throbbing as it pushed farther into his body. His cock was aching, leaking against his stomach and flexing when the tentacle curled deep within. "Oh, fu... oh, Loch...."

Loch kept Sloane's legs firmly parted, kissing along his chest and beneath his chin, murmuring, "My love... tell me what you need."

"More," Sloane pleaded, desperately raking his fingers up into Loch's hair. "Please, I just, I just need more... by all the fuckin' gods, I can't believe what you do to me... it feels so damn good!"

The second of Loch's slitted tentacles moved to join the first, swirling around in the slick lubricant before slipping inside. Sloane cried out pleasurably, every nerve ending firing off from an overload of sensation. He slid a hand down over his stomach, and he could *feel* Loch's tentacles moving there, and he groaned from the heavy ache of being so full.

Sloane rolled his hips down for another explosion of bliss, gritting his teeth as he fought to keep going. It was beyond ecstasy, somewhere between too much and not enough, meeting Loch for every thrust. His cock had softened from the intensity, but he was still so unbelievably turned on.

Loch caught Sloane's mouth in a passionate kiss, his teeth nipping at his lip as he warned, "I'm going to come, Sloane... I can't... mm, you feel too perfect, my love."

"Come on, come on," Sloane urged, gasping as Loch's tentacles slammed into him with more force. They were swelling with every thrust, hitting the same tender spots over and over again until Sloane couldn't stand it. "Loch! I'm, I'm—"

"Come with me," Loch growled, and his shoulders trembled as he hit his climax. "Yesss, come with me, my sweet Starkiller!"

The flood of hot come made Sloane scream, every muscle tensing up as he was pushed right to the very edge of climax. He gritted his teeth, zeroing in on the pulsing sensation inside of him, and the next wave shoved him right into oblivion. "Ohhh, Azaethoth!"

His half-hard cock shot all over his stomach, and he collapsed against the bed as Loch's tentacles kept on fucking him. The shivers of his orgasm went on for several moments, strung out by every twisting thrust in his sensitive hole. He sobbed loudly as another impossible wave of pleasure came over him and screamed as he came again.

Loch's tentacles pushed as deeply as they could go, leaving him completely stuffed. Sloane had to move, had to grind down against him to chase the perfect feeling of being so full that he ached.

"I love you," Loch whispered again, panting and smiling down at him. "I love you so much."

"I love you," Sloane whimpered, his hips still rutting down on Loch's thick tentacles. His body was heavy, and he was absolutely exhausted. "Mmmph... damn, Loch."

Loch cuddled up to Sloane's side, petting his chest and grinning smugly. "Ah yes, I know. I bring you physical pleasures that your mortal mind can barely comprehend."

"Definitely." Sloane laughed and kissed Loch's hair. He gasped as Loch withdrew his tentacles, and he stretched his aching body with a low groan. "Wow."

"Do you require more of my seed, my love?"

"I'm so good." Sloane grinned wide. He knew that monstrous tentacock was ready and willing, but he was already quite satisfied. "My mortal mind has definitely been pleasured beyond comprehension."

"Now we cuddle?"

"Absolutely." Sloane hugged Loch, and he smiled as his tentacles curled all around him. He loved when Loch held him like this, and there was nowhere else in the whole world that he felt so safe and loved. "Mmm, we're sleeping here, right?"

"Unless you want to share the couch with Jay?"

"Uh, no." Sloane scrunched up his nose. "We really need to find that damn Asra and wake him back up! How serious is the threat of war if you go to Xenon?"

"Pretty explicit. The Asra are not very fond of us."

"The rebellion was sort of a clue. Well, shit. I guess we just wait and keep Jay at Lynnette's. The wards there are safe...." He looked around for a moment, asking, "Wait, why don't we bring Jay here?"

"I thought you didn't want to share with him. You really need to make up your mind."

"No, not right now! I mean tomorrow!" Sloane playfully poked Loch's hip. "Only gods can get into these places, right? Forgotten by time and all that?"

"Unless they're a very special mortal who happens to have a god who's madly in love with them and teaches them the spell," Loch replied cheerfully. "It's perfect."

"No, not perfect!" Sloane corrected. "You do realize what you just said also describes Alexander and the god he's bound to?"

"Ah!" Loch held up his hand. "While Alexander and his little godly beau may be able to travel to these worlds, they would need to have the exact coordinates to come here specifically."

"And these are pretty much infinite, right?"

"Yes. It would be like trying to find a needle in a sandwichstack."

"You mean a haystack."

"Why would you stack hay?" Loch wondered out loud. "That's just silly."

"Why would you stack sandwiches?" Sloane countered with a smirk.

"To create a tower of delicious sandwiches for visual pleasure and later consumption, obviously."

"Right, anyway." Sloane did his best not to laugh. "We'll bring Jay here before we go to the department. And Loch?"

"Yes, my love?"

"Can you… try to behave tomorrow?"

"As if I've ever given you any reason to expect otherwise!" Loch scoffed.

"Right," Sloane groaned. "It's not like you threatened to turn the mailman inside out—"

"I told you what he did to my catalogues!"

"Or when you tried to steal a stop sign, or that time you tried to attack the guy at the mall."

"First of all," Loch huffed, "I did not *try* to steal anything. I very successfully stole that stop sign, and you made me put it back. And that man at the mall sprayed me with poison!"

"It was cologne! He was trying to sell you cologne!" Sloane took Loch's hand, pleading, "Can you please try? For me?"

"Yes," Loch conceded, and he kissed Sloane sweetly to seal his promise. "For you, my love, I will be on my best behavior… however…."

"What?" Sloane frowned.

"I can make no promises for my mother."

AFTER BRINGING Jay to the garden the next morning and taking a small sample of his blood, Sloane and Loch returned to Lynnette's to meet up with Urilith and Milo. The drive over to the precinct was eerily familiar to Sloane, and it made him remember all too well when he used to make this trip every day.

He had no regrets about losing his job, having been fired for repeatedly abusing the police department's resources to research his parents' murder case. After all, he reasoned, if he hadn't been fired and took up a career as a private investigator, he may have never met Loch.

The thought made him smile as he pulled into the parking lot behind Milo and found a space in the visitors' section.

"Okay, now listen very carefully," Milo said as they all marched together toward the rear staff entrance. "I want you guys to stay close. Like super close. I want you to know what kinda deodorant I'm using. And if anyone asks, it's Bring A Former Coworker To Work Day, and uh…." He glanced at Urilith. "You're my new therapist!"

"What about me?" Loch asked eagerly.

"You're my… eh… manicurist?" Milo groaned. "Fuck! This is never gonna work! We're gonna get caught, and then we're gonna get murdered!"

"It'll be fine, Milo." Sloane patted his shoulder reassuringly. "We'll be in and out so fast, no one will even notice that we're here, and we'll destroy the blood the second we're done."

"This is all so exciting!" Urilith gushed, taking Loch's arm. "This is where mortals bring their criminals?"

"Not exactly." Sloane chuckled. "This is where the police officers work and do their research to find the criminals."

"With the assistance of sexy and talented magical forensic experts such as myself," Milo added, swiping his ID badge at the door. He cautiously ushered everyone inside, warning, "Okay, to get to the lab—"

"Down the hallway by the break room, make the next right," Sloane recalled.

"Yeah, and try to get there with no one questioning my new posse."

"This will be fun!" Urilith cheered.

Milo did not look convinced, his whole body tense as he tried to walk as quickly as possible with the merry trio trailing behind him. He saw an officer coming up the hallway toward them and immediately cringed.

The officer paused as if to say something, but his phone rang and he turned away to answer it.

Milo scooted faster still, breezing by the break room because everyone was singing "Happy Birthday" and fussing over a big cake.

As they made the final turn to the lab, Milo nearly smacked into a large pale redhead and a handsome black man, squeaking in terror, "He's just my manicurist! Please don't kill me!"

"What the hell, Milo?" the redhead scoffed, eyeing him suspiciously and glancing over the others with a deep frown. He recognized Sloane, blinking as he asked cautiously, "Sloane Beaumont? Is that you?"

"Uh, yeah! Hey, Chase!" Sloane grinned and reached out to shake his hand. "How's things?"

Detective Elwood Q. Chase—Sloane remembered him well. A bit of a slob and a smartass, but a good man. He didn't know the other man, but he was glaring at Sloane as if he was a speck of mud on his shoe.

"All visitors have to sign in at the front desk and wear visible passes on their person," the man said sternly. "You are aware of the department's policy, are you not, Mr. Evans?"

"Oh, so very, very aware, sir," Milo stuttered.

"This charming little muffin with the stick up his ass is my partner, Detective Merrick," Chase said with a strained smile. "Don't think he was around before you got the can."

"Yeah, I think I'd remember," Sloane said, certain that Merrick's steely blue eyes were burning a hole into his soul. "Nice to meet you."

"There is also a limit on two visitors per employee," Merrick went on, ignoring Sloane and turning his harsh gaze on Milo. "Three is more than two, Mr. Evans."

"I'm not a visitor, I'm a therapist!" Urilith announced, and she pouted at Merrick. "Perhaps you need a healer? A physician of some sort?"

"Excuse me?"

"To see about the stick in your ass," Urilith replied innocently. "It must be causing you great pain… or does your face always look like that?"

Merrick was visibly boiling, and Loch cackled, "Oh, nice one, Mother!"

"Hey, down, boy," Chase scolded, smacking Merrick's arm lightly. He gave Milo and Sloane a pleading look. "Look, whatever it is you're fuckin' doin'… just be done with it by the time we're all done eating cake, okay?"

"Can do!" Milo exclaimed, zipping by the detectives and swiping his ID card to open the laboratory door. "Come on, guys!"

"But there's cake." Loch gazed down the hallway longingly. "I like cake."

"We can have cake later!" Sloane hissed, pushing Loch through the door. "Bye, Chase! Bye, Detective Merrick!"

"This is extremely unorthodox and a blatant violation of our department policies," Merrick snarled at Chase as he dragged him to the break room.

"You're blatantly violating my fuckin' patience," Chase snapped back. "If I miss a piece of fuckin' birthday cake because you were running your damn mouth, I swear…."

Sloane shut the lab door with a big sigh of relief.

"That went much better than I thought it would," Milo confessed. "Like, way better. I'm still alive, and no one's been arrested."

"You carry Galgareth's blessing," Urilith reminded him with a kind smile. "She's a goddess of serendipity. Happy accidents, you know."

"Oh. Right."

"We should do this before our luck runs out." Sloane handed Milo the vials of Alexander's and Jay's blood. "Let's hurry the hell up and get out of here."

"You got it." Milo slipped on a pair of gloves and opened the vials. He grabbed a pipette, taking some of the blood and squirting each sample into a test tube. To that, he added another mixture and stirred it up inside the tubes.

"What's he doing?" Loch asked loudly. "Why is the tube turning colors?"

"He's testing the blood," Sloane replied. "In a moment, he'll be able to run them through the computer and read what type they are."

"Ah."

"It'll only take a minute." Milo sat at the computer terminal and booted it up.

Loch was eyeing another rack of test tubes, and when Sloane glared at him, he said innocently, "I was only looking."

"Your tentacles are showing," Sloane noted.

Holding up his hands and sliding his tentacles back into hiding, Loch protested, "I'm just excited!"

"Ding, ding," Milo said, clicking something on the computer screen. "Here's something to really get excited about. We have a winner! Both Jay and Alexander are definitely AB negative!"

"I was right." Sloane wasn't smiling.

"What's wrong?" Loch asked. "You don't look happy."

"Yes, I've confirmed that all the missing Silenced people, including Alexander, have the same blood type. But this still doesn't give us any direction as to what god is behind this or anywhere else to go."

"Oh, but wait," Milo declared. "We haven't seen what's behind door number two!"

Loch looked around suspiciously, his tentacles whipping back out as he hissed, "There is only one door! What kind of witchcraft do you speak of?"

"It's just an expression," Sloane soothed, grabbing one of Loch's spiraling tentacles and squeezing. "It's okay. Milo, what's up?"

"Familial match," Milo replied quickly. "There's a match in the system, okay? Someone related to Alexander did a bad-bad and their DNA is in the system!"

"Who?" Sloane pressed.

Keys clicked rapidly, and Milo replied, "Just wait a second! I'm freakin' looking! Whew, everyone just hang on to their butts and respective god parts!"

Loch retreated to the corner of the lab and pouted. He crossed his arms, his tentacles slipping back out of sight as he spat, "Fine."

Sloane gave him an appreciative smile, turning back to Milo. "Okay. So, the match, what do you have?"

"Milton Ward," Milo said, reading out loud. "Got popped for an assault, but the charges were dropped… and oh… oh no. He and his wife, Dianne, were both murdered seven years ago. Ouch."

"Found at home after a neighbor called for a welfare check," Sloane read, picking up where Milo had stopped. "Autopsy revealed single stab wounds to the heart, no weapon recovered, no witnesses, no evidence except…." His eyes widened. "A blue residue of unknown origin."

"The goo," Milo whispered excitedly. "Holy shit."

"The Wards' son… oh fuck. Their son, Landon Ward, aged seventeen, was never found." Sloane took the mouse from Milo, frantically clicking over to the next page of the file. "Do you think it could be…?"

There was a family photograph of the Wards posing in front of a large oak tree in a park. There was a young boy standing between them, and even though his hair was brown, Sloane recognized him immediately:

"Alexander."

"That's him?" Milo asked. "That shrimp is the crazy powerful god guy?"

"Yes, that's totally him… wait." Sloane looked around worriedly. "Why are we an immortal short? Where did Urilith go?"

"Oh, she wanted cake," Loch said casually. "I told her to bring me back some too."

"You *what*?"

CHAPTER 8.

"WHY DID you tell your mother to go get cake in the middle"—Sloane raised his voice—"of a fucking police station!"

"Because she wanted cake!" Loch replied, hopelessly confused. "You don't just refuse a goddess cake!"

"I'm sure she's fine!" Milo said anxiously. "Can we get back to the mysterious god of blue goo who probably murdered home-guy's parents and kidnapped him?"

"Unless Alexander is totally in on the deal," Loch suggested in a conspiratorial whisper. "Maybe he's the one who killed his parents and summoned the god after he whacked 'em!"

Sloane stared.

"What? It was just a thought!" Loch protested, adding sheepishly, "I may have been watching some mafia films recently. There's this really spicy one about a man named Roderick who has a really big—"

"Focus!" Sloane urged. "We have to go get your mother before she does something!" He looked back at Milo desperately. "Is there anything else in the Wards' case file that might help us?"

"Uh." Milo whirled back around to click through the various pages, shaking his head. "The case is frozen cold. The Wards didn't have any known enemies. They were both Lucian, Milton was registered as Silenced, uhhh… even the assault didn't turn up anything. Just some drunk fight from his college days."

"What did they do for a living?" Sloane pressed. "There has to be something."

"Boring. They were both doctors, hematologists who worked for…. Huh." Milo turned to look at Sloane, his brows quirked. "Hazel Medical Research."

"That's where Jay's donor card was from!" Sloane grinned triumphantly and snapped his fingers. "How much you wanna bet all the other missing Silenced people donated blood or plasma through Hazel?"

"Look, I can run the list for you," Milo said earnestly. "Just email it to me. Now, can you please destroy all of this blood and go see what Urilith is doing before I get fired and or murdered?"

Sloane disintegrated the blood samples with a snap and gave Milo a quick hug, promising, "There! Your precious mortal body is safe! Thank you so much! You're the best!"

"I know. Now go!"

"Farewell, dear mortal," Loch called out. "Thank you for your assistance in our investigation."

"It's always a pleasure, your godliness," Milo said, bowing his head respectfully.

Sloane took Loch's arm and hastily exited the lab, jogging back down to the break room. His heart thudded with dread when he saw there was quite the crowd.

"Mmm, guess everyone wanted cake," Loch observed. "Hope there's still some left."

"Come on." Sloane urged him through the cluster of people to see what was going on.

Detective Chase waved, munching on a highly coveted piece of birthday cake. Detective Merrick was sitting at the small table and totally enraptured by Urilith, who was perched across from him and gently petting his hand.

"And you see," she was soothing, "that's why you're so unhappy. You're looking for perfection, and you've set your standards so high that no one will ever be able to reach them."

"I am expecting too much?" Merrick asked.

"Yes," she said. "You need to accept that something not perfect could actually be perfect for you. Stop creating excuses for every little thing and be with the person who makes you happy. Otherwise you'll be alone for the rest of eternity."

Merrick looked as if he was about to cry.

"Hey," Chase said cheerfully, "your therapist sure is a hell of a lady. She got Rico and Bonnie over in dispatch back together, Ed finally asked out Robin, and she just figured out why Merrick is single. She's great!"

"In my younger days, I was a love goddess," Urilith said with a bashful shrug.

The cluster of police officers all chuckled at that, and Chase chimed in, "Shit! Me too, sister!"

"Love goddess?" Merrick looked skeptical. "Oh really?"

"She means she used to be a relationship therapist," Sloane interjected.

"Did you save me any cake?" Loch asked hopefully.

"Of course!" Urilith said, offering Loch a small slice. "What kind of mother do you think I am?"

"We should probably get going," Sloane said with a big smile. "Uhm, come along, Mrs. Love Goddess."

There was a wave of disappointed booing, and Chase protested, "Hey! Come on! I was about to get my love reading!"

Urilith stood up with a sweet smile, and she patted Chase's scruffy cheek. "Oh, dear boy. The love of your life is right in front of you. You just have to be brave enough to take it."

Chase's jaw dropped, then slowly shut, his fair face flushing. "Uh... yeah. Sure thing, sister."

Urilith was practically glowing as they left, and Loch swallowed down his cake with a happy grin. He offered some to Sloane, but he declined the thoughtful gesture. He was too eager to get the hell out of the precinct before anything else happened.

He was still half expecting Alexander to appear and attack them again.

"That was fun!" Urilith cheered as they hit the door. "Oh, how I've missed congregating with mortals! I'm determined to make a new effort to be a more active goddess! Even after the wedding, I want to stay here for a while!"

"That's very lovely, Mother," Loch cooed. "We would love to have you and show you all around the city!"

"There's a lot of great restaurants and museums," Sloane offered, getting into his car and plugging in his phone to charge. He accessed the list of names he'd compiled and emailed it over to Milo.

"And there are entire stores full of sexual toys and pornographic videos," Loch went on, fastening his seat belt. "Mortals act very prudish in public, but privately they're quite debauched. It's amazing."

"People like to keep their love lives to themselves," Sloane said, unable to resist a small grin. "Ahem."

"Seat belt, Sloane!" Loch reminded him. "And you shouldn't be on your phone in the car."

"We're parked! I'm not driving. I'm just trying to get those names over to Milo—"

"Texting plus driving equals death," Loch recited. "Do you know how many accidents the AVPD has responded to because people were on their phones?"

"How many of them were parked?" Sloane retorted dryly.

"Hmm, that information wasn't on the poster I saw in the break room."

"There, look." Sloane dropped his phone into the cup holder. "I'm putting my phone down. Happy?"

"Can we get more cake?"

"Later."

"More cake would make me happy."

"Speaking of cake," Urilith piped up from the back, "I could make my cake for your wedding."

"The one you made for the first Dhankes?" Loch gasped. "Oh, Mother. Yes, please. That would be wonderful."

"I guess we do need to start making some plans," Sloane said, backing out of the space and driving back toward Lynnette's house. "A date, our guests… uh…."

"Do wedding registries accept sacrifices?" Loch asked urgently.

"Nope, sorry."

"Have you even decided where you want to get married?" Urilith asked. "What do mortals do these days?"

"Sages still try to follow the old ways," Sloane replied. "Our friends Lochlain and Good Robert had a Sagittarian ceremony with handfasting and—"

"It was so boring," Loch griped.

"They got married out in the trees by their home, had a big reception inside their house," Sloane continued, ignoring Loch's commentary. "Maybe there's a park or somewhere like that we could go. There wouldn't be very many people, uh…."

He was hit with a faint pang of sadness, knowing he had absolutely no family to invite. He had a few dear friends like Milo and Lynnette, perhaps even Fred, but he was struggling to think of anyone else who would come.

Urilith's yellow tentacles gently curled around the seat to pat Sloane's chest. "It doesn't have to be a grand event. It's whatever you and Azaethoth want."

"Truly, I just want Sloane to be happy," Loch said, smiling gently and resting his hand on Sloane's thigh. "I'll marry you anywhere you like, anytime."

"Thank you, Loch." Sloane was touched. "That's so sweet—"

"As long as there's a fire."

Sloane laughed suddenly, the sadness ebbing as he begrudgingly agreed, "Okay, yes. There can be a fire."

Loch looked very pleased.

"Oh! What about the garden you gave me? Why don't we get married there?"

"Would that make you happy, my love?"

"Well, I only have three people to invite, five if I include Robert and Lochlain, so it's not like we'd be trying to transport a whole crap ton of mortals over there. Your family, heh, they're all gods, so they can travel there on their own."

"My love," Loch said, one of his tentacles curling around Sloane's knee, "it's not a matter of convenience. If you wanted to take a thousand people there, I would gladly do it. But is that really what you want?"

"It's beautiful." Sloane recalled the dreamy blue sky and all the glowing flowers, and he smiled. "It's… it's perfect. Yes, I would love to get married there."

"It's settled, then," Loch said, giving Sloane's knee another squeeze. "I'll build the wedding arch myself, just for you. Oh, and a table for us to feast at, and a wedding couch for our guests to watch our consummation—"

"Maybe not so much on the wedding couch?" Sloane squeaked, exhaling sharply as he came to a stoplight. "I'm sure everyone coming already knows we've got the consummation part taken care of."

"Indeed." Urilith chuckled fondly. "Which reminds me, Azaethoth. Who else do you want to come?"

"Aunt Shartorath, Uncle Yeris, mmm…. Grandpa Baub." Loch paused to think it over. "Maybe Uncle Babbeth if you could wake him up? Or Uncle Gordoth?"

Shartorath was the Goddess of Marriage and the Home, Yeris was the God of the Oceans and Hidden Things, Baub was the God of War and Divine Wrath, Babbeth was the God of Death and Lost Children, and Gordoth the Untouched was the God of Justice and Righteous Wrath.

Sloane knew all the names, and the casual way Loch listed them off as potential wedding guests was surreal.

"I don't want to be greedy, and I don't know who hasn't gone completely mad up there." Loch fidgeted. "If possible, perhaps my idiot brothers as well. That is, if they're not too busy conspiring to wake up Father and destroy the world."

"I'll be more than happy to wake Uncle Gordoth for you," Urilith said cheerfully. "He was always a morning person. Shartorath may be a bit cranky, but not insane... not yet anyway. I'll check on the others when I return home to fetch your wedding present."

"Thank you, Mother."

"How soon are we planning this wedding?"

Loch looked to Sloane, asking, "Well, my love? How soon do you want to be properly mated?"

"Well, uh, you've only just asked me." Sloane chuckled nervously. "I'd want to wait for Lochlain and Robert to come back from their honeymoon—"

"Next week, then?"

"Wow, that's kinda fast, don't you think?" Sloane flushed, always flattered by Loch's obvious love for him.

"Why wait?"

"How about," Sloane mused thoughtfully, "we wait until Urilitha? That's only a few weeks away!"

"My sabbath!" Urilith gushed. "The spring equinox! Oh, that would be so lovely!"

"Start our new life together with the start of a new season," Sloane said, more certain of his decision now. "And we'll have Urilith herself there to bless our union!"

"For you, my darling Starkiller, anything," Loch confirmed. "On Urilith's Day, we shall be married."

Sloane was filled with a rush of excitement and nerves, all smiles as he parked in Lynnette's driveway. Having a date made the wedding feel tangible, and he still had no idea what he was doing, but with Loch at his side, he knew he could manage.

Together, they could do anything.

As they headed back into the house, Sloane heard his phone ding and retrieved it from his pocket. It was a message from Milo.

"Hey, guys!" Lynnette called out from the kitchen. There was a thick smell of incense perfuming the air, and something was boiling on the stove. "How did it go?"

"Awesome," Loch replied smugly. "We had cake."

"And the testing?" Galgareth asked, smirking as she checked on the bubbling pot.

"Went off without a hitch thanks to your sweet blessing." Sloane paused to read Milo's message aloud: "Confirmed. Every Silenced dude and dudette donated at Hazel."

"Hazel?" Lynnette wrinkled her nose. "The medical place that gives away mugs for donating blood?"

"That's the one," Sloane replied. "Alexander's parents used to work there before they were murdered seven years ago. Alexander's real name is Landon Ward, and he's been missing ever since."

"Murdered?" Galgareth clasped a hand to her chest.

"Yes. And our mysterious blue goo was found at the crime scene. It's gotta be the same god we're looking for."

"How did you find out about Alexander's family?"

"When Milo was running the blood, he found a familial match in the system," Sloane explained. "Alexander's father was in there, and that's what led us to him."

"A familial match?" Galgareth looked thoughtful and eyed the bubbling pot for a long moment.

"What is it, my daughter?" Urilith quizzically peered over at the mixture.

"I have an idea," she said, one of her lavender tentacles unfurling from her arm. She picked up a knife and used the blunt end to scrape along the slick skin.

Lynnette seemed to catch on to what she was doing, and she brought over a little bowl of the blue goo.

Galgareth took the end of the knife and stirred it into the goo. She held the knife over the boiling pot and it melted into glittering slime, blade and all, splashing as she dropped it in. "There!"

"There what?" Sloane asked curiously.

"I'm making my own familial match test." Galgareth gestured at the pot. "This was going to be a purification potion, but I can use it to see if me and the other god are a match."

"Clever!" Loch exclaimed. "If you are, the potion won't have anything to do...."

"But if it smokes, that means we weren't a match," Galgareth finished with a proud smile. "Well, at least not a very close one. It will at least rule out our brothers and uncles and aunts. She cocked her head. "I think...."

"It's worth a try," Sloane said earnestly. He texted Milo back to thank him and stuffed his phone back in his pocket as he asked, "How long will it take?"

"Mmm, maybe a few hours," Galgareth said. "You usually need to wait for a full moon for this kind of purifying power, but I can speed it right along."

"So! What do we do now?" Loch asked. "Jay is safely tucked away, potion's bubbling... are we going to go make a big crack in the case?"

"I hope so," Sloane said. "I think we're gonna go take a little trip to the Hazel Medical Research Facility."

"They're, like, a huge international company," Lynnette chimed in. "They have places all over the world! They have blood drives after earthquakes and all kinds of do-gooder crap. You really think they're involved?"

"Our god of the blue goo has probably been using Hazel's vast resources to track down and select their targets," Sloane replied. "It's our best lead."

"So we can go down there and I can unleash my godly wrath?" Loch asked with a distinctly hopeful tone.

"Not yet," Sloane warned. "He or she may be posing as an employee like Bad Robert was, so it could be anybody."

"Fine. We poke around, find him or her, and then I can unleash my godly wrath?"

"Strong maybe."

THE HAZEL Research Facility was a mammoth skyscraper in the middle of downtown Archersville. It was one of the tallest buildings in the city, with hundreds of floors, a giant monolith of steel and glass looming over the sidewalks below.

The lobby was clean and white, and there were directories offering various paths to their donation center, laboratories, and offices. The donation center was the only part open to the public, and Sloane decided to start there. With Loch tagging along, he was planning to pose as a potential donor and nose around.

"Do they really give you a mug for donating your bodily fluids?" Loch flipped through a brochure he'd snagged in the lobby.

"Yes," Sloane replied patiently, following signs to the elevators.

"So, for what amounts to a blood sacrifice, mortals are gifted a plastic piece of drinkware?" Loch scoffed in disgust. "Really? They gave up our worship to go pray to their little Lucian god because ooohhh, blood and tentacles are gross, but they'll split open their veins for meager bits of plastic!"

"Well, they're donating their blood or whatever to help people. It's not about the cup."

"Hmmph." Loch sniffed. "Maybe we would have kept more followers if we offered toasters."

"Loch...."

"Or beach towels! Look! You can get a beach towel after ten pints! Oh, the orgies and good harvests weren't good enough, but neon synthetic fabric is?"

"Azaethoth!" Sloane hissed, hoping no one was listening too closely. He stroked Loch's back. "Listen, I know it's probably very upsetting, but these places really are meant to help people."

"It's ridiculous," Loch huffed as he jabbed at the elevator button.

"It's okay." Sloane took Loch's hand and squeezed it reassuringly. "I haven't given you any blood sacrifices, you know."

"So?"

"Does that make me a bad follower?" he teased, stepping inside the elevator when the doors opened. He pushed the button for the third floor. "Or are you going to start a new beach towel incentive to entice me?"

"Well, you do offer me plenty of other bodily fluids." Loch coyly slid a hand over Sloane's ass. "You've gifted me often with your come, your sweat, your tears of pleasure…."

"Does that earn me a towel?" Sloane asked, trying to remain calm even as a blush crept up his neck. "Or am I at toaster status?"

"Definitely a toaster." Loch leaned in to nuzzle Sloane's neck.

Sloane playfully swatted him away when the doors opened, clearing his throat and trying to appear professional. "Now it's time to behave and…."

Standing in front of the open doors was Alexander, and he was glaring at them heatedly. "So lovely to see you both again so soon."

His mind racing, Sloane stared at the elevator pad. This was supposed to be the third floor, but there was only an empty room behind Alexander.

"You," Loch snarled, lunging forward to attack.

"Wait, Loch!" Sloane grabbed Loch's shirt and tugged him backward. He looked to Alexander, saying urgently, "Landon? That's your real name, right?"

Alexander flinched.

Sloane swung up his hand to keep the elevator doors open. "Landon Ward? Look, we want to help you."

They know….

"Yes, we know!" Sloane said urgently.

Alexander's scowl faded into obvious shock.

He… he can hear me?

The mysterious voice sounded particularly surprised.

"Yes, I can hear you!" Sloane groaned. "We know you're working for a god, that—" Something grabbed him and wrenched him forward, off-balance and falling.

The building flashed away, a bright light blinding him, and he cried out as he crashed into something hard. Ground, he was on the ground.

Sloane managed to pull himself up to his knees, now finding himself in a vast field. The grass was dried and dead, and it crunched beneath him as he moved.

Alexander was standing over him, pressing his hand against Sloane's forehead.

Sloane felt a faint burn, struggling to push Alexander away and throw up a shield. The magic fizzled and sparked, but he couldn't summon a shield. "What the…?"

"You're silenced," Alexander snapped. "Now, explain to me how you can hear him."

He's a starlit witch… but there's something else….

Sloane gasped as something cold pushed inside his chest, squeezing down until he could barely breathe. "What, what are you doing?"

"Hold still," Alexander snorted. "No one can hear him. No one. How are you doing it?"

"I, I don't know!" Sloane wheezed, staring down at the faint vision of tentacles digging into him. Oh, by the gods, it was inside him and pushing so hard and he was feeling faint. "Please… stop…."

"Tell me how!" Alexander demanded, his eyes bright red and narrowing angrily. "What are you?"

"I'm… a private… investigator…?" Sloane croaked. He was about to pass out, falling down onto his hands and groaning softly. "Stop…."

There was suddenly a large flapping of wings and a terrifying roar, and then Sloane heard Loch's voice screaming, "Prepare to feel my godly wrath!"

CHAPTER 9.

LOCH WAS here in all of his dragon glory, wings outstretched and teeth bared, his long tail furiously whipping around him.

There was no sign of his human vessel, only his true godly form.

Sloane gasped as Alexander pulled away. The phantom tentacle left his body, and he could breathe again. He watched as Alexander strolled across the field toward Azaethoth, a tiny mortal and a god about to do battle.

It was a ridiculous display. It was like watching a lion about to devour a mouse. Alexander was powerful, certainly, but there was no way....

Sloane looked up.

And up.

He stared stupidly upward and onward as he realized he could finally see the monstrous deity attached to Alexander.

It was like looking at a mirage, the image shimmering and translucent, but it was big. Bigger than even Loch's magnificent dragon, it was a beast with a huge upper body and massive arms like a gorilla, but there was a thick array of giant spikes cascading down its back from the top of its head.

It dragged its lower body on the ground, a thick tail made out of spiraling tentacles, and more tentacles hung from its long, jagged snout. It roared in reply, and it swung one of its great arms out at Loch.

Loch gracefully dodged out of the way, snarling and snapping his teeth at the beast. He missed, diving forward again.

"Look out!" Sloane screamed, watching the beast's tail whipping around to strike.

The mass of tentacles smacked Loch right across his face, sending him off-balance and stumbling back a step with his wings flapping wildly.

Alexander calmly walked forward, and the mammoth thing connected to him lumbered ahead and hurled itself at Loch again.

Loch skidded and roared, baring all of his giant teeth and biting at the air around him with a wretched snarl of frustration. He tried lunging down at Alexander's minute form and got a vicious blow right in his jaw for his efforts.

He can't see him, Sloane realized in a panic. Loch was fighting completely blind, and he was losing ground quickly. "Loch! Come on! I can see him, come on!"

Loch whirled around, bolting toward him and bowing his head. "Get on!"

"Oh fuck!" Sloane's stomach lurched as Loch's giant head dove between his legs, and he fought to wrap himself around Loch's long neck and hang on tight.

Loch stretched out his great wings and leaped into the air, flapping them hard as he rose above the fields. He circled Alexander and the ghostly beast, snarling, "If it's too bloody hot in the kitchen, you need to get the fuck out!"

"You've been watching way too much Gordon Ramsey!" Sloane yelled.

Loch replied with a roar of flame, flickering streams of magical fire bursting from his mouth and scorching the fields below them. The ground was instantly incinerated, the dry grass catching quickly, and the fire spread in seconds.

Alexander lifted his hand, deflecting the flames with a glowing shield. The shield was weakening beneath the godly fire, and Alexander's nose began to bleed. The beast quickly grabbed him around his middle and slithered them both out of the way.

Sloane tried to squint against the rush of wind and heat. "Left, left, left!"

Loch turned his head sharply, following Sloane's directions. "No! Too much! Right! Go back right!"

"You are terrible at this!" Loch complained.

"Pay attention!" Sloane groaned. "Now, turn around and drop down! Quick! He's right underneath us!"

Loch pumped his powerful wings, whirling in the air and tucking them close to his body as he dove. He roared triumphantly, Alexander in his sights and headed right at him.

The fields were on fire, and there was so much smoke, Sloane coughed hard as he tried to peer around Loch's head to see what was happening.

Alexander wasn't moving, standing among the glittering flames with his shield redirected over himself. When he saw Loch and Sloane coming at him, he didn't budge. He held his ground with a slight smirk curling his lips.

All too late, Sloane realized the beast was no longer behind Alexander. It had disappeared! But as Loch let loose another blast of flame, the beast rose out of the very ground where it had been hiding with a fierce snarl.

"Loch!" Sloane tried to warn him, but the beast struck with enormous strength and knocked Loch right out of the sky.

Loch landed with a thunderous crash, and Sloane went flying, skidding through some of the burning grass and cursing loudly.

The beast circled around Loch and began to strike, Loch's furious roars making the very ground shake as he quickly went on the offensive. At first Loch was able to drive the beast and Alexander back, but his advantage didn't last.

The beast lashed out, a powerful blow that made Loch growl furiously. Another hit sent him reeling, and he swung his long tail around to put some distance between them as he backpedaled.

Sloane raised his hands to throw a magical missile at Alexander to drive him and the beast away, but nothing happened.

Fuck!

Alexander's ward!

Sloane struggled to stand and desperately clawed at his forehead. He could feel the edge of the ward Alexander had used to silence him. It was magic and very strong, but Sloane was stronger.

He dug in his nails, focusing as hard as he could and screaming from his efforts as blood dripped down his face.

He had to hurry! He had to get to Loch and help him!

Loch roared again, but this time in pain, dragging Sloane's attention to the battlefield. Alexander was directing the beast expertly, leaping and flying out of the way every time Loch tried to crush him. After all, Alexander was the only one Loch could see, and the clever little jerk was using himself as bait.

There was black blood leaking from a gash in Loch's shoulder, and he was starting to limp.

Alexander lured him in for another cheap shot, the beast's clawed hand opening up another tear in Loch's chest.

This time, Loch had been expecting it. His jaws snapped down around the beast's wrist, but his teeth landed on nothing but thin air. He couldn't hit the beast at all and roared in frustration.

"Shit! Loch! Hold on!" Sloane closed his eyes, trying to focus again. He scratched and dug, fighting through his fear to find the edge of the ward.

There.

There was an explosion of sparkling light as the ward shattered, and he grunted as he leaped to his feet. He took off, running right at Alexander and the beast. He summoned all of his magic, squinting through the blood running down into his face.

"Mom, Dad, please! Please hear me!" Sloane pleaded, his broken voice turning into a vengeful roar as he screamed, "Great Azaethoth! You listen the fuck up! Help me now! Don't you dare take Loch away from me!"

The sky darkened, impossibly bright bolts of lightning crackling all across the swirling clouds. Light flowed between Sloane's hands, and he dropped them down to his side as he ran. He could feel it, the weight, the familiar shape against his palms.

A sword of starlight.

Sloane raised it over his head, aiming for the beast's massive tail and swinging with all of his might. Alexander turned, too slow, and the beast roared in absolute agony as the blade made contact.

The shimmering image faded in and out, retreating and howling miserably.

Sloane bared his teeth, rushing to stand between Loch and Alexander, pointing his sword at the awful beast above as he shouted, "My name is Sloane Beaumont, son of Daniel and Pandora Beaumont, betrothed mate of Azaethoth the Lesser! I am a Starkiller amongst mortals, and if you touch him again, there is no power in the universe that can save you from where I'm going to fucking send you!"

"Wait!" the beast snarled. It sounded different this time, loud and clear. "Starkiller...?"

"Yes," Loch growled in reply, bowing his head down next to Sloane as one of his great wings curled protectively around him. "*My* Starkiller."

"I killed Tollmathan, God of Plagues and Poetry!" Sloane yelled back, and he tightened his grip on the brilliant sword. "I don't know who you are, but I'll end you too, if you don't back the fuck off!"

"Starkiller! I yield!" the beast said, lying down on the ground. He made no other move, except to wind a ghostly tentacle around Alexander's outstretched hand.

"Wait, what?" Sloane blinked. He stared stupidly, glancing back at Loch, who seemed equally confused. This didn't make any sense.

"What are you doing?" Alexander hissed, apparently in agreement.

"Trust me," the beast soothed. His ghostly image became more solid, no longer a clear mirage but a visible creature whose skin was flooded with rich reds and purples.

"Who are you?" Sloane asked, looking over the spectacular monster.

"My name is Rota," the beast said.

"Rota?" Sloane scoffed. "I don't know of any god named Rota."

"It's the name I gave myself," Rota replied. "We have much to discuss, Starkiller. Please. I don't want to do battle any longer."

The sword of starlight began to fade away in Sloane's hands, which were aching from the strain of trying to hold on to so much magic. He finally let go, and he rubbed his throbbing fingers together as he demanded, "So, out with it. Who are you really?"

"I don't know," Rota said, his colorful image fading. He dissolved until he was nearly invisible, pleading, "Alexander... I...."

"Rest," Alexander said, reaching over to pet the shimmering beast. *You didn't have to show yourself... it wears you out.*

I need them to believe us, was Rota's exhausted reply.

"They will," Alexander said, reaching into his coat to retrieve a pack of cigarettes.

"Will what?" Loch griped.

"Right now, you will listen." Alexander held his hand up to the end of the cigarette, and Sloane could see the end of a shivering tentacle sliding up his hand. Together, tentacle and fingers produced a flame to light the cigarette.

Waiting patiently, Sloane moved closer to Loch to inspect his wounds. While Alexander puffed away, Sloane slid his hands up over Loch's smooth skin to offer his magic. "How'd you find me? Infinite worlds between worlds, right?"

"You're my mate." Loch's eyes glittered. "No matter where you are, I will always find you."

Just as the first gash in Loch's skin closed, Alexander spoke again.

"Neither of us have any memory of who we were before we woke up at Hazel." Alexander's bright red eyes glanced back at Sloane and Loch as he exhaled a cloud of smoke through his nose. "I've been there for as long as I can remember, but I didn't meet Rota for a few years. They had to get me ready, you see, to be his conduit."

"A conduit?" Sloane asked.

"That's what they call me," Alexander replied. "A mortal body controlling an immortal spirit. I can channel Rota's energy with my thoughts alone, or I can use my own body to focus his power."

"A weapon," said Sloane, his jaw getting tight. "That's how they made you into a weapon."

"Yes."

"Why?"

"If you really killed Tollmathan, you already know why." Alexander flicked his cigarette with a roll of his eyes. "There are gods who mean to wake Salgumel and remake the world."

"You mean destroy it," Loch growled.

"Potato, potahto." Alexander shrugged. "Look, Tollmathan was far from alone. There's an entire faction of old gods working together to make it happen."

"What?" Sloane's heart sunk into his stomach. "All the gods are supposed to be asleep! The dreaming—"

"It only took one," Alexander cut in. "Once Tollmathan woke up, he started waking up others he knew would be down for the cause. Yeah, some of them went right back to sleep, but they're ready to rise when the time comes. There's no telling how many there are now."

Sloane's stomach twisted up in a wretched guilty knot. He was the one who inadvertently woke up Tollmathan with a prayer that was meant to save his parents when he was a child. "Okay, but then why make weapons? Why take all these innocent people?"

"To fight the other gods." Alexander used the end of his cigarette to light another. "The faction is strong, but clearly they're worried about winning the war. That's why they're going to all this trouble... to enslave their enemies."

"You mean take the gods who actually want to keep Salgumel sleeping and turn them to their cause whether they want to or not," Sloane clarified, clinging to Loch's side for comfort. "Fuck."

"Now you're getting the idea." Alexander leaned back against Rota's shoulder. He looked as if he was pressed up against nothing, his body cocked at an impossible angle, and it only added to the weirdness of it all.

"Don't you still want Jay?"

"I don't want him," Alexander snorted. "He was just the next name on my list, all right?"

"Then who does?" Sloane pressed.

"Gronoch. Azaethoth the Lesser's brother."

Loch said nothing, and he curled around Sloane tighter.

"Toll went to his brothers first," Alexander said. "Well, all except Azaethoth, obviously. Some sibling rivalry there, eh?"

Loch bared his teeth.

"Here's the million-dollar question." Sloane took a deep breath. He kept petting Loch's smooth scales, trying to soothe him as he asked, "Why are you telling us all of this?"

"Isn't it obvious?" Alexander cocked his head. He flicked his cigarette ash and took a deep drag. "You are a Starkiller. You kill gods. We're currently being 'employed' by one." He held up his hands and made little air quotes. "Pffft. You're supposed to be a detective, right?"

"Well," Sloane mumbled indignantly, still not putting the pieces together, "yeah?"

"We want you to kill a god," Alexander snapped. "Duh."

"Wait, what?"

"Look, if I'd known you were a Starkiller, I would have never attacked you," Alexander said dryly. "I knew you were a powerful witch of starlight, but I never thought you'd actually be strong enough to help us."

"What is it exactly that you want?" Sloane pressed, his suspicions immediately raised. "Who do you want me to kill?"

"I want you to kill Gronoch."

"I'm not an assassin!" Sloane protested in disgust. "If we could have talked sense into Tollmathan, I wouldn't have killed him either. There has to be another way to stop Gronoch!"

"Come on! I don't want to see the world destroyed any more than you do. Plus, you'll get the added bonus of keeping little Jay and the other Silenced people of the world safe. If Gronoch is dead, no more conduits, so no more hunting. No more building an army, okay?"

"And what are you getting out of it? Really?"

"My freedom isn't enough?" Alexander challenged.

"I don't trust you." Sloane took a bold step toward him. "If you were so worried about just being free, you would have found a way by now to get away from Gronoch. You have the power of an old god at your disposal! You could easily escape him into realms like these!"

Just tell him, Rota urged.

And risk having someone else trying to hold your body hostage? No fucking way! Alexander's thoughts were positively volatile, but his expression remained calm.

"You know I can hear you when you two do that?" Sloane said with an amused smile.

"What?" Alexander's eyes widened, anything but calm now. He looked afraid.

"He's a Starkiller," Rota realized out loud. "He's been touched by Great Azaethoth…."

"Guess it had some side effects?" Sloane shrugged and scratched the back of his neck.

"How about we all talk using our outside voices, hmm?" Loch piped up, sitting back on his hind legs, his wounds fully healed now. "I'm getting tired of being left out. It's boring, not to mention rude."

"Yeah, no more secrets," Sloane agreed. "Tell us, Alexander. What's this about a body?"

"Gronoch." Rota spoke up while Alexander silently stewed. "He has my body. He found a way to put gods to sleep, like in the dreaming, and pull their soul away to bind to a mortal using the magic from Asran bones."

"Can't you just poof back to Zebulon?" Sloane asked.

"No, my soul is tethered to Alexander," Rota explained. "I cannot return without first reclaiming my body."

"And breaking the bonds?"

"No," Rota said firmly. "It would kill Alexander. There are bindings you can't see. Inside his head, on his heart—"

"They get the idea," Alexander cut in with a grimace.

"Even if breaking the bindings wouldn't hurt him, I could only return to Zebulon as a spirit," Rota said, his ghostly tentacles curling around Alexander's waist. "Unless my body dies or is destroyed, I cannot reincorporate a new one…. And Gronoch has hidden it from me."

"And of course, you're a god," Loch drawled. "You're not likely to starve to death anytime soon."

"I understand you want your body back, but wouldn't reuniting with it also break the bindings?" Sloane frowned. "Alexander could still die. Kind of a big risk, don't you think?"

"I wouldn't let that happen," Rota said passionately. "Once I'm fully restored, I would be able to heal him. Then we'd finally be together."

"Rota," Alexander hissed.

"You two, are… uhm." Sloane grinned, glancing at the way Alexander's hand brushed over Rota's tentacle, so tender and familiar. "Uh, dating?"

"None of your fuckin' business," Alexander replied coldly. *Lalala, lalalala, get out of my fuckin' head!*

"Ah!" Loch grinned wide, his sharp teeth shining. "Now it all makes sense! That's why you're both so desperate to get his physical body back!"

Alexander scowled.

"They wish to mate!" Loch said proudly. "As a soul, god or not, Rota can only physically manifest himself for brief spurts of time! Certainly not long enough to be very satisfying."

"Okay, we get it." Sloane cleared his throat.

"Why don't you just take over a fresh corpse? It works wonderfully! Speaking from personal experience, it can be quite pleasurable. Oh, hmm. Or is it because Rota's soul is already tethered to Alexander. Can he not possess another body?"

"Hey, come on."

"Trying to focus his power through Alexander only hurts Alexander, so that doesn't work, although I'm sure they've already tried that," Loch went on shamelessly. "I imagine that only a few moments of penetration at a time are possible, and that just sounds awful—"

"Shut up," Alexander growled, his cheeks turning as red as his eyes.

"Loch," Sloane urged. "This is private for them, okay?"

"Maybe that's why he's so angry." Loch dropped his voice down to a hushed whisper. "He hasn't been able to mate yet."

"On second thought, forget the whole getting you to help us thing. Let's keep fighting," Alexander snapped, standing up straight and incinerating the spent cigarette butt in his hand away to nothing.

"Loch, leave it alone," Sloane warned, giving him a dirty look.

"What?" Loch gazed down at Sloane with his big starry eyes wide in confusion. "You tend to get cranky if you haven't had a good helping of my seed. Maybe it's the same for him!"

"Loch!" Sloane blushed angrily.

"Well, you do."

"*Azaethoth!*"

"Ulgh, fine!"

"Alexander, Rota." Sloane turned to face them with a strained smile. "How about we meet back at my office? Talk some more?"

"Does this mean you're going to help us?" Alexander asked flatly, still singing away in his head in an effort to keep Sloane out of his thoughts.

"Of course," Sloane insisted, "but I do want to try something other than more godly murder."

"Mmm, I need to go find my vessel," Loch remarked absently.

"Wait, where did you leave it?"

"Oh! I left it somewhere very safe!" Loch promised, and he beamed proudly.

Smothering his face in his hands, Sloane already knew he wasn't going to be happy with the answer as he groaned, "Oh, by all the gods… where?"

"At the post office."

"What?"

CHAPTER 10.

"YOU DON'T even trust the post office with your stupid catalogues, but you left your body there?" Sloane shouted, tires screeching as he zoomed through downtown traffic. The car door was thankfully still attached, but it made an awful creaking sound every time he made a left turn.

While horribly disfigured, they do arrive on time, Loch's voice protested. *I couldn't very well leave my body at Hazel, could I? Once you went through the portal, I knew I needed to leave it somewhere safe so I could take on my true godly form to come do battle and rescue you!*

"This is the stupidest idea you've ever had."

Why? You've never objected to me being inside you before—

"Okay, but this is freakin' insane!"

Loch had taken them out of the mystical fields and brought them back to the earthly plane, but a giant dragon was a bit much to take on a little trip down to the post office.

Out of ideas, Sloane did the only thing he could think of:

He offered his body as a vessel to a god.

The process was over in a blink, and Sloane wasn't even sure what had happened. One moment Loch was there, and the next, he wasn't. Sloane didn't feel much different, except now he had Loch's voice chatting away inside his head.

"How does this even work?" Sloane grumbled. "Sucking it in on a godly scale, right?"

Exactly so, Loch said cheerfully.

"What about what's happened to Rota? Can you separate your soul from your body like him? Like, astral project?"

I suppose if I really wanted to, Loch huffed, *but I don't see what the point would be. I don't need to separate my soul from my body for magical travel. I can simply take my body with me.*

"But it could be done?"

Rota did say they were using the bones of Asra to power the process. Humans used to raid Asran graves for their magical powers, including astral projection.

"Think it would be enough to project a god's soul out?"

If you had enough bones, yes.

"Can you possess someone with just your soul?"

Mmm, thinking of Rota and Alexander, are you?

"Yes," Sloane confessed. "I was trying to think if there would be any possible way to help them. I'm sure they've already tried everything, but it's just so sad."

Your compassion is quite admirable, my love, Loch said sweetly. *Unfortunately, Rota needs his body to transition to another human body. With his soul tethered to Alexander, he's trapped. Hmm... unless....*

"Unless?"

When my mother was a love goddess, eons ago, she used to have the most spectacular fertility celebrations with Sages who had starsight.

"People who've been touched by Great Azaethoth," Sloane murmured thoughtfully.

Witches who had starsight were blessed with a variety of amazing gifts, like communicating with the dead and predicting the future. The gift was so rare that Sloane couldn't think of ever meeting anyone who had it.

Yes. She could share her soul with them, possess them by the dozens, and they would have the most incredible orgies that would last for days.

"Wait, so it is possible?"

Orgies that last for days? Most definitely—

"Rota possessing another body!" Sloane interrupted with a dark blush.

Only with witches who have starsight, Loch clarified. *She would stay in her own godly body, but she could extend her soul to take control of them and enhance their pleasures.*

Pulling into the cramped post office parking lot, Sloane paused to think for a moment. "And this, what we're doing right now, is this like what you do with your ghoul body? Just… hanging out in a body with your own actually inside?"

The very same, Loch replied, a slight smirk in his tone. *Although I'm allowing you to remain in control….*

"Wait. Are you saying that you could just take over whenever you wanted?"

You're the one who let me in, Loch said innocently, suddenly seizing Sloane's hands and sliding them up his thighs.

It was a very bizarre sensation, having his limbs tugged around without his control, and Sloane gasped, "Whoa! That's freakin' weird!"

Loch moved Sloane's hands higher, palming his crotch and pulling at the fly of his pants.

"Hey, hey!" Sloane protested, glancing around the parking lot. "What are you doing?"

Taking over. Loch slid Sloane's hand inside his underwear to squeeze his cock.

Sloane dropped his head back against his seat and groaned. The feeling was definitely his own hand, his own touch, but there was an undercurrent of distant electricity that made his fingers curl around his shaft and stroke all on its own with a new, exciting level of pleasure.

The energy had to be coming from Loch, and Sloane experimentally tried to pull his hand away, finding that he was totally powerless.

Loch must have felt him trying to resist and immediately stilled Sloane's hand, asking quietly, *Do you want me to stop?*

"No," Sloane said, groaning when a deep shudder of lust rumbled through his loins.

Do you want me to keep going?

"Fuck." Whining with need, Sloane couldn't believe how hard he was already. It was like hitting a switch, and he couldn't sit still now. He tried rocking up into his own hand, panting, "Loch, please… don't stop."

Is that a yes? Loch teased, so cruel, keeping Sloane's fingers in a loose grip that offered no satisfaction.

"Fuck!" Sloane grunted, glancing around again to make sure no one was paying any attention to him. The parking lot was crowded, but he didn't see anyone looking their way. "Just, just let me grab my coat!"

Loch freed Sloane's hand long enough for him to reach into the back seat for a forgotten jacket, which he draped over his lap to hide his throbbing cock peeking out of his pants. As soon as he was hidden, Loch took over again and began to stroke.

"Oh, Loch," Sloane groaned, letting himself give in and melt into the seat. It was eerily good, and he was already much closer than he'd like. He wanted to savor it and bit his lip as he fought not to come.

Mmm, I can feel you. You're right there.

"Loch!" Sloane gasped, feeling something inside of him shift, and there was suddenly pressure on his prostate from within. It was impossible—*fuck, did it feel good*—and he couldn't stop himself from coming.

Loch kept pushing from inside of him and jerking Sloane's cock through a spectacular orgasm, and all Sloane could do was moan and twitch. He became sensitive all too quickly, and he whimpered as he struggled to get control of his hands back.

"Okay, okay, stop stop stop!" Sloane pleaded, now red-faced and sweating.

Mmmm… fine. Loch sounded like he was pouting, but he released Sloane's hands.

Sloane wiped himself up and tucked the coat back into the rear floorboards to clean up later.

We should do that again, Loch said gleefully. *It was fun.*

"Later," Sloane grunted, trying to make himself look presentable. He swore he could feel Loch's smugness resonating in his bones. "Now, where did you leave your body?"

Right outside. I didn't put any stamps on it or anything, but I'm sure they kept it safe.

"Oh, by all the gods."

Apparently the post office's idea of keeping his body safe was not what Loch had expected. Their response to what they perceived to be a corpse was to immediately call the local police. Paramedics arrived first and quickly determined Loch's lifeless body to be a ghoul.

Seeing as how any form of necromancy was illegal, the police confiscated the body and were holding it at the county medical examiners' office. With a little bit of truth magic and a sweet smile, Sloane found out that Crosby-Ayers Funeral Home downtown had an exclusive contract with the county for all indigent and abandoned cases.

That included ghouls.

With Loch yapping away in his ear, Sloane drove them to the funeral home and tried desperately to think up a plan. He walked into the plush lobby and smiled politely at the receptionist.

"Hello," she said, "can I help you?"

"I need to see someone," Sloane said hesitantly.

"Has someone passed away?" she asked, frowning in sympathy. "I'm sure I can get one of our directors to come speak to you. Miss Kitty York should be available—"

"No. I mean, yes!" Sloane fidgeted. "They were brought here from the post office? Uh…."

The receptionist's eyes widened.

She knows! Loch exclaimed.

"Look, he was a dear friend of mine," Sloane tried. "I just really need to see his body."

Dear friend? Loch scoffed.

Sloane grunted, hoping Loch would take the hint.

He did not.

"We were more than just friends, you see," Loch said, using Sloane's voice and taking over to lean against the desk. "We were lovers. He was like a living god, and oh, how we'd make love for hours...."

"Oh my!" The receptionist blushed.

"We would stay up all night together, and he would worship my body until I was a quivering, dripping mess," Loch went on with a lovesick sigh. "I will never again know such rapture."

Dead! You're so dead! Sloane screamed inside his head.

"Have you ever known a love like that, Doris?" Loch tilted his head at her name tag. "I bet you have, hmmm?"

"A very long time ago," Doris said with a bashful smile.

"I knew you were a woman of passion," Loch declared. "I could tell the moment I looked at you. You must know how desperate I am to see him...." He held Sloane's hand over his chest. "One last time."

"Wait here." Doris stood up and patted Sloane's shoulder. "I'll see what I can do, okay?"

"Thank you ever so much, Doris," Loch gushed sweetly, waving after her as she headed into the back through a private door.

"I am going to strangle you!" Sloane snarled as soon as Loch gave him back control.

Why? Loch's voice sounded offended. *It worked, didn't it? They're going to bring my body out for you to say goodbye.*

"And then what? You're just gonna walk out with it?"

Well, it is mine!

"Ghouls are illegal, Loch! I'm surprised the police aren't here—"

There was a jingle as the front door opened, and Sloane turned around to find Detective Chase and Detective Merrick walking in.

"Oh shit," Sloane hissed.

"Hey there, Sloane," Chase greeted, quirking his brows in surprise. "Didn't expect to see you again so soon."

Ah! Let me handle this, Loch said, eagerly seeking out control of Sloane's body again.

"No!" Sloane shouted before he suddenly realized how insane that seemed because no one else could hear Loch. He cleared his throat, taking in Chase's shocked expression and calmly replied, "No, I didn't either."

"You okay?" Chase asked carefully.

Merrick said nothing, but he was staring Sloane down with an intense ferocity.

"Fine, fine, just… uh… you know." Sloane gestured around them. "Grieving."

Grieving the wonderful lover who always left your sweet body flooded with bountiful seed? Loch suggested.

"Sorry for your loss," Chase took off his hat respectfully.

"Thanks," Sloane said with a strained smile. He really didn't like how Merrick kept staring at him, and he sighed in relief when Doris finally returned.

"Oh! Hello!" Doris greeted, smiling politely. "I'll be with you gentlemen in just a moment." She waved for Sloane to follow her. "This way, sir."

"Later, Chase," Sloane said. "Merrick."

"Detective Merrick," he corrected sourly.

Sloane didn't bother to reply, following Doris around the desk to a set of viewing rooms. She patted his arm with a sweet smile, urging, "You take all the time you need, sir."

"Thank you," Sloane said gratefully, stepping into the viewing room and shutting the door behind him.

Loch's body was laid out on a table with a blanket drawn over him. His eyes were closed, and he looked peaceful, as if he was only sleeping.

"Go on," Sloane said urgently. "We need to get out of here."

"Oh, look at that!" Loch suddenly exclaimed from his body, swinging his feet off the table. "I'm not dead! Isn't that fun?"

"Any bright ideas for how we're going to escape?"

"Oh, ew! They put these awful little plastic things in my eyes!" Loch complained, flicking away a pair of eye caps. "Hmmph. How rude."

"Focus," Sloane pleaded, pulling Loch down into an urgent kiss. Physical affection was usually very effective for getting Loch's attention. "Ulgh, wait! What is in your mouth?"

"Cotton and some string," Loch said, turning his head to spit it all out. "They sewed my mouth shut."

"Gross!"

"Well," Loch huffed, "they had to get me ready to see you! Couldn't have my dead mouth just hanging wide open. That would have been awful."

"Okay, listen. There are cops right outside. I can't just waltz out of here with a corpse! They're already acting suspicious as hell!"

"You know I could just transport both of us out of here," Loch scoffed.

"Yeah, except they're going to be expecting me to walk back out!" Sloane groaned in frustration. "They're gonna know I came here to see you! And when you disappear, they're gonna come ask me about it!"

"Well, I can't very well stay here and pretend to be dead," Loch sniffed. "Can you imagine how boring that would be?"

"Ulgh, fine!" Sloane waved his hands. "We'll figure something out. I'll go first, and just meet me in the car. We've gotta get back to my office."

"Right," Loch said with a curt nod, "because we have to plan to kill my other brother."

"We don't know that we're going to kill anyone yet!" Sloane insisted.

"Probably for the best."

"We will discuss this later. I'm going to leave now. I will see you in the car."

"Very well, my love. Remember to look sad!"

Sloane resisted the urge to groan again, hastily leaving the viewing room and glancing around for Merrick and Chase. He didn't see them, but he made sure to thank Doris before hurrying outside.

As soon as he sat down in the driver's seat of his car, Loch magically appeared beside him and cheerfully reminded, "Seatbelts!"

"Yup, got it! Now let's get the hell out of here," Sloane muttered, drumming his fingers on the steering wheel as he drove back to his office.

"What's troubling you, sweet Starkiller?" Loch reached out with a slick tentacle to hold his fidgeting hand.

"Chase isn't stupid. If he goes digging around, he's gonna figure out who you're a ghoul of, and I can't possibly explain any of this to him."

"Why not? Is he Lucian?"

"No, I actually don't know. He might be a freakin' atheist for all I know. This isn't just about illegal magic. There's that whole teeny, tiny murder thing."

"You mean Kunst?" Loch's brow scrunched, and he offered another tentacle. "My love, it was his choice to sacrifice himself."

"Yeah, I'm sure the cops will love to hear that," Sloane mumbled. "The worst part is now that I'm thinking about it, it's like he died for nothing. We destroyed the totem that would wake up Salgumel, but there are still other people, other gods, trying to find a way!"

"And we shall stop them," Loch said confidently.

"You're always so sure. Why?"

"Because we're together." Loch smiled. "And together, my love, we can do anything. We obviously have Great Azaethoth's blessing. What more could you want?"

"I guess a sword of starlight is a pretty big sign that we're on the right track," Sloane said, managing a tired laugh. "Glad to know we have a fan."

"I think it's safe to say he ships us," Loch added gleefully.

"How do you even know what that means?"

"Milo told me, because he ships Han Solo with General Leia. I believe he also said they're his OTP, which is a title of great prestige."

"Right."

"We're probably Great Azaethoth's OTP. I'm still his favorite great-great-great-grandson, you know."

"I know you are."

"He might even show up to our wedding!"

"You really think so?" Sloane asked, quirking a skeptical brow.

"My dear Starkiller," Loch said smugly, "anything could happen. You just need to have faith."

"Right." Sloane's phone rang, and he reached for it. "It's Fred."

"Ah-ah! You're driving!" Loch scolded, using a tentacle to snatch it away from Loch. He answered it on speaker, saying politely, "Azaethoth the Lesser here, how may I be of assistance?"

"You guys okay?" Fred asked gruffly.

"Everything is just peachy," Sloane replied. "Uh, why do you ask?"

"Because I got a call from a good friend of mine who works down at Crosby-Ayers Funeral Home," Fred explained. "Kitty York? Maybe you met her."

"Shit. No. I don't think we met her. What now?"

"She's part of a little network of people who like to help ghouls. Told me, uh, that they just had a ghoul's body vanish from the funeral home after some nice-lookin' guy with big eyebrows came in to see him? Sounds a lot like you."

"Did she say anything about the ghoul?" Loch asked. "Maybe mention how dashingly handsome he was? That he exuded an immortal charm despite being a lifeless corpse?"

"No," Fred said flatly.

"We're fine," Sloane promised. "Thanks for checking on us."

"No problem."

"Did you still need help with your penis?" Loch piped up. "You never did call me back, and I was just wondering—"

Click.

"—if you needed... hmmph." Loch made a face and set Sloane's phone back in the cupholder. "All I ever want to do is help people, and they're so rude."

"Whatever Fred wanted, I'm very sure that one, it had nothing to do with his penis, and two, he figured it out or he would have called you back before now."

"Hmmph. As if anyone else's advice could possibly be better than mine."

Sloane did his best to soothe Loch's bruised ego and stay positive, but his heart was currently thudding in his stomach for what was ahead of them. He still felt sick when he and Loch walked into his office. The door was unlocked, and Alexander was lounging in his chair at the desk.

"What took you so long?" Alexander asked dryly, lighting up a cigarette with a snap of his fingers.

"Don't ever leave a body at the post office," Sloane quipped, and he moved to open a window to air out the smoke.

"I'm going to leave them a scathing review online," Loch promised.

The room behind Alexander shimmered, Rota's invisible body settling in there with a soft laugh.

"So, to business," Alexander said. "Gronoch has taken the body of a man named Peter Myers. He's the lead researcher for Hazel Medical."

"Is the real Peter Myers alive?" Sloane asked.

"Yes. He's a devout follower of Gronoch. He's a willing vessel for that bastard. Fitting for a doctor, you know. Worshipping the God of Healing and Attrition."

"Is there somewhere else we can try to find him? Talk to him?"

"He's out of the country," Alexander replied, flicking his cigarette. The ashes disappeared before they could hit the floor. "Hazel Medical is having a big summit in London, but he'll be back early tomorrow morning for a press conference."

"I was hoping for something a little less public?" Sloane cringed, and he sat down in one of the chairs by his desk. "Don't you know where Gronoch lives when he's not at Hazel? You found my home, after all. You must know some sort of tracking sorcery."

"Sorcery?" Alexander actually laughed. "I found your office address on Jay's calendar, and once I knew who you were, it wasn't hard to look up your home address."

"Well, shit. I guess you weren't divining Jay's blood to track him down either, were you?"

"No?" Alexander frowned. "Who even does that? Divining is crap."

"Right."

"Why don't we just go back to the shiny building that promised towels and mugs?" Loch nodded his head at Alexander. "That's where we found you, yes?"

"Yes, it's where we live," Alexander said curtly. "There's nothing there."

"Even in the labs?" Sloane pressed. "I'm sure a god's body would be quite the prized specimen."

"We've already looked," Alexander snapped.

"Even down in the restricted levels, we've only ever found human material," Rota added, trying to be helpful. "My body isn't there."

"Human material?" Sloane echoed, exchanging a worried glance with Loch. "Alexander, where are the people you took before going after Jay?"

"If any of them are alive, they're probably in the labs," Alexander said calmly. "Gronoch may snatch people from all over the world, but his nasty little experiments only happen here."

"What the hell is everyone's fascination with this town?" Sloane mumbled under his breath. He quickly got back on track. "So you're telling me that there's potentially innocent people trapped down there right now?"

Alexander sat up straight, his eyes narrowing as he hissed, "Oh, don't even think about it."

"Wait. What are we thinking about?" Loch rejoined the conversation with a grin. "Because I'm thinking about my very strongly worded review for the post office. What's happening?"

"There are innocent people trapped at the Hazel Medical building down in their labs," Sloane explained urgently. "We have to help them."

"No," Alexander corrected. "What we need to do is hunt Gronoch. He'll be back tomorrow, and we can follow him after the press conference, and then you can whip out that beautiful sword of starlight and make him tell us where Rota's body is!"

"Thought you wanted me to kill him," Sloane drawled.

"After he tells us!"

"This first!" Sloane argued passionately. "You said this is the only facility where Gronoch is doing the experiments, right? We can shut him down and save all those people!"

"That's stupid!" Alexander seethed. "The labs are heavily protected, and trying to go down there would be fuckin' suicide!"

"How can you be so sure?"

Growling in frustration, Alexander reached for another cigarette. "This is fucking ridiculous. The last time Rota and I tried to go down there, Gronoch almost killed us! It's idiotic, it's…." He paused, exhaling a long puff of smoke. "It's perfect."

Alexander…? Rota sounded concerned.

"Ohhh, is it going to be dangerous?" Loch asked eagerly.

"Very," Alexander confirmed with a wicked smile. "You want to go save those people? Let's go."

"Wait, wait, what was that about Gronoch almost killing you?" Sloane demanded.

"Here's the plan." Alexander inhaled deeply. "My clearance can get us down to the first restricted level where the staff quarters are. Beyond that, where you want to go rescue people, is going to be a challenge…."

"How much of a challenge?"

"Armed security teams, all expert witches, and dozens of silencing ward traps," Alexander replied. "Rota and I made it down all the way to the very bottom level before Gronoch came."

"You want him to come," Sloane realized out loud. "You don't care about those poor people, you just want to draw him out!"

Skillfully blowing a smoke ring, Alexander snorted, "Duh." He smirked. "What are you worried about, Starkiller? With all of our power combined, it shouldn't be a problem."

"I still haven't agreed to kill anyone," Sloane warned. "I want to help those people, and I want to try reasoning with Gronoch."

"Trust me," Alexander said. "Once you meet him, you'll very quickly learn there is no reasoning with him."

"Well," Loch snapped, "we have our own plan."

"We do?" Sloane asked under his breath.

"Please, Little Azaethoth," Alexander drawled. "Tell us what your great plan is."

"We have something that even a mighty god like Gronoch fears," Loch said dramatically, rising up to his full height and brandishing a dashing smile. "Something that will call him to heel, that will make him shake with terror in his fleshy disguise…."

"What?"

"His mother."

CHAPTER 11.

"ABSOLUTELY NOT," Urilith bellowed, her hands planted firmly on her hips as she glared at Loch.

"But Mother!" Loch protested.

"You want me to kill my own son? My child?"

"Our own brother?" Galgareth spat.

"Now wait a moment! That's not what I said!" Loch argued smoothly.

"Yes, you did!" Urilith yelled. "You said that—"

"I said that Sloane is going to kill him!"

Urilith glared at Sloane, and Sloane grimaced.

Oh, this wasn't going well at all.

They had regrouped over at Lynnette's, and introductions were strained. Alexander didn't want to meet anyone, and Rota was equally hesitant. They popped right up on the roof to avoid everyone and so Alexander could smoke.

Loch was trying to convince Urilith to help them, but the conversation was turning disastrous very quickly.

Lynnette was hiding in the kitchen but occasionally peeked into the living room to see what was going on.

"Urilith," Sloane pleaded, "I know it sounds really bad, but I don't want to hurt anyone! That's why we want you to come with us! We want to try to talk Gronoch down, see if he'll stop!"

"Ha!" Urilith scoffed. "You're trying to set a trap for him!"

"Just a tiny one," Loch said with a sweet smile. It withered when Urilith turned her angry glare on him. "Mother, please listen. Gronoch doesn't like me. None of my brothers ever did. He's not going to listen to me, but he might listen to you!"

"What am I supposed to say to him?" Urilith snarled, her anger beginning to weaken. "How he's completely broken my heart... how he's betrayed the very mortals we were supposed to nurture and protect?"

"That would be a good start!"

Urilith scowled, and she bopped Loch on top of his head with one of her tentacles.

"Ow!" Loch mumbled, rubbing his head. "Well, it would be."

"I'm sorry, my sweet child," Urilith said. "I can't help you. Whatever the circumstances, I can't choose between my children. I know what's at stake... I just...." She wrung her hands and shook her head. "I can't."

"Then I'll go." Galgareth stood up abruptly from the sofa.

"Galgareth?" Urilith frowned with worry. "My sweet daughter, why?"

"Because Gronoch needs to hear these things," Galgareth replied firmly. "He may have already chosen to side against us and mankind, but he's still our family. He deserves a chance to change his mind."

"I pray that he does," Urilith whispered, and she pulled Galgareth into a close embrace. She reached for Loch and dragged him into the hug too.

Sloane took a few steps back to give them space, but he found a yellow tentacle tugging him over.

"You're one of my children now," Urilith said, stroking Sloane's hair. "Before you leave on your quest, I want you all to have my blessing."

"Thank you." Sloane smiled shyly.

He hadn't had a family in so long, his heart ached in a way that was strange and unfamiliar. It made his knees feel like spaghetti, but he also felt like he could take on the whole world with one noodly step.

With arms and tentacles wrapped all around him, he hadn't felt so loved in decades:

The adoration of a spunky sister.

The affection of a kind mother.

And the undying love of a beautiful soul, a god, who would do anything for him.

Sloane was crying before he realized it, an awesome sensation flowing through him from so much tenderness and divine contact. It was surreal, his new family and faith, both wrapped around him like a warm blanket.

He jerked his head up when he heard someone else crying, seeing Lynnette at the doorway.

She was sobbing into her hands, wailing, "I'm sorry! It's just so beautiful!"

"Come, mortal child." Urilith beckoned her over and pulled Lynnette into their massive group hug. "Join us… both of you."

Lynnette wiggled into their embrace, and she was still crying. "Both…? Both of us?"

Urilith's arms wrapped around her, and a stray tentacle petted Lynnette's long hair. "Yes, my child. You and the babe you carry inside of you."

"Huh?" Lynnette's head snapped up. "I'm pregnant?"

"What?" Sloane gasped.

"You didn't know?" Urilith smiled warmly. "Ah, then I am pleased to hear the news if you are, dear one."

"Yes! I think! Holy shit!" Lynnette slapped her hands over her mouth. "Oh wow. I knew I hadn't been feeling right, and I was late, but I'm, like, always late—"

"Are you happy?" Urilith asked.

"Yes," Lynnette said with more certainty. "I'm happy. I love Milo so much, and ugh, I've been so awful to him. Oh! Milo! I have to tell him!"

"Congratulations!" Sloane exclaimed, and he hugged Lynnette tightly. "I'm so happy for you! Milo is gonna freak out!"

"Freak out?" Lynnette frowned.

"Happy freak out! Totally happy!" Sloane promised. "You have any idea how much he's gonna love being a father?"

Lynnette laughed, caught up in an emotional wave of tears.

"If it's a boy, just be prepared. We both know he's gonna wanna name him Han Solo!"

"Maybe not!" Lynnette defended. "It could be Luke!"

Sloane grinned. "Seriously, congrats."

"I'm going to go tell him right now!" Lynnette declared, sweeping her hair back and smiling at all the gods before her. "Thank you all. For all your blessings."

"I can't take credit for this one." Urilith chuckled, and her tentacles reached out to reverently touch Lynnette's stomach. "Ah, but this... this is from me. Thank you for your hospitality and all your kindness. May your pregnancy be gentle and your sickness vanish."

"Thank you!" Lynnette gushed, and she rubbed her stomach excitedly. "Hear that, little Han-or-Luke-or-possibly-Leia? We've been blessed!"

"Congratulations!" Galgareth gave Lynnette a big hug. "Now! Go see your mate and share the news!"

Waving frantically, Lynnette took off running to the door.

"Think she'll have any trouble getting into the precinct?" Loch mused, the first thing he'd said in several minutes.

"Nah," Sloane said. "Lynnette's pretty fierce, and with that baby on board? They'd better just let her in to see Milo." He paused and tried to catch Loch's eye. "You okay?"

"Fine," Loch said all too quickly.

"I'm going to prepare a feast," Urilith announced. "To celebrate the new life growing inside our hostess and to bless you both on your quest tomorrow. Hmm, I don't suppose there are cows available for humane slaughter and feasting?"

"No, but there's a grocery store down on Fifth Street according to Toby." Galgareth took Urilith's arm and brandished a wallet chain. "Inside this is a device called a 'Visa' that we can use to purchase what we need for the feast."

"Will you two be all right with Alexander and the godling?" Urilith asked.

"I'm sure we'll be fine," Sloane replied. "I'm pretty sure he doesn't intend on coming down from the roof anytime soon."

Urilith kissed them farewell. "Tonight will be a wondrous celebration! There's so many dishes I'm going to cook." She patted Sloane's arm. "Maybe even a few I'll make again for your wedding!"

"That sounds great! Thank you!"

Galgareth hugged Sloane and Loch, assuring them, "And before you ask, I promise we'll be fine. The grocery store is close, and I'm much better suited to navigating the mortal realm."

"Be safe," Sloane still cautioned, waving goodbye as the goddesses departed. When they were alone, he turned to address Loch. "Hey, seriously. What's going on? You're never this quiet unless Gordon Ramsey is on."

Loch frowned, and he took Sloane's hands in his and curled a few tentacles around his wrists to deepen the connection. "I'm… troubled."

"Talk to me, Loch," Sloane encouraged, pressing closer and kissing his cheek. "We're mates, right? We're getting married in just a few weeks. You can tell me anything."

"My family," Loch tried, uncharacteristically awkward, clearly struggling to find the words. "I'm going to miss them."

"I'm sure they'll come visit after the wedding," Sloane soothed. "We'll definitely see your sister every winter solstice." He scanned Loch's furrowed expression. "Is this about your brother? Gronoch?"

"Gronoch was never particularly kind to me," Loch scoffed. "None of my siblings were except Gal. The pains of being the youngest, I suppose. But there were times with Gronoch… I thought he was different from the others. But now knowing he's following Tollmathan's madness…."

"I'm sorry," Sloane said earnestly. "I really am, but you know there's still a chance that we can talk to him. I don't wanna hurt anyone, Loch. Especially your family."

"Oh, my sweet Starkiller." Loch grimaced. "Gronoch is a god, and while we are prone to being a bit whimsical, I'd say he's pretty sold on taking over the world. Ripping souls out and all that is pretty hard to come back from."

"Still…."

"It's all right." Loch's eyes turned black, glittering with stars as he gazed down at Sloane. "We will get through it together, one way or another."

"Thank you for telling me," Sloane said as he hugged him close. He enjoyed the warmth of Loch's arms around him, adding, "For a second, I thought you were upset about Lynnette's baby."

"Ehhh. Possibly."

"Why?" Sloane didn't understand and reached up to stroke Loch's hair. "I thought you liked kids!"

Loch pouted more, and then the answer clicked.

"Loch, I've already told you that I would happily have children with you. Whatever that means for us. I mean, what does that mean for us?"

Brightening back up, Loch replied, "As a god, I could easily spawn on my own. Like dear Chandraleth, my half sister, who was born of Salgumel alone. But I always wanted to share a child with my mate. Together, you and I could spawn in a variety of ways."

"Such as?" Sloane smirked, amused by how excited Loch was.

"With your seed, I could carry our child. Or, if you wanted to…." Loch actually blushed. "You could."

"Really?" Sloane slid a hand over his belly without thinking about it, and he laughed. "I just… wow. I never thought…." The idea of carrying a child, Loch's child, was making his face warm. "That would be incredible."

"I'm in no rush," Loch assured him. "I'm just thinking of it more often now. And our wedding being so close, it feels inescapable."

"It's okay, Loch!" Sloane brought him over to the couch to sit down. "I think about that stuff too."

"You do?"

"Of course! I think about our future all the time!" Sloane grinned. "You know, like getting out of my apartment and actually buying a house together. Do I change my last name when we get married? Or hyphenate? Sloane Beaumont-Azaethoth?"

"Mmm.... Sloane Beaumont-Azaethoth does sound rather lovely," Loch mused as he leaned back and got comfortable. He pulled Sloane up on his chest, curling his tentacles around his shoulders to keep him close. "Only if you want to, though."

"We'll see." Sloane laughed, kissing Loch's neck with a contented sigh. It wasn't hard to find himself in the mood, being so close to Loch. There was also something about discussing children that excited him.

Maybe it was the thrill of knowing they had such a bright future ahead of them.

He kissed Loch's neck a little harder and slid his hand up his chest, hoping he'd take the hint.

"Please forgive me," Loch murmured, laying his hand over Sloane's. "Although this would be an opportune time to ravage your tight mortal body... could we just...."

His expression was strained, and his eyes were pleading.

"Cuddle?" Sloane suggested.

"Yes."

"Of course." Sloane got settled in Loch's embrace and stretched his legs over the end of the couch.

"You're not angry with me?" Loch asked hesitantly.

"What? Because you don't wanna ravage my tight mortal body?" Loch scowled.

"I'm not angry." Sloane chuckled. "I promise. There's gonna be a day that maybe I won't be in the mood, and I expect the same respect when I politely decline your advances."

"Of course," Loch promised, but there was a small pause. He smirked, seemingly unable to help himself as he amended, "Although, I'd first make sure you were feeling all right, because obviously you'd have to be quite unwell to refuse my physical pleasures."

"Oh, obviously." Rolling his eyes, Sloane reached for the remote and flipped through the channels. "Mmm, no Gordon. But ah, *Chopped* is on."

"Ted?" Loch perked up, smiling when he saw the spectacled host on screen. "Ah, he pleases me."

"I know."

"Sloane?"

"Yes?"

"I love you," Loch said, wrapping himself around Sloane even tighter. "I love you so much."

"I love you too. No matter what happens tomorrow, I know we'll be fine."

"Mm?"

"Because we're together."

They watched television until Urilith and Galgareth returned from their grocery trip to start working on the feast. Sloane got swept up into the kitchen to assist while Loch hung around the sidelines, occasionally snagging a bite to eat.

Alexander poked his head in briefly, perhaps drawn in by the smell, but he only stayed long enough for Rota to help him steal a bottle of Lynnette's wine before returning to the roof.

"Gordon says you're supposed to let the meat come to room temperature before cooking," Loch was scolding, his nose firmly turned up as he watched his mother cook.

Bopping Loch smartly with one of her tentacles, Urilith griped, "I've been cooking for thousands of years, eons before the first mortal man ever took his first step. Don't tell me how to cook, little one!"

Galgareth and Sloane shared a good snicker over that, then left the kitchen briefly to set up the dining room table. As they were smoothing out a new tablecloth, the front door opened.

"Can you hear me in there, little space general?" Milo was cooing, walking in all hunched over as he talked to Lynnette's stomach. "You want your name to be Leia, don't you?"

Lynnette ruffled Milo's hair. "We still don't know if it's a boy or a girl yet! Are we really set on Leia? Because Mara would be pretty too."

"Ohhh!" Milo gasped. "What about Mara Organa?"

"I take it he's excited?" Sloane opened his arms to give Lynnette another big hug.

"So very excited!" Milo gushed, embracing Sloane next. "I can't believe it! I'm going to be a daddy!"

"Congratulations!" Sloane cheered. "I'm seriously so stoked for you guys. Get off work early, huh?"

"Hell yes!" Milo laughed. "I might have spazzed out a tiny bit and took the rest of the day off."

"He screamed 'I'm gonna be a daddy!' repeatedly and knocked over a table," Lynnette said with an affectionate smile. She tilted her head and sniffed eagerly. "Mmm, what is the smell?"

"Urilith is preparing a feast to honor your new child," Sloane replied.

"Wait, I smell lavender," Lynnette gasped. "Is she giving me a Neun Monde feast?"

"Of course!" Galgareth replied. "She hasn't had the chance to cook for one in a few hundred years. She's very excited."

"What's that?" Milo asked.

"Uh, it's like a Sagittarian baby shower?" Sloane offered.

"Is this like the naming thing? Like what I did when I converted?" Milo scratched his chin. "We haven't decided officially on a name, but I mean, Mara Organa is pretty wicked."

"No, that won't happen until the baby is born," Lynnette explained excitedly. "We celebrate the pregnancy with the Neun Monde. Nine moons for nine months. Lavender and other soothing herbs are burned to help relax my new mommy mojo, we eat lots of fruits and meat that are good for the baby, and we get gifts that we'll use for the birth."

"The birth?" Milo struggled to keep up. "There's other stuff to do?"

"Yes. Stuff that you will do as my partner!" Lynnette beamed. "Don't worry, I'll teach you. It's going to be beautiful, baby."

"Okay," Milo said, taking a deep breath. "Shower stuff, birth stuff, and then naming stuff?"

"You got it," Sloane confirmed. "I remember the birthing gifts. My mother kept my bell for me. I still have it somewhere."

"A bell?" Milo frowned.

"The ring of a bell so the first sound upon your ears is music," Sloane recited.

"But babies can totally hear in the womb, right? So the bell wouldn't technically be the first thing they'd hear."

"It's just part of the ritual," Lynnette whispered loudly, kissing Milo's cheek and swishing into the kitchen.

"Oh, okay."

"Don't worry, mortal child," Loch soothed. "You will not have to travel this path alone."

"Thank you, your great godliness," Milo said, obviously relieved. "I don't wanna mess anything up!"

"Even if you do, we'll all be right here," Sloane promised.

Soon the table was set with a massive assortment of food: steaming roasts, juicy fruits, and savory vegetables. There was also a collection of colorful bottles, a small box, and a large jar filled with honey.

Urilith made a crown of lavender for Lynnette's hair, placing it upon her as she said, "I've brought you a bell so your child's first sound will be music, honey so your child's first taste will be sweet, herbs so their first smell will be calming, blankets so their first touch will be tender, and this crown so that when they look upon you, their first sight will be your beauty as their mother."

"Thank you," Lynnette gushed, instantly tearful and cradling the crown on her head. "It's perfect. It's all so perfect. Thank you, Urilith."

"I helped her make some milk potions for you too," Galgareth said proudly. "Fennel, basil, and thistle. And for the new daddy, ginger and chamomile."

"For me?" Milo blinked. "What do I need it for?"

"To help you stay calm and focused while you're helping take care of your new baby," Galgareth scolded. "Trust us. You're going to need it."

Sloane felt someone watching them and turned his head to spy Alexander snagging a plate of food and trying to slip back outside undetected. He tapped Loch's shoulder to let him know he was excusing himself for a moment and followed Alexander.

As he came outside, he saw Alexander's feet as he floated up to the roof, no doubt being carried up there by Rota's ghostly tentacles. Sloane clapped to make himself a ladder of starlight, carefully climbing up to the edge of the gutters. "Alexander?"

"What?" Alexander sourly retorted, settled on the very peak of the roof and frowning down at him.

"You know you and Rota are more than welcome to come eat with us," Sloane offered. "You don't have to hide up here."

"We're not hiding. We're preparing ourselves."

"For tomorrow?"

"Yes," Rota mumbled, his massive form curled up behind Alexander. Part of his body appeared to be sinking into the house, his tentacles wound around Alexander's legs to keep him safely on top of the roof.

Don't speak... rest. Alexander petted Rota before addressing Sloane shortly, "You do realize how dangerous this is? The secured levels we're going to were almost too much for me and Rota."

"So?" Sloane bristled a little. "Loch is powerful, and so am I!"

"Ah, but you're the one risking your life over some people you've never met," Alexander reminded him. "You value human life so much that you're willing to die for a stranger."

"Compassion isn't weakness, Alexander."

"It is when someone is holding a gun in your face," he dryly replied. "You'd hesitate to kill someone—"

"If they're trying to hurt me or my loved ones, that's different!" Sloane argued. "I'll do whatever needs to be done."

"I'll remember you said that," Alexander said with a nasty smirk. "Funny thing... I once overheard Gronoch talking about a totem they'd found that would wake Salgumel up, but it kept getting destroyed in a pretty nasty ritual."

Sloane's heart sunk.

"Seems some innocent person had to sacrifice themselves to power the spell," he went on casually. "You wouldn't know anything about that, would you? Maybe doing whatever needed to be done?"

The ritual Alexander spoke of was the same that had killed Sloane's parents when he was a child. He'd repeated it as an adult to destroy the totem once and for all, and Professor Emil Kunst had offered his life.

Sloane shivered as he remembered the horrible moment when he'd pushed the knife into Kunst's chest as if it was yesterday.

Huffing in annoyance, Sloane said, "Look, I was just trying to be nice. Forget it. You can sleep up here for all I care. We'll leave first thing in the morning."

"Very well, Starkiller." Alexander leaned back on Rota's invisible bulk. "Tomorrow I suppose we'll really find out how well you wield that little sword of starlight, won't we?"

"If it comes to that," Sloane said firmly. He climbed back down the ladder without another word to find Loch back inside the house.

"What is it, my love?" Loch asked.

"Could we go lay down?" Sloane whispered.

"Oh!" Loch grinned lecherously. "Eager to mate? I understand completely. I wasn't feeling quite like myself earlier, but all of this talk of children has put me in the most amorous mood."

"Loch, it's not that." Sloane shook his head. "Could we... I mean, could you just...?" He felt sick, trying to get Alexander's words out of his head.

Loch frowned and reached for Sloane's hands. He kissed his knuckles, asking gently, "Do we need to cuddle?"

"Yes," Sloane sighed.

"Absolutely, my love."

CHAPTER 12.

SLOANE WOKE up in Loch's arms, nestled comfortably against his chest with a warm blanket of tentacles wrapped around him. He stretched his legs and tried to wiggle free as he yawned. "Loch… it's time to get up."

"The sun isn't up," Loch argued. "Therefore, I do not need to be up."

"We need to get going," Sloane said, smirking as Loch's tentacles squeezed a little tighter in protest.

"Now, if you please," Alexander's voice called from the doorway. He was leaned against the frame with his arms crossed, Rota's giant form hovering behind him.

Rota was so big that parts of him were dipping into the floor and up into the ceiling. Being intangible had its perks when one was of godly proportions.

"Just give us a second," Sloane said, trying to hang on to the warmth of Loch's embrace for a little longer. He grumbled when Alexander didn't budge. "Fine."

"Come eat! All of you!" Urilith called out from the kitchen.

Still rubbing sleep out of his eyes, Sloane forced himself up from the couch to find Urilith. He was met by the savory scent of sizzling bacon and eggs, and his mouth instantly filled with drool. "Wow, that smells amazing."

"Come on! Eat your breakfast!" Galgareth handed Sloane a plate. "It's chock-full of Mother's strongest blessing of protection."

"Thank you," Sloane said, gratefully digging in.

"You too." Galgareth thrust a plate at Alexander.

Alexander made a face and picked at it with his fork, but he started to slowly eat after deeming it acceptable.

"When you're done eating, we'll head out," Galgareth said brightly. "I've been talking to Alexander, and the guards change shifts at eight o'clock. It may be the best time to make our move."

"Mmm," Sloane grunted through a mouthful. "Milo and Lynnette still sleeping?"

"Yes," Urilith said with a sweet smile. "I made them a special potion to help them rest so they can bond today."

"But they have work... eh... never mind." Sloane wasn't about to explain the nuances of taking sick time to a well-meaning goddess. He tried to finish eating quickly and took a deep breath. "Okay."

"I'll meet you there," Alexander said briskly, turning and promptly vanishing with Rota.

"Wait! Well... shit." Sloane frowned. "So much for having a plan or anything."

"But we do have a plan," Loch said confidently. "You're going to stay back, look ravishing, and let three gods unleash their mighty wrath."

"On unsuspecting and possibly innocent mortals who just happen to work for a very evil company?"

"Okay, just a smidge of wrath."

"Thank you."

THE DRIVE over to Hazel was tense, and it only grew the closer they got. By the time Sloane parked, he was ready to start chewing his nails off. His godly companions remained at ease, but Sloane couldn't help the state of his nerves.

Loch's warm tentacles in his lap helped, but he still couldn't shake the feeling of dread gnawing at his gut. He knew what he might have to do if things took a turn for the worse.

He'd have to kill another god.

Putting on a brave face, he led Galgareth and Loch inside to the elevator.

There wasn't much of a crowd, and the single patrolling security guard did not pay them any mind.

When the elevator doors opened, Sloane jerked back in surprise to see Alexander waiting inside. "Uh, hi!"

"Are you ready?" Alexander asked dryly.

Rota was nowhere to be seen, his massive form doubtlessly hiding somewhere above or below the elevator.

"Yes!" Loch slid into the elevator with a bounce in his step.

Even Galgareth looked a little more peppy than usual, and she was smiling. She nudged Loch, saying, "This is just like when we used to steal the sacrifices from the other gods' altar before the rituals were over."

"Ah, good times." Loch sighed fondly. "We had so much fun."

Sloane didn't think what they were about to do even compared to some godly shenanigans, and he stepped into the elevator with a heavy feeling in his stomach still nibbling away.

"Going down." Alexander waved his hand over the panel and pushed a button marked B7.

As the elevator descended, Loch suddenly swept Sloane into a tight embrace and kissed him firmly.

"Loch!" Sloane mumbled, his cheeks flushing from such a passionate kiss in front of an audience. He kissed back nonetheless, losing himself in Loch's lips. "Mmm, Loch…."

"I love you," Loch said. "Fear not."

"I love you too." Sloane tried to smile. Out of the corner of his eye, he saw Alexander staring at them.

At first he thought it was disgust for such a blatant public display of affection. A closer look showed something else.

The pain in Alexander's eyes, the draw of his mouth, it was the pain of longing.

One day, Rota's voice promised, *I'll kiss you like that.*

Alexander looked away, a sad smile appearing and draining his young face. *Keep telling me your beautiful lies…. They're all I have.*

The elevator lurched to a stop, and an alarm went off.

"Shit," Alexander hissed.

"What is it?" Sloane demanded.

"Time to get off." Alexander moved in front of the doors and raised his hands. With a loud groan of metal, Rota's tentacles came up from the floor to follow his lead and pry the doors open.

"What's going on?"

"Hazel has cameras," Alexander replied. "They saw us coming and decided we don't look friendly."

"Okay." Sloane's thoughts raced as he stepped forward. "We can put up shields, maybe a few not-so-legal sleeping spells—"

"Too late," Alexander said when a troop of armed men appeared to line the hallway before them.

They were wearing tactical gear, and some had rifles. However primitive, ballistic weapons could still be quite effective. Sloane quickly noticed the men who didn't have guns were weaving spells with their hands.

There were at least a dozen of them, and again Sloane pleaded, "We can find another way to do this! No one has to get hurt—"

No sooner did he speak that the guards opened fire and a chilling wind full of hail rained down on them.

Sloane hurled up a quick shield to combat the icy chunks and bullets, but it was Loch who froze them all in midair with a thought.

"Now," Loch called out, "that's not very nice."

Though clearly stunned, the guards kept moving. A few continued to fire, and a large grenade sailed over to clatter at their feet.

Galgareth grabbed the grenade and closed her eyes, the device thunking harmlessly to the ground a moment later. She winked at Sloane, explaining, "Goddess of Serendipity. Happy accident that the one grenade they threw at us was a dud!"

Five more grenades joined the first.

"Well, shit."

Loch opened up a portal on the floor, a window into another world, and frantically kicked the grenades into it as he hissed, "Couldn't just have them all miss? Maybe throw them at each other?"

"You know my magic doesn't work that way!" Galgareth growled.

Sloane expanded his shield to block the entire hallway to keep them safe, the magical barrier fending off another volley of grenades. They exploded promptly and shook the entire hallway, forcing Sloane to take a knee to keep his balance.

"They're not going to stop!" Alexander barked, glaring at Sloane. "Not until we're dead!"

"Please!" Sloane shouted at the guards. "You have to stop!"

The hail increased, and a spear of starlight thunked into the center of Sloane's shield. The shield began to crack, and Loch raised his hand to heal it.

"Persistent, aren't they?" Loch grumbled.

From behind them in the broken elevator, there was an innocent clinking sound. They turned around to see another cluster of grenades dropping down from the roof of the elevator.

"Loch!" Sloane yelled.

Loch turned to block the new explosions from them with a shimmering white barrier of his own, but more were still coming.

Sloane's ears were ringing, and he watched as another spear hit his shield. It cracked again, splintering rapidly down the sides. He struggled to hold it, but he couldn't concentrate, and everyone was yelling so angrily.

Galgareth's foot had somehow gotten caught in one of Loch's portals, and now the two of them were cursing at each other as she struggled to break free.

Sloane's pulse became a pounding drum inside his head, and his hands ached from the strain of maintaining the shield. More spears of starlight were striking his wall, and the cracks were growing.

"Enough!" Alexander screamed, his eyes glowing brightly as he stormed through the disintegrating shield toward the guards.

"Alexander!" Sloane shouted. "No!"

As Alexander stalked forward, all the gunfire and magic was directed right at him. Rota's ghostly bulk rose up from the floor where he had been hiding to defend him. Bullets and hail bounced off his invisible flesh, and an errant chunk of ice ricocheted as well, striking the first guard in the chest. It pierced through his armor, and he teetered backward with a desperate cry.

As he fell, Alexander raised his hand to direct Rota's tentacles to deflect a bullet into the second guard's neck right in between his helmet and the edge of his armor. The man collapsed with a spray of blood, Alexander sidestepping his corpse as he pushed onward. One of Rota's tentacles swept sharply to the right and smashed the next guard into the ceiling with a gut-wrenching crunch.

The gunfire was staggered now, the hail vanishing almost completely, and the sounds of weapons and magic spells were replaced by frantic screams of pain and death.

Alexander was relentless, and it was all happening in mere seconds. He stretched out his hands in a fierce push, Rota's tentacles moving with him to strike the last group of guards and shove them backward.

Sloane dropped his shield and struggled to chase after him, but Loch grabbed his arm. "Hey!"

Loch's expression was dark, watching Alexander and Rota tear the guards to pieces. "No."

Alexander lifted the last guard, growling frantically, and the man's head crushed inward like a grape. Rota's tentacles kept squeezing and twisting until there was nothing left. Alexander was panting, his chest heaving and his arms trembling as Rota dropped the remains on the floor.

The guards were all certainly dead, and Sloane's anger had reached boiling. This was exactly the kind of mindless slaughter he'd wanted to avoid. He jerked away from Loch, stomping up to Alexander, and reached for his shoulder, snapping, "Hey! We had it under control! We—"

As soon as he touched Alexander, he was struck by a wave of violent pain. He saw Alexander strapped down to a bed, screaming and sobbing as the guards beat him. The guard he'd crushed against the ceiling was holding him down, and the one who'd died by deflected ice was hitting him and laughing.

There was another flash, and he was naked in a shower while the guards cranked the water up to scalding and laughed cruelly as he was burned. The last guard whose head he'd smashed was leading the torture, shouting disgusting insults and vulgar insinuations....

If only you'd be a good boy for us, L-X-I-X! Come on, we just wanna play!

Alexander was writhing in agony, all of his bonding circles fresh from being cut into his skin and burning beneath the hot water. He wanted to die, anything to end the pain....

And then there was Rota....

No more pain... no more....

Alexander shoved Sloane away to sever the connection, hissing, "It's done. Let's go before more come."

Sloane watched Alexander sprint away with Rota right behind him, at a total loss for words. He could still feel Alexander's pain as if it was his own, and he whispered urgently, "What they did to him... they...."

"I'm sorry, my love," Loch urged, arriving at his side to cradle him close. "I'm so sorry... he needed it."

"How, how did you know?" Sloane stammered.

"I didn't, not exactly," Loch replied. "But I'm a god of divine retribution. I know an act of revenge when I see it."

"We need to keep moving," Galgareth said. "If Gronoch didn't know about us coming before, he definitely knows now."

"Right." Sloane struggled to focus. "We've got to get into the lower floors of the lab to find the Silenced people. We just have to keep moving."

There was a loud crash up ahead, and they all rushed toward the sound. They passed by another dead guard and around the corner found Alexander waiting for them by another elevator.

He was holding the door open and waved for them to step inside. "They've locked the elevators. We have two more levels before we're at the bottom. We have to climb up on top of the elevator and drop down the shaft."

"Oh, goody," Sloane grumbled.

Rota's tentacles had already opened up the hatch in the ceiling and grabbed Alexander, effortlessly lifting him up and out of sight.

Galgareth followed, her tentacles reaching up to grab the edge of the opening and pull herself up.

"I've got you, my love." Loch hugged Sloane around his waist and went up after the others. His tentacles lifted them through the hatch and over the top of the elevator, squeezing the two of them down the sides.

Alexander and Rota were already at the bottom, fighting with the doors. Rota was tirelessly pounding into the metal, and when an opening finally appeared, he seized upon it to pull the doors apart.

Sloane's stomach still felt sick as he and Loch landed safely on the floor behind the others. He stayed close, magic brimming on the tips of his fingers, and followed everyone through the twisted opening Rota made.

The final floor was a cavernous space. It was easily the size of a football field, and Sloane couldn't believe all of this was hidden beneath Hazel. Several metal tables were covered in laboratory equipment, but it looked like someone had been interrupted packing it into boxes. There was a long walkway lined with large cages leading away from the tables, and beyond that was nothing but empty space.

It was like looking at the inside of a giant metal egg, and Sloane couldn't begin to imagine what it was all for.

"What is this…?" Galgareth asked quietly.

"This is where I brought them," Alexander replied, Rota rising up to his full size beside him. He stopped midstep when Rota swept a tentacle in front of him.

"What's wrong?" Sloane frowned.

Alexander bowed his head. "It's already too late."

"We just got here!" Sloane stomped forward to check the cages. The first few he came to were empty, but he stopped in his tracks when the next one was filled with blood.

There was no sign of a human being, only a large splatter where one used to be. It appeared fresh, still dripping, and Sloane thought he might throw up.

He ran to another and found more blood, panting erratically as he searched for any sign of life. As he reached the last cage and saw it was empty, he dropped to his knees with a miserable groan. "Fuck...."

"I'm sorry." Loch kneeled beside him and hugged him close.

"But... but why?" Sloane demanded, his heart sinking. "Why would they do this?"

"Because we're going to be closing down this operation," a voice called out from the mangled elevator.

"Gronoch," Alexander hissed, his eyes flashing brightly.

Sloane jumped to his feet to face the man approaching them, his hands curling into tight fists by his sides. Starlight was making his fingers glow and shake, and he fought to keep himself under control.

No, this wasn't a man. It was a god.

Gronoch appeared as a mortal in an expensive suit, strolling toward them with a sharp smile. He was carrying a large trunk that he set down on one of the metal tables and then dusted off his hands. "Ah, L-X-I-X! Mm, I see you've failed to bring the new conduit. Now, I wonder who your friends are." He grinned at Galgareth. "Is that you, little sister?"

"You recognize us, brother?" Galgareth scoffed. "How?"

"You do look so very different in your funny little meat suits," Gronoch laughed, "but who else would you be? No one else is awake that I wouldn't be expecting." He eyed Loch. "Except you, little brother."

"Don't suppose there's any way to end this peacefully?" Loch drawled.

"End what?" Gronoch looked surprised. "The conduit program will continue in another location, since this one has been compromised. L-X-I-X will come with me, of course. Nothing changes."

"Never," Alexander growled and slowly backed away. "Never again."

"We're going to stop you," Sloane snapped. "All of those poor people? You just killed them! Why?"

"Ah, so this is the mighty Starkiller." Gronoch ignored the furious questioning. "Hmm. Thought you'd be taller or something. You do sort of look like that Vulcan guy."

"Hey!" Sloane snarled, his hands sparking erratically. "Are you listening to me? I want to know why you killed these people!"

"Best to start over with a new crop." Gronoch shrugged. "They weren't showing much progress, and I like to travel light. We'll be opening a new facility soon—"

"No! No more!" Sloane shouted. "You're not going to hurt anyone else ever again!"

"And who's gonna stop me?" Gronoch laughed. "You, little Starkiller?"

"I killed Tollmathan," Sloane warned. "I'll do what I have to do."

"I think you'll find I'm much more clever than Toll was," Gronoch cautioned.

"Mm, that's what Mother used to say," Loch chimed in casually. "You know how much she loves you."

"Of course, she—"

"And you know how this is breaking her heart," Loch went on. "I don't think she's really mad at you for torturing innocents and trying to wake up our father. I think…." He sighed dramatically. "I think she's just disappointed."

"Oh, shut up, Azaethoth." Gronoch groaned. "She won't be upset for long once we've remade the world. She'll understand. You all will!"

"You already know what Father will do if he wakes up." Galgareth shook her head in disgust. "You just don't care at all, do you?"

"Sacrifices must be made, little sister," Gronoch said firmly. "Starting with you."

"What?"

A long blue tentacle lurched out from Gronoch's body, and it slapped the ground beneath Galgareth's feet. Her human body dropped to the floor, Toby regaining control and scrambling away with a scream.

In the vast space behind them appeared a large tentacled beast. It had a full beard of writhing tentacles and giant wings like a bat. It rose up on its clawed feet and charged forward, running smack into an invisible wall.

It was Galgareth's true godly body, and she couldn't break through the barrier surrounding her.

"No!" Loch roared, diving toward Gronoch in a violent rage.

"Wait! Loch!" Sloane tried to warn him.

Gronoch's tentacles lashed out again, and Loch's body dropped lifelessly to the floor. His forward momentum carried it onward, skidding to a stop at Gronoch's feet.

Sloane watched in horror as Loch's magnificent dragon form appeared behind the invisible wall alongside Galgareth, both of the gods now equally trapped. "Loch!"

"Sloane!" Loch roared, frantically slamming himself against the wall. It did nothing. Whatever the barrier was, it wouldn't budge.

"Now we have two more gods to create new conduits," Gronoch said gleefully as he clapped. "L-X-I-X has been our only success, and I've been so desperate to prove to the others that my operation is viable. Mmm… what's your blood type?"

"Let them go!" Sloane barked. "There's not going to be any more experiments! This is going to end, right now!"

"Ah." Gronoch gazed up at his siblings. "Isn't this wonderful? All of us together… one big happy family."

"Sloane," Alexander hissed. "He's not going to stop. He won't let any of us go now. You know what you have to do, don't you?"

"Yes," Sloane said, raising his hands out in front of him as starlight burned between his palms. "I have to kill a god."

CHAPTER 13.

GALGARETH AND Loch were still fighting to escape the barrier, Toby was hiding over by the elevator, and Sloane quickly advanced toward Gronoch with starlight glowing in his hands. Alexander was a few steps behind him, and Rota's tentacles were lashing like whips across the floor all around them.

Gronoch did not look impressed. "You really think your little puny sword of starlight is going to be enough to kill me?"

"Good enough to kill your brother," Sloane reminded him. "It's good enough to kill you."

"We'll see."

Gronoch kneeled down, and behind his human host appeared a staggering reptilian behemoth with dark scales and sharp teeth. The human host then calmly stepped aside as the real Gronoch bellowed, "I am the great and mighty Gronoch! Brother of Tollmathan, Xhorlas, and—"

"Oh, shut the fuck up!" Sloane glared up at the monstrous god. "Let Azaethoth and Galgareth go! Right now!" He took a deep breath, a hilt forming between his palms. "Last chance."

"No, I'm afraid it's *your* last chance," Gronoch said, the tentacles on his back whipping about. "You can either join the cause or die. Be a shame to waste a Starkiller, but without your godly mate? You're just another sack of meat."

"That's not true!" Sloane argued. "I'm a fuckin' witch of starlight, the proud son of Daniel and Pandora Beaumont, and I swear to Great Azaethoth himself that I am going to kill you if you don't stop!"

"You're welcome to try." Gronoch chuckled cruelly. "Come along… let's see what you're made of."

"Hey, Gronoch!" Alexander suddenly called out.

All their attention was directed to where Alexander and Rota were now standing by the row of cages, and there was a loud screech of metal as Rota's tentacles ripped the bars apart. He was collecting them into a bundle while Alexander snarled, "Heads up!"

Rota hurled the bars like spears, aimed by Alexander's quick eye. They struck Gronoch's face and throat, making him roar with anger and lash back. A row of them stuck in his flesh like a metallic mohawk, black blood oozing from the depths of the punctures.

Gronoch reached out, screaming angrily as he pulled them from his scales and sent a giant fist smashing into one of the cages, swinging at Alexander.

Alexander was quicker, propelled by Rota's tentacles, and nimbly moved out of harm's way, shouting, "Jump in any fucking time, Sloane!"

"Shit! Sorry!" Sloane closed his eyes and reached down deep, trying to summon the sword. He could hear a distant hum of power, Loch's furious screams from inside his prison, and his own heart pounding in his ears.

There, in the space between each pulse, he could feel the power bubbling up inside of him.

He pulled as hard as he could, baring his teeth as he brought the sword to life. It burst forth from his hands, a blade of pure starlight, shimmering and glowing brightly. It lit up the enormous room with brilliant light, and Sloane had to concentrate to keep a hold of it.

Alexander was leading Gronoch right to him, and Sloane held his ground, preparing to strike.

"This is the end, Gronoch!" Sloane shouted, raising the sword high. "This is—" One of Gronoch's tentacles smacked him right in the chest and sent him flying.

"Sloane!" Loch screamed.

Sloane crashed into the metal tables, glass tubes shattering around him and the trunk Gronoch had brought in popping open as it fell over next to him. He quickly scrambled out of the way as large fragments of bones scattered everywhere. He stumbled up to his knees, and though the sword flickered, it did not go out.

"Okay! I'm good! I'm fine!"

"Stupid fuckin' idiot!" Alexander groaned. "Can't you dodge?"

"Fuck! I'm sorry!" Sloane gasped.

Gronoch turned now on Alexander and Rota, his clawed hands being held in Rota's invisible grip. Alexander was trying to keep it going, his arms outstretched alongside Rota's. He was channeling all of Rota's raw power into the hold, screaming, "Sloane! Now!"

Sloane shook off the blow, eyeing the line of Gronoch's hunched back. He switched to holding the sword in one hand and focused his thoughts.

If he could hear Alexander, then maybe....

I need to get up on his back!

"Then come the fuck on!" Alexander hollered, blood gushing down his face from his nose. He was weakening, and all of Rota's tentacles were tied up trying to keep Gronoch pinned.

Sloane broke into a run, sprinting as fast as he could toward them.

Every second seemed to tick by at slow speed, and it was like Sloane was running through water. He saw Alexander drop to a knee, screaming in pain as more blood flooded down his face.

Alexander! Rota wailed, his tentacles writhing and flexing to fend off Gronoch. His grip was breaking, his voice cracking as he cried, *Don't! You have to stop! I'm losing you!*

"Don't let go!" Alexander screamed back. "Don't you dare! He has to die!"

I love you, you stubborn boy, Rota roared, heaving his massive body from the floor and forcing Gronoch back a step.

"I love you!" Alexander panted, his head jerking back to Sloane. "Sloane?"

"Now!" Sloane shouted, finally reaching them and leaping into the air.

"Rota!" Alexander thrust his hand up to direct a ghostly tentacle at Sloane.

Sloane grunted as it wrapped around his waist, air whipping by him as he was launched higher. He began to fall, aimed right at Gronoch's head, the blade set to strike his throat.

Yes.

This was it.

One hit and it would be over.

"Not quick enough, little mortal," Gronoch sneered, suddenly breaking a tentacle free from Rota's compromised grip and swiping at Sloane.

"Oh, fuck meeeee!" Sloane screamed as he went soaring back toward the elevator.

"Sloane!" Loch roared from behind the barrier, clawing and pounding his head into it. It was useless; Loch was still trapped and screaming helplessly, "Sloane! My love!"

Sloane grunted as his back hit the wall, and he threw up a shield to help break his fall as he slammed into the ground.

"Sloane!" Galgareth cried, trying to join Loch's efforts to break through the wall around them, but nothing was working. "Sloane! Are you okay?"

Groaning, Sloane managed to lift a hand to weakly wave. The room was spinning and his shoulder was throbbing. The shield had helped catch him, but it broke as soon as he landed.

Rota's hold shattered as Alexander collapsed, bloody and defeated onto the floor. He was still trying to hold himself up, and Rota's tentacles were wrapping all around him to help lift him.

Gronoch reared back and pounded his fists against Rota's invisible mass.

Rota's skin turned bright purple and red, his body taking on its physical version to fight back against Gronoch's attacks. Alexander could barely sit up, wiping blood off his face and struggling to move.

"Oh, what the fuck are you doing?" a very familiar voice whined. "Really? Fighting a god? This is so lame!"

"Asta?" Sloane jerked his head over to see a giant black cat monster now standing beside him.

No, not a monster—an *Asra*.

Asta was now as big as a Clydesdale, with a huge mouth full of pointed teeth, tentacles spiraling out from the tip of his long tail and more hanging by his pointed ears. He was as thin and sleek in this body as his human form was, flashing his fearsome teeth in what might have been a smile.

"Miss me, Starkiller?" he cooed.

"Where the fuck have you been?"

"Okay, so I didn't exactly go straight home to Xenon," Asta confessed, bowing his giant head down and helping Sloane stand up. "Backstreet Boys, all very complicated! But I'm here now!"

"We could definitely use your help." Sloane got back on his feet with a loud groan. "Alexander. Over there! Please go help him!"

"What the fuck is an Alexander?"

"Go!" Sloane shouted impatiently.

"On it!" Asta crouched down and took off, gracefully leaping into the air and sinking his teeth into Gronoch's arm.

Gronoch roared in pain, his attention diverted to the giant cat attacking him. He swung his fist to strike Asta, but Asta quickly opened a portal and dropped safely through to dodge it. A second later, he popped out of another portal and landed on Gronoch's head, clawing at his eyes.

Sloane grunted when a hand tugged at his waist, whirling around to see Gronoch's human vessel grabbing at him.

"It's inevitable!" the mortal hissed. "Salgumel will rise! He will wake and remake the world—"

There was a distinct thunk, and he collapsed.

Toby stood over him with one of the broken bars Rota had thrown earlier, and he was wielding it like a baseball bat. His eyes snapped up at Sloane, and he pleaded, "Go! Now! Kill that son of a bitch!"

"On it!" Sloane summoned a new sword of starlight, and in a panic, he hurled it as hard as he could at Gronoch.

Gronoch had just pulled Asta off his face and thrown him aside as the blade struck his shoulder and made him howl in pain. "You insignificant little worm!"

Rota had managed to drag Alexander away while Gronoch was distracted, both of them clearly exhausted from battle, and Sloane wasn't even sure if Alexander was conscious.

Asta was up, shaking off his impromptu flight and crouching for another attack.

The sword in Gronoch's flesh faded, and Sloane focused his magic to create another one in his hands. It was harder now, the hilt burning his skin, but he kept at it.

It wasn't enough, not yet.

Asta took off, roaring as he lunged up at Gronoch's throat. He sank his teeth in, and black blood sprayed out in a wet gush.

"Fuck yeah!" Sloane cheered.

Gronoch snatched Asta away, blood pouring down from the deep wound left behind. He squeezed him like a little toy and hurled him against the wall. Asta collided with a horrible smack, fell to the ground, and didn't move.

"Oh fuck no!" Sloane used his anger to fuel the sword's summoning.

There!

"You nasty little fools!" Gronoch roared, turning his mammoth body to attack Sloane.

As Gronoch's fist came down, Sloane swung the fully formed sword up with a scream. It hurt to hang on to it, but he couldn't stop. He watched the blade effortlessly pass through Gronoch's hand and drop some of his fingers onto the floor.

He had to keep going.

Gronoch roared in pain and lunged at him again, his tentacles whipping around to strike.

Sloane swung the sword with one hand to meet Gronoch's fist, quickly throwing up a shield with the other to fend off the whipping tentacles. The blade cut, the shield held, and he kept on fighting.

He could already feel the drain on his body from using so much magic, and trying to fight something the size of King Kong was almost laughable. Blow after blow, he was making mincemeat of Gronoch's hands and managing to block the swipe of his tentacles.

Alexander was up on his feet, but barely. He was hacking up blood, clinging to Rota's ghostly appendages and staggering to join back in. "Sloane... I'm coming!"

"Be right... there!" Asta groaned, weakly lifting himself up. "Delivery in thirty minutes or less... or it's free." He collapsed.

"Stay back!" Sloane urged frantically. "Both of you just stay back—"

The moment he turned his head, Gronoch struck. His bloody fist punched Sloane squarely in the chest and all of his starlight faded. He couldn't breathe, coughing violently and finding blood all over his hands as he lurched backward.

He tried to inhale and his ribs burned like they were on fire, wheezing as more blood splattered onto his palms.

"This ends!" Gronoch snarled. "Now!"

Sloane fell to his knees, trying to call on his powers. He had to do this. He had to win. His thoughts were flooded with bloody cages and helpless cries. He could hear Loch screaming and Alexander's desperate shouts.

He had never felt this weak....

He only had enough magic for one more spell.

Grinding his teeth from the agony, Sloane called on the sword one last time. He had an idea. It was a long shot, but he was out of options.

This would work. It just had to.

"Think that's going to do anything?" Gronoch sneered, scoffing at the way the blade flickered in and out. "Ha! You couldn't hit me with that puny little thing right now if you tried!"

"Not… gonna try…." Sloane groaned, flashing a quick grin. He lifted the sword and hurled it as hard as he could at the barrier holding Loch and Galgareth.

"No!" Gronoch howled as the wall shattered. "Impossible!"

Loch came flying out of the broken prison and launched himself right at Gronoch, his long jaws wrapping around his neck as he tackled him to the ground.

Galgareth swept Sloane into her giant arms, asking urgently, "Are you okay? Are you hurt?"

"I'm fine!" Sloane protested. "Loch! We have to help Loch!"

At the moment, Loch didn't seem to need any help. He was chewing away at Gronoch's throat and clawing at his chest as he snarled, "You will never hurt anyone ever again! Not my mate! Not our sister! No one!"

"Sloane…." Alexander called for him, weak but alive.

"I'm here!" Sloane called back. "Alexander?"

"Rota's… body…." Alexander pleaded. "We need to know…."

"Gal, come on," Sloane urged. "Let's finish this."

Galgareth gently set Sloane down, and she lumbered over to help Loch pin Gronoch to the ground. Gronoch was too weak to fight them both, and Galgareth said quickly, "Whatever you need to ask, do it now!"

"Gronoch!" Sloane called. "Rota's body! What did you do with it?"

"What?" Gronoch groaned incredulously, ceasing his struggling for a moment. He actually laughed, scoffing in disgust, "You have me at your pathetic mercy and that's what you ask of me?"

"Answer the question!"

"Between the stars and the veil of dreaming, at the everlasting fountain of the Kindress," Gronoch sneered. "That's where I stashed it!"

"The Kindress?" Sloane couldn't believe it. "That's just a freakin' myth!"

Even the most faithful of Sagittarian worshippers denied its existence and claimed it was just a silly story. The legend said that the Kindress was the first child of Great Azaethoth, not the beloved twins Etheril and Xarapharos.

Shortly after its birth, the Kindress died in Great Azaethoth's arms, and the mighty god's tears of mourning flooded the skies. The tears were so great that they had threatened to drown the world, and so Azaethoth trapped them in a fountain.

Speculation about the fountain's possible power varied, but the myth surrounding the Kindress was always the same: Just as Great Azaethoth had brought life to the universe, the Kindress could only bring death.

"That's bullshit!" Alexander snapped. He was standing upright, staring hatefully up at Gronoch. "There's no such place!"

"I found it," Gronoch declared. "That's where I hid that worthless chunk of flesh after setting his soul free! Ha! The legends are all true, and you will never see that body again!"

"Tell us where it is!" Loch barked, snapping his sharp teeth at Gronoch.

"Never!" Gronoch said gleefully.

"He's not going to tell us," Galgareth scoffed. "Even if the fountain is real, he would never share its location."

"Wait." Sloane rubbed his forehead. "You guys are gods… and you don't even know if it's a real place?"

Loch and Galgareth exchanged a sheepish look, tough to do with tentacles and fangs, but they pulled it off.

That moment of levity was short-lived, however, as Gronoch seized the moment of distraction. He twisted his strong arms and broke free in mere seconds. He came charging right at Sloane, screaming, "You're mine now, Starkiller!"

"Shit, shit, shit!" Sloane screamed, not thinking and simply reacting. He didn't think he had any strength left, and his hands were blistered from using the sword so much, but he had nothing else to attack with.

He flung his arms forward, calling on the magic deep within, and heard a soft whisper in his ear. It was over before he could understand what it was saying, but he was overwhelmed with a massive surge of power. Before his eyes, he saw a new sword of starlight materializing in thin air, spinning wildly….

And sinking right into Gronoch's chest.

Gronoch staggered and collapsed on his side with a low groan. "No… impossible!"

Sloane lunged forward, grabbing the hilt of the sword even as it scalded him, and ran down the length of Gronoch's body with a pained scream.

Gronoch was split wide open, and his body started to deteriorate and fade away into nothing. "This isn't the end… not yet… there's so many more of us… we'll find the Kindress… we will awaken Salgumel… and then you'll all die…."

Alexander kicked Gronoch's snout and nearly fell back over from his efforts. "You fucking bastard! Tell me where Rota's body is! If you can do one fucking decent thing before you die, just fucking tell me!" He was hysterical, his voice cracking as he desperately screamed, "Please!"

All Gronoch did was laugh.

Loch had reassumed his human body, his strong arms embracing Sloane and holding him close. Sloane fell against him, surprised to find that he was shaking all over.

Gronoch's body was consumed in a brilliant light, and it exploded into a giant burst of glittering bits before vanishing completely.

Sloane wrapped his arms around Loch's neck to steady himself, whispering, "It's over."

"Yes," Loch said with a slight nod, his voice strained. His brows furrowed in concern as he took Sloane's blistered hands in his own. "Oh, my love, you're hurt."

"I'm okay," Sloane swore, but he was grateful when Loch healed him. The blisters faded beneath Loch's glowing fingers, and there was a slitted tentacle hovering at his lips.

"Here," Loch urged. "Drink."

"But that's, it's—" In spite of the pain Sloane was in, he had his reservations about guzzling down one of Loch's magical loads in front of an audience. Magical healing or not, it was... weird.

"What?" Loch asked flatly, oblivious to the reason behind Sloane's embarrassment. "Galgareth has seen me share my seed before!"

"True," Galgareth piped up. She was back inside Toby's body and dusting herself off.

"Asta still appears to be asleep," Loch went on, "and Alexander and Rota probably don't mind—"

"Ulgh," Alexander grumbled. "Whatever."

"Just be quick." Sloane opened his mouth as his face turned bright red. He swallowed, unable to hold back a low groan as the sweet fluid hit his tongue. He could feel the aches in his chest and shoulder fading, his body slowly rejuvenating from the divine liquid.

"There," Loch said smugly. He turned to Alexander, offering, "If you'd like some—"

"No," both Sloane and Alexander snapped in unison.

"Hmmph, I was just trying to help."

"I'll be fine," Alexander snorted, turning to gaze up at Rota. He reached for him, and he cradled Rota's massive head and held him close. *I love you.*

I love you too. Rota materialized, very briefly, the purple-and-red beast fully revealed.

You shouldn't, you need your strength. Alexander pressed his cheek against Rota's snout. *By all the gods, you feel so good... I just wish....*

When I'm fully restored, you can have all of me that you want, Rota promised.

Kisses?

Those too....

Alexander smiled sadly, pressing a tender kiss to Rota's nose.

Sloane watched as Rota's solid form melted away, and the heartbreak in Alexander's face was clear. He recalled that Loch had said Rota might be able to possess a witch who had starsight, and he wished he knew someone who had been touched by Great Azaethoth who could help them.

Wait....

He glanced back at Loch, saying quietly, "Look, I know that I don't have starsight, but I'm a Starkiller, right?"

"Yes, my love. We've known that for some time."

"What I mean is that I've been touched by Great Azaethoth!" Sloan jerked his head toward Alexander and Rota. "So, if I wanted to try and let Rota borrow my body... for, like, sixty seconds... would you be okay with that?"

"Sixty seconds isn't enough time to really do anything," Loch scolded. "If you're going to let him take it, at least give them, like, an hour. Maybe two."

"Ugh, you're disgusting. Forget I said anything."

"You just got mad at me for trying to share my seed, and now you want to share your body?"

"It's stupid, just... drop it."

Loch glanced over to where Alexander and Rota had stepped away from each other and frowned. He hugged Sloane. "One minute. That is all."

"Thank you," Sloane said, kissing Loch's cheek and then walking over to Rota and Alexander. "Hey, so, maybe this is weird, but I wanted to... I wanted to offer you something."

"What?" Alexander was instantly suspicious.

"I'm not sure if it will work, but Rota can try to take over my body for a minute," Sloane said, smiling bashfully. "It sounds weird when I say it out loud, but I just thought...."

Alexander? Rota's voice was hopeful.

Alexander was blushing a very vivid, spectacular shade of red, mumbling, "Yeah, okay. Sure."

"Go ahead," Sloane said, holding his arms out expectantly.

Here goes nothing. There was a long pause, and Rota suddenly gasped. *It's.... Yes! It's working! It's really working!*

As Rota slipped inside of Sloane, he was reminded of when Loch had possessed him. It was warm and weird, and he could feel an immense power just as before. It did feel different than Loch: older, deeper somehow.

Rota moved Sloane's hands to touch Alexander's cheeks, and he reverently wiped away the blood from their battle.

"Rota," Alexander whispered in awe, staring up at Sloane's eyes and smiling with an open joy he hadn't shown before. "It... it's really you."

Sloane knew it was, because Alexander wasn't looking at him. He was looking at Rota, the god he loved, and Sloane could feel the love Rota felt for this young man in return.

Rota slid one of Sloane's hands into Alexander's pale hair, the other holding him at the small of his back.

There was a strange tension in Rota, like he was feeling a new and incredible pressure.

Alexander's red eyes seemed almost pink, his lashes fluttering as his lips parted. He was trembling in Sloane's arms, his hands folding between them as if he didn't know what to do with them.

Finally, urgently, Rota leaned in and kissed Alexander.

Alexander's eyes closed, and for a moment, it was nothing but a chaste press of lips, sweet and precious. He made a quiet sound, and their lips finally began to move.

I... I can feel you, Rota....

I'm here, my love... I'm yours.

The kiss deepened quickly, Sloane's arms moving to crush Alexander's slim body against his own. The passion was dizzying, and it had to have been longer than a minute before Sloane realized Loch was standing right beside them.

Rota pulled away with one last departing kiss, leaving Alexander flushed and breathless.

Thank you.

Sloane gasped as Rota left his body, stepping back to take Loch's arm to steady himself.

Alexander looked embarrassed now, saying quickly, "So, we should go. Now. Like, right now."

"Wait…. Were you guys just making out?" Asta asked, his voice a bit slurred as he staggered up to his feet. He stretched and grunted, padding over toward them.

"Don't worry about it," Sloane said. "How's your head?"

"Haven't had any complaints," Asta teased.

"Cute."

"I'm very cute, thank you, and…." Asta trailed off, his eyes finding the scattered bone fragments. He immediately transformed into his human form, kneeling down to reach inside the trunk. He pulled out a giant skull that had no business being able to fit inside.

It looked like a tiger or a lion, but much bigger. The large fangs were all capped in gold, and the rims of the eye sockets had been gilded as well.

"Is that what I think it is?" Sloane trailed off, staring in amazement.

"Yes." Asta looked as if he might be about to cry, but he was smiling. "An Asra."

"Those are what Gronoch was using to power his experiments," Sloane realized, turning the trunk right side up and clapping. All of the pieces magically returned, and the lid snapped shut.

Asta was still holding the giant skull against his chest, whispering, "Thank you."

"Are…. Are you okay?" Sloane didn't know if he should try to hug him, pat his head, or simply do nothing. He had no idea what acceptable comforting behavior was for an Asra. It was obvious that the skull meant a lot to Asta.

"What if I say no?" Asta suddenly grinned in spite of his damp eyes. "Gonna let Azzy give me another squeeze?"

Groaning loudly, Sloane shook his head and refused to answer the question.

"If you'll excuse me," Asta said as he placed the skull back inside the trunk, "I have some personal business to take care of." He picked up the trunk and opened a portal. He gave a little salute, saying cheerfully, "Later, bitches!"

"Wait!" Sloane shouted. "What about Jay? What about his roommate—"

Asta was already gone.

"Damn him!" Sloane threw up his hands in frustration.

"He's an Asra," Loch drawled. "I'm surprised he even stayed to fight." He wrapped a tentacle around Sloane's waist to comfort him. "Don't worry. He'll be back."

"You really think so?"

"No, not really." Loch grinned wide. "But it made you feel better, didn't it?"

"We'll sort out what to do about the Asra later. A more pressing question is what are we going to do with him?" Galgareth asked, nodding at the human vessel Gronoch had previously occupied, who was still unconscious on the ground.

"We'll take him," Alexander said, his eyes now red once more. "See what he can tell us about the Kindress." He looked to Sloane and Loch. "I do appreciate everything you did…. Thank you."

"Of course," Sloane replied. "Maybe go easy on the guy? I'm sure Gronoch brainwashed him pretty good. Maybe there's hope for him now that his master is dead."

He'll survive, Rota's voice promised.

"Mostly." Alexander cleared his throat. "We have a lot of questions that need answers."

"I have a question," Loch declared, glancing slyly between Alexander and Sloane. "Seeing as how we're having a wedding coming up and it's going to be on Urilith's Day, who you know is a goddess of fertility—"

"No!" Sloane immediately argued, laughing. "Just because I let Rota use my body to kiss Alexander does not mean we can have an orgy!"

Loch pouted, huffing, "You're no fun."

"Nope, I'm just the worst."

"Fine," Loch sighed dramatically. "I'll just have to be content worshipping your body and yours alone for the rest of eternity."

"You sure you're gonna be okay with that?" Sloane asked, chuckling as Loch leaned in to kiss him.

"Always, my sweet Starkiller."

CHAPTER 14.

"So, RUN this Kindress thing by me again?" Milo asked, busying himself with setting the table for dinner. "What is it exactly?"

"Ehhh?" Lynnette frowned. "It's complicated."

"Right." Sloane scratched his chin. "It's sort of a long story."

A few days had passed since the battle at Hazel, and the wedding was fast approaching. There was absolutely nothing on the news about the medical facility being attacked or any deaths. Sloane wasn't surprised that it was being covered up, and he was still saddened that he hadn't been able to save anyone.

The news did announce that Hazel's CEO would be taking an early retirement, and Sloane wondered if he was alive or if this was another potential cover-up. If Alexander had learned anything from Gronoch's mortal vessel, he hadn't been forthcoming.

Sloane hadn't heard anything from him or Rota since the conclusion of the battle. Whatever their plans were, moving forward, he had no idea. He hoped, however, that they would reach out if they needed help.

Urilith had left to mourn her lost son but promised she'd return in plenty of time to assist with the wedding. Galgareth went with her and assured them that their vessels would be safely returned. There was no sign of Asta the Asra, and Jay remained safely tucked away in the garden. Milo had put in for an emergency leave of absence on Jay's behalf, and Loch had been more than happy to assist with forging the applications.

Sloane was grateful for a few days of quiet, and he was secretly relieved that the only god he had to deal with was his own.

They'd invited Lynnette and Milo over to Sloane's apartment for dinner to catch up from the chaotic week, and Loch had left to grab more garlic for the meal. Enough time had passed that Sloane was getting worried, and he said a quick and silent prayer for the staff at the grocery store.

"You know how Sages believe Great Azaethoth created the universe?" Sloane said, checking on the sauce lightly bubbling away on the stove. "Azaethoth has always been, always was, and will always be."

"He took his first breath, and into his hands were born Etheril and Xarapharos," Lynnette chimed in. "His second breath brought forth the Asra and so on, blah blah blah."

"Right!" Milo said eagerly. "And then came the Vulgora and the Eldress and everybody else!"

"Like human beings." Sloane smiled, pleased that Milo had been taking his Sagittarian studies so seriously. "We were the last of Great Azaethoth's children."

"And the twins, Etheril and Xarapharos, were the first?"

"Unless you believe the legend of the Kindress." Sloane fumbled around the cabinet, glancing at the time. He'd wanted fresh garlic for the sauce, but he would have to make do with dried powder since Loch still hadn't returned.

"Which is?"

"That Great Azaethoth had a child before the twins." Sloane sprinkled a bit into the sauce and grabbed another pot to boil water for the noodles. "His firstborn was a being of pure starlight, but it died. It was in his child's memory that Great Azaethoth made the stars, and from his tears came the Kindress Fountain."

"Which does…?"

"Some people say it's, like, a fountain of youth," Lynnette said, sitting down at the table and rubbing her stomach. "Others say it's some sort of plague."

"And still more people say that the Kindress *is* the fountain." Sloane snorted. "Something to do with the translation from the godstongue or whatever."

"And Gronoch said he'd found it?" Milo glanced between Lynnette and Sloane.

"He claims he found the Fountain because that's where he hid Rota's body," Sloane explained, and he thought for a moment. He tried to recall Gronoch's final words, saying carefully, "And he said they were going to find the Kindress, but...."

That would mean the Kindress and the Fountain were not exclusively the same thing, since Gronoch had claimed to have hidden Rota's body at the Fountain. It still didn't explain why Gronoch or any of the other gods would *want* to find the Kindress, though. Whatever it or the Fountain really were, Sloane had the distinct feeling they were bad news.

There was a loud knock at the door, and Sloane jumped. "Oh! Huh."

"Loch?" Lynnette asked with an arched brow.

"He wouldn't knock," Sloane said, wiping off his hands and heading over to answer it. "I mean, even if he lost his keys, he's a god. He could get in."

"Good point."

Sloane opened the door and immediately cringed when he saw the rumpled ginger visage of Detective Chase standing on the other side. "Uh... hey! How are you?"

"Fine, Sloane," Chase said with a wry smile. He saw Milo and Lynnette and gave a friendly wave. "Look, I don't mean to interrupt, but you got a second to chat?"

Glancing around Chase into the hallway, Sloane asked, "Where's Detective Merrick?"

"Not here," Chase said flatly. "This is kinda personal, you know. Considering you're such good friends with Milo and all, I wanted to talk to you on my own."

"Oh." Sloane turned to Lynnette and Milo, asking, "Can you guys keep an eye on the food? I'm, uh, just gonna step outside real fast."

"Sure thing!" said Milo. "You go do... uh... whatever it is you're doing."

Sloane stepped out into the hallway, and he looked around to ensure they were alone before he asked, "So what's up, Chase?"

"I always liked working with you, Sloane." Chase got settled against the wall opposite him. "Thought it was really shitty the way they canned you."

"I appreciate that," Sloane said, "but you wanna tell me what this is really about?"

"This has been a really interesting week," Chase replied casually. "Like, it was super interesting that I just happened to see you at the funeral home where a ghoul went missing. And how very interesting it was when we ran the ghoul's fingerprints. Turns out, they don't belong to nobody dead."

Sloane felt sick.

"Some cat by the name of Lochlain Fields. He's a suspected rogue witch and apparently likes to take things that don't belong to him. According to our records, he just got married. Asked around, and he's off on his honeymoon. Pretty strange that a living guy would have his own ghoul, don't you think?"

"Oh, very strange." Sloane tried to keep his voice from cracking.

"It gets fuckin' weirder," Chase assured him. "Fields and his new hubby were gifted some property recently, property that actually belonged to you. You remember, don't you? You inherited it from Professor Emil Kunst."

"He was... uh... a friend of my mother's," Sloane said weakly.

"Oh, that's kinda weird since he killed her, right? I remember when you came in to finally close the case with his little confession. And it's really weird that after being missing for several weeks, it turns out that he actually passed away in his sleep at that very house."

Sloane saw the flash of a knife and a bright splash of blood. "Yeah, it was really peaceful."

"Weird because I found a redacted report that actually says they found his decomposed corpse somewhere out in the woods."

"Uh. Hmm."

"I did some more lookin' around, and it turns out that his body was never viewed by a medical examiner prior to his cremation," Chase went on, his expression growing grave. "Super fuckin' weird, right? Since he was a pretty devout converted Sage, from what I understand, it's hard to imagine why he got cremated."

His thoughts reeling, Sloane tried to think of something to say. Chase didn't have any actual evidence or Sloane would be under arrest right now. This was all circumstantial.

"So, I got a criminal running around with his very own ghoul that mysteriously disappeared, the same criminal who is living at the home of a professor whose body was cremated without the proper procedure and against his religious beliefs, and right in the middle of it all is you," Chase concluded with a grimace.

"Huh," was all Sloane could think to say.

"And not that I wanna drag Milo into this," Chase added, "but I'm pretty sure his baby mama is Lochlain Fields's sister and also a rogue witch." He pinched the bridge of his nose. "I really, really need you to explain what the fuck is going on, Sloane."

"I really, uh, can't say…?" Sloane clapped his hands together, panic creeping in and making his breath catch. "That all sounds super crazy, and uh… I don't know what to tell you."

"Sloane," Chase urged, "please give me something. This is reeking of conspiracy."

"Uh…."

I'm engaged to an old god who took over the body of that very same thief you're talking about after he'd been murdered by another old god for a piece of an ancient relic… yeah, this sounds way too crazy even in my head!

"It's… it's really complicated."

"Try me," Chase said, his eyes pleading.

Sloane could tell that Chase wanted to help him. It was why he had come here alone and was asking for answers. He tried to think of something to say, his heart thumping awkwardly, when he heard the elevator ding.

The doors opened to reveal Loch holding a grocery bag and dragging a giant fake palm tree behind him. Sloane recognized the fake tree as part of the welcome display in the lobby of their local grocery store, and he wanted to scream.

"I had some difficulties," Loch announced, boldly strutting forward with his head held high. "Do not fear, all is well. I was victorious."

"Lochlain.... Lochlain Fields?" Chase scoffed, staring at Loch with a very confused frown. "You're not here, you're supposed to be... wait, okay, no more games! What the fuck is going on, Sloane?" He threw up his hands. "And why the fuck does he have a fucking tree?"

"Ah! It's a most valiant tale!" Loch marched proudly up to them and patted the tree. "You see, I went out on a quest given to me by my beloved mate for fresh garlic—"

"Sloane," Chase grunted. "Is this Lochlain Fields? Or is this the damn ghoul from the funeral home?"

"It's the ghoul, but it's a lot more complicated than you think!" Sloane said quickly, frantically trying to clamp his hand over Loch's mouth. "My love, my dearest one, please stop talking right now."

"Mmm, brmmmm hmmmph?" Loch kept talking and groaned as he pried Sloane's hand away. "This is important! The grocery store is nothing more than a bunch of lying vile fiends! There was garlic in a jar that they called 'Italian Garlic,' but after closer inspection, the package revealed it was made in Spirit Lake! In Idaho!"

"Are you or are you not Lochlain Fields?" Chase barked.

"Is that really important right now?" Loch complained. "I'm trying to tell my story!"

"Answer the question, sir."

"Hmmph." Loch scowled, narrowing his eyes suspiciously. "Who wants to know?"

"Detective Elwood Chase, AVPD." Chase flashed his badge with a stern grimace. "Now tell me, are you Lochlain Fields or not?"

"No," Loch retorted impatiently. "I'm Azaethoth the Lesser, brother of Tollmathan, Gronoch, Xhorlas, and Galgareth. I am the son of Salgumel, he who was spawned by Baub, the child of Zunnerath and Halandrach, they who were born of Etheril and Xarapharos, descended directly from Great Azaethoth himself!"

Sloane cringed while Chase stared blankly.

"Now," Loch huffed, "when I spoke to the staff about their fraudulent advertising, they were very rude to me. So I took their tree, and I told them that their welcome sign was dishonest because they did nothing to make me feel welcome the entire time I was there!"

"Thank you." Sloane grimaced as Loch handed him the grocery bag. He looked worriedly at Chase. "Don't mind him, he's just a regular ol' clown! Always kidding around, aren't ya, Loch?"

"But Sloane, I'm not a clown! I'm a god—"

"Oh, look at the time! We really need to go. Great seeing you, Chase!"

"Sloane." Chase grimaced. "I really hate to do this, but you know ghouls are illegal. So is aiding and abetting one. I'm gonna have to call this in."

"Call who?" Loch asked.

"Call dispatch and inform them I'm about to make an arrest," Chase replied somberly. "I'm sorry, but if it's not me, it'll just be somebody else."

"Shit," Sloane hissed.

"Mmm, I don't think so." Loch shook his head. "We're about to have dinner, and getting arrested would just ruin our evening."

"Look, *Azaethoth*," Chase drawled, emphasizing the godly name and making it clear he didn't believe Loch's claim, "you two come quietly, or I can call for backup."

Loch suddenly burst out laughing. He was laughing so hard his eyes were wet with tears, and he had to lean against the fake tree for support.

"Loch!" Sloane wanted to strangle him. "This is freakin' serious! We're both about to be arrested! Do you understand?"

"Oh, pffft," Loch snorted, wiping at his eyes and taking a deep breath. "You worry too much, my love." He reached out with one of his tentacles and poked Chase right in the middle of his forehead.

"What the...." Chase's eyes rolled back in his head, and he collapsed to the floor. A portal opened up beneath him, and he disappeared.

"Loch, what did you do?" Sloane gasped.

"I fixed it!" Loch protested. "Now he won't bother us."

"Fixed it how?" Sloane demanded.

"Oh, I erased his memory," Loch replied. "He'll get up, go to bed, and in the morning, he won't remember anything about why he came here."

"Where did you send him?"

"To the safest place I know!" Loch replied with a happy smile.

"If you say the post office, so help me...."

"No!" Loch pouted. "Home! I sent him to his home."

"Well... shit." Sloane ran a hand through his hair. "I feel kinda bad. Chase was always so nice to me." He paused. "Wait, how did you know where he lived?"

"I stole his wallet." Loch beamed, holding it up proudly.

"Give it back!" Sloane pointed at the floor. "Right now!"

"Fine!" Loch opened up another portal, tossing the wallet in and sighing as if he was in deep pain. "I'm really doing my best here. You didn't want to be arrested, and you've made it very clear I'm not supposed to reveal my true godly nature because of potential mass panic and religious hysteria. This seemed to be the easiest option."

"Unless he puts it all together again," Sloane mumbled, leaning to hug Loch tight. "Then what do we do?"

"Then I'll just erase his memory again!" Loch said cheerfully as he kissed his hair. "Don't worry, sweet Starkiller. I have this completely under control."

From inside the apartment, Lynnette screamed.

"Oh, what now?" Sloane broke away to hurry back inside, summoning a shield of starlight and ready to attack.

Lynnette had her chair in her hands and raised above her head as if to strike. Milo was trying to take the chair from her, standing in between her and her target perched on top of the table.

"Baby!" Milo was shouting. "Come on! You're not supposed to be lifting anything! Put the chair down!"

The cause of the commotion was Asta, sitting down right in the middle of the table and helping himself to a plate of spaghetti. He was in his human form and totally naked. He turned his head when Sloane and Loch came rushing back in, and he waved. "Hey, guys!"

"Oh, gross," Loch groaned, fussing as he shut the door behind them. "It's just Asta."

"Hey! Where the hell have you been?" Sloane demanded. "And don't you ever wear clothes?"

"What is it, what does it want, and why is it eating my pasta?" Lynnette snarled.

"It is an Asra, it wants some grated Parmesan, and it's hungry," Asta replied, shamelessly slinking off the table and heading to the fridge.

Lynnette lowered the chair, eyeing Asta suspiciously. "This is the Asra? Asta the Asra?"

"Yup, this is him." Sloane stomped over to slam the fridge door shut and thrust an apron in Asta's face. "Hey! Put this on and answer me! You never came back!"

"Uh, yeah, I did." Asta wrapped the apron around his hips. "I seem to remember me coming to the rescue when you were fighting a god."

"After that! You never came back for Jay!"

"Uh, hello, had to put my family's bones back?" Asta scoffed. "I was a little busy. So what's up? Where's my ol' buddy Jay at?"

"Safe," Sloane grumbled. "He's still not awake from your little sleeping spell, or do you even remember doing that?"

"Oh, right! Yeah, just bring him over here and I'll get right on it."

"Loch?" Sloane asked.

"Yes, my love. I'll go get the little mortal." Loch pointed a finger at Asta. "Don't you dare touch the breadsticks while I'm gone."

"Wouldn't dream of it," Asta said sweetly, dumping a large helping of Parmesan on his plate and munching away.

Sloane watched Loch disappear, and he turned his attention back to Asta. "So, uh, the bones belonged to your family?"

"Yeah. Wasn't able to put everybody back together, though." Asta glumly took a big bite of pasta. "They used up all the ancient ones first, but I got my mom and, like, half my grandpa. It's better than nothing, I guess."

"How did the bones get taken anyway? I thought gods couldn't enter Xenon."

"Some fuckin' scumbags were stealing the bones for 'em and murdering the fuck out of each other," Asta replied. "I missed a lot of crazy shit while I was babysitting Jay. Like, fuckin' wow, there's this super annoying snotty dead professor that appointed himself Royal Occult Advisor."

"Snotty dead professor…." Sloane narrowed his eyes. It couldn't be, but then again, anything was possible when dealing with gods and monsters. "Was this professor named Emil Kunst?"

"*Kunst*? Oh yeah, that's him. I've been calling him Cun—"

"Right," Sloane said quickly, "but he's okay? He's… he's happy?"

"Happy?" Asta laughed. "He's all but trying to run the whole fuckin' kingdom now and driving my dad absolutely insane. He's having the fuckin' time of his undead life."

"Yeah?" Sloane was incredibly relieved hearing that, and some of the guilt he'd been carrying for so long ebbed. "Thank you."

"No problem." Asta gave a little salute before pouring more Parmesan on his plate. "Happy to help."

"Now, are you gonna tell me where Jay's roommate is?" Sloane took the jar of Parmesan away and crossed his arms. "The whole point of you going back was to bring him so Jay wouldn't freak out, remember?"

"Yeah, okay, I got a little distracted!" Asta whined, pouting over the loss of cheese. "After I left your stupid office, I happened to find out about the awesome Backstreet Boys reunion tour that I've been predicting for months was finally starting, and I maybe followed them around for a few days."

Sloane put his hands over his face and sighed.

"Hey, Backstreet's back and better than ever, motherfucker," Asta declared. "So anyway, when I finally got home, that's when I found out about all the bones being stolen for Gronoch. I saw the shit going down on the bridge when all the Silenced souls came through, and yeah, okay, I got a little worried about Jay."

"Oh?"

"Well, obviously something crazy went down! Took me a little while to find you guys, and oops, I ended up having to fight a god for you. A little 'thank you' would be nice."

"Why didn't you stay to help Jay?" Sloane demanded.

"Do you know what a good way to say 'thank you' is? A breadstick. Breadsticks are very thoughtful."

"Fine!" Sloane grabbed a breadstick and handed it to Asta. "Now, why didn't you stick around to help Jay? We haven't been able to wake him up!"

"Uh, getting my family's bones back was kind of a priority. Hello." Asta rolled his eyes as he nibbled on his breadstick. "I came back as soon as I could! I knew he'd be safe with you guys!"

"Okay, so where is Jay's roommate? You still need to bring him back here!"

"I can't do that."

"And why not?"

"He's busy."

"Busy doing what?" Lynnette piped up.

"Probably getting married," Asta replied, taking a big bite of spaghetti and continuing to talk through it. "He made thith really big impresshun on the king. So." He gulped. "The king is gonna go on and put a ring on it."

"Wait, huh?" Sloane blinked. "Are you serious?"

"He's getting married to the king?" Lynnette gasped. "He's gonna be a prince? Aw, how romantic!"

"Who's getting married?" Milo asked in a hushed whisper.

"Jay's roommate, uh…." Sloane blinked. "You know, I don't think I even know his name."

"Tedward of Aeon, Kicker of Cats," Asta said with a snort. "He's gonna be my new step-daddy. Isn't that fun?"

"You said he was gonna marry the king," Sloane accused. "How does that make him your step-anything?"

"Oh, right! Prince Elysian, the powerful and wise? The super cool dude I told you about?" Asta pointed at himself. "That's me."

"By all the fuckin' gods. You lied to us!"

"Only a little."

Loch reappeared with Jay in his arms and dropped him off on the couch. "What did I miss?"

"Asta is actually a prince, and Tedward is getting married to the king of the Asra," Sloane replied.

"What's a Tedward?"

"He's Jay's roommate, your godliness," Milo called back.

Asta left his plate on the counter and came over to kneel by the couch, smoothing his hand over Jay's hair. "Thank you, guys… for taking care of him."

"Yeah, of course." Sloane smiled.

"Hey." Milo frowned. "What happened with Chase? He didn't end up in a portal, did he?"

"Well, technically." Sloane grimaced. "He might have maybe been here to possibly arrest me because he figured out Loch was a ghoul, so Loch erased his memory and sent him through a portal back to his place… and yeah, it's fine now."

Milo did not look convinced.

"Shit, Jay needs his glasses. He can't see crap without them." Asta snapped his fingers, and a pair of glasses appeared in his hand. Gently, he slid them onto Jay's face. "There."

Sloane frowned when he spotted something shiny around Loch's neck. "Loch, what is that?"

"Oh! I stole this from Detective Chase when he was trying to arrest you earlier." Loch beamed proudly, holding up a police badge. "Isn't it neat?"

"You have to give that back!" Sloane tried to grab it from him. "Come on!"

Loch passed the badge to one of his tentacles and raised it high up where Sloane couldn't reach. "But I like it!"

"If you give it back, I'll let you keep the tree you stole."

"Hmmm…."

"What the fuck?" Jay's voice suddenly squeaked. He was sitting up, clumsily trying to back into the far corner of the couch. He stared up at Loch's tentacles in horror. "Wh-what the fuck is going on?"

"That's just Azzy," Asta said dismissively. "Don't worry about him. Hey, are you okay?"

"Who…." Jay stared, reaching out to gently touch Asta's sunglasses. "Mr. Twigs? Is that you?"

"Yeah." Asta grabbed Jay's hand as if to push him away. He hesitated, and their fingers slowly laced together. "Uh… surprise?"

"There's a lot we need to explain, Mr. Tintenfisch," Sloane said, gesturing for Loch to put away his tentacles.

"I could always zap his memory," Loch whispered loudly. "One little poke and problem solved!"

"No!" Sloane growled.

"I'm still not really sure if I'm awake or dreaming," Jay said, scrubbing at his eyes. "Milo?"

"What's up, dude?" Milo waved cheerfully.

"Fuck, my head hurts." Jay suddenly gasped. "Ted. Where's Ted? Did you guys find him?"

"I can take you to him," Asta promised, standing up and helping Jay get to his feet. "He's fine, I swear."

"Mr. Twigs?" Jay's face turned bright red. "Why... why are you only wearing an apron?"

"I'd rather not be wearing anything. Have you ever jumped through a portal naked?" Asta winked. "It's the best."

"Jump... through a what?"

"Uh, would you guys like to join us for dinner?" Sloane gestured to the dinner table. "We have plenty of food—"

"You gave away one of the breadsticks!" Loch hissed.

"We can get more!"

"Not at that grocery store," Loch lamented. "They're very unhappy with me over the recent loss of their beloved tree."

"You guys wanna sit down, take a breath, and I can try to explain what's going on?" Sloane pulled out his chair for Jay.

"Definitely gonna need a drink." Jay ran his hands through his hair. "And I really, really need to pee."

"I got you, buddy," Milo assured him, heading into the kitchen to pour some whiskey while Sloane showed Jay to the bathroom.

When Jay came out, he sat down at the table and downed the whiskey. He took a deep breath. "Okay. I might need a few more of those, but I'm ready."

"Right, so," Sloane began, "this handsome guy is Azaethoth the Lesser. Yes, he's *that* Azaethoth. This all started last Dhankes at a Halloween party I went to last year...." He went on to tell Jay the whole story of how he'd met Lochlain and his subsequent murder, then being courted by Azaethoth in Lochlain's body as they worked together to solve the mystery.

Although Loch was eager to share details of how their romantic relationship had blossomed, Sloane did his best to keep the conversation modest. Jay listened intently, often asking questions or requesting a refill on his drink. Sloane explained what

Gronoch had been planning and why Jay was a target, and that's when Jay simply took the bottle and turned it up.

"Gronoch was going to use the bones of the Asra to force a god's soul out of its body and bind it to mine to make me into a weapon to use in battle?" Jay took a breath. "A battle that will come if they're actually able to wake up Salgumel because the gods will try to stop him and the other bad gods from destroying the entire world?"

"Yeah, that pretty much sums it up," Sloane said with a sympathetic sigh.

"Fuck," Jay muttered, and he glanced over at Asta, who was sitting on the edge of the table next to him—still naked aside from the apron. "And Mr. Twigs is not actually Mr. Twigs."

"Nope," Asta replied with a click of his tongue. "Mr. Twigs is Asran royalty, baby."

"Your visions made you come find me, to protect me?"

"Maybe."

"Yes," Sloane supplied, "and he apparently had a little tiff with your roommate."

"There is a strong possibility that I sent him through a portal to Xenon after he viciously attacked me," Asta declared, swinging his legs cheerfully.

"That's exactly what he did." Sloane rolled his eyes. "Ted is in Xenon with the Asran king."

"And he's really okay?" Jay pressed. "He's... he's getting married?"

"Totally gross, right?" Asta complained.

"Wow. So, uh, yeah. This is a lot," Jay leaned back in his chair and inhaled slowly. "I mean, I always had faith in the gods. Always. I just never thought I'd be hanging out watching one eat pasta."

"Life can be quite unpredictable," Loch agreed, twirling some noodles around his fork. "I came to find a murderer and also found my eternal mate!"

"Uh, so, who else knows about this?" Jay asked cautiously.

"Everyone here plus Lynnette's brother and his husband," Sloane replied.

"Ahem." Lynnette cleared her throat. "And Fred."

"Right, sorry, and their friend Fred! But that's it—"

"Oh! And Fred's cute little ghoul doctor," Lynnette continued to chime in. "We've also gotta count that Silenced guy. Alexander, right? And the god that he's bonded with."

"Yes, them too." Sloane paused, eyeing Lynnette expectantly. "Anybody else?"

"That depends." Lynnette grinned and rubbed her belly. "Are we counting the unborn?"

"Technically," Milo teased, draping his hand over Lynnette's, "the baby can't hear until eighteen weeks, so we've got some time."

"Wait, you're pregnant?" Jay sputtered. "Wow! Uhm, that's awesome! Congratulations, guys!"

"Thank you!" Lynnette beamed.

"Okay!" Sloane laughed. "*Now* that's everybody who knows."

"It's still a very exclusive club." Milo grinned. "I'm working on T-shirts."

"I guess we need to get one for Ted too." Jay chuckled nervously. "I can't even imagine what he's been through over in Xenon."

"We can go see him now if ya want," Asta offered. "Just a quick portal away."

"Yeah," Jay said, standing up. He swayed a little, but Asta was right there to steady him. He smiled shyly. "I want to. It's not that I don't trust you or anything—"

"You really shouldn't," Loch advised.

"—but I want to see my friend."

"Sure thing." Asta stripped off the apron and tossed it over to Sloane. "Hey, Azzy. Sloane." He flashed a big toothy grin. "You ever need anything, you've got one hell of an IOU with the Asran royal family."

"Do you have cake?" Loch asked hopefully.

"Loch," Sloane warned, trying to shield his eyes from Asta's naked body with the discarded apron.

Too late.

He couldn't unsee it now.

Asta definitely had two dicks.

"But I want cake," Loch fussed, distracting Sloane from the bizarre anatomical revelation.

"I will get you a cake later, I promise."

"Thank you both," Jay said sincerely. "Thanks for keeping me safe and finding out what happened to Ted. I'm still trying to get a handle on all of this, but… I appreciate it."

"It was our pleasure," Sloane said with a warm smile.

"You'll get our bill in the mail." Loch wrapped his arm around Sloane's shoulders.

Sloane elbowed him.

"You're so mean to me. I'm going to have a boner to pick with you later."

"It's 'bone,' not 'boner.'"

"With me, it can always be—"

"Shush! We're trying to have a nice, *normal* goodbye!" Sloane lowered the apron as he waved to Asta and Jay. "Take care of yourselves!"

"You've got another week left on your leave," Milo said, giving Jay a big hug.

"Leave?"

"I had to tell the precinct something! Try not to stay gone too long, okay?"

"Thank you, Milo." Jay hugged him hard. He turned to hug Lynnette, though much more gently. "And congratulations again! I'm seriously so happy for both of you!"

"You be careful over there," Lynnette teased.

"I will."

"Hey, I'll bring him back in one piece, I swear." Asta reached out for Jay's hand and opened up a portal. He glanced back at

Sloane and Loch with a smirk, peering over his shades as he said, "Thanks for helpin' me save the world. Later, bitches."

Away into the portal they went, the opening closing behind them with a bright flash of light and a loud swoosh.

"Fuck," Sloane exhaled, flopping down at the table and laying his head next to his plate.

Milo patted his back. "So, the dinner entertainment has been super cool!"

"Cops, naked cat people, magic portals," Lynnette listed off. "It's been a very fascinating evening! Ten out of ten, would definitely recommend."

"And I stole a tree," Loch said proudly, taking his seat next to Sloane.

"We're gonna have so much to tell Lochlain and Robert!" Lynnette giggled. "They're not gonna believe it!"

"Killed another god and foiled a new attempt at destroying the world," Sloane said, lifting his head with a wry smile.

"New bundle of joy on the way!" Lynnette grinned, rubbing her stomach eagerly.

"Met a Silenced guy who can cast magic," Milo added.

"And Sloane made out with him," Loch declared.

"Wait, you did?" Milo stared.

Sloane's head dropped back down with a loud groan. "Oh my gods. Loch, please stop talking."

"They absolutely did," Loch went on salaciously. "There was almost certainly tongue."

"Azaethoth!" Sloane griped. "Please!"

"I'm just trying to tell a story." Loch fidgeted. "Can I keep the badge?"

"Will you stop telling the story if I say yes?"

"The chances vastly increase."

"Yes. You can keep it."

"Oh, how I love you, my darling Starkiller." Loch pulled Sloane into his lap for a tentacle-filled embrace and an adoring kiss.

Sloane laughed in spite of himself, giving in and kissing Loch back. "I love you too."

"Forever?"

"And always."

CHAPTER 15.

"SLOANE?" URILITH called.

"Yes?"

"It's time." She gave Sloane's hands a warm squeeze. She was back in the same body as before, wearing a flowing dress, with her thick hair braided back with fresh flowers. "Are you ready, my little love?"

"I'm ready." Sloane smoothed out his jacket and kilt. His coat and shirt were black, and his tie was purple to match his kilt. They were both a deep violet, a traditional wedding color for Sages because of its affiliation with Great Azaethoth. He'd combed his hair at least three times, and he was worried he'd put on too much cologne.

Looking at Urilith and knowing she was here to take him to the garden for his wedding filled him with a new set of fears.

Sloane took a deep breath, hesitating as he tried to find the right words. He was about to marry this goddess's son after having killed two of them. It was awkward, it was weird, it was—

"Sloane," Urilith soothed. "I forgive you."

Startled, he asked, "Can you... can you read my mind?"

"No." She chuckled. "But I know when you're troubled, and the issue is obvious." She kissed Sloane's forehead and promised, "You're forgiven, dear one. I know Gronoch could not be saved any more than Tollmathan."

"Thank you." Sloane sighed in relief. "There's not exactly a Hallmark card for this, you know?"

"Now—" She smiled ever so sweetly. "—should you be foolish enough to break Azaethoth's heart... then you will know my wrath."

"I wouldn't expect any less."

"Come," Urilith said with a satisfied smirk. "It's time."

Through a portal they went, appearing in the lush garden. There was a small crowd waiting for them, and Sloane was instantly swept up in a giant round of hugs.

Lochlain and Robert were there to congratulate him, and Robert made Lochlain promise not to bring up any potential heists that might distract Loch from the honeymoon ahead of them.

Lynnette smothered Sloane with kisses, and Milo gave him a rib-bruising hug. He was surprisingly emotional, wiping away tears when he told Sloane how happy he was for him.

Fred didn't say much, but he mumbled a very heartfelt congratulations and introduced his date, a beautiful young man named Ell. Sloane remembered him from Lochlain and Robert's wedding but had forgotten his name.

"Oh! This must be the one you wanted me to look at your penis for!" Loch suddenly exclaimed as he wiggled his way over to Sloane's side.

Sloane was too busy staring at Loch to correct his crude comment, gawking at his shapely legs peeking out beneath his kilt and the strong cut of his jacket, in matching colors to Sloane's own. He was positively edible, and Sloane resisted the urge to jump on him right there in front of everyone.

"He's a real talented ghoul doc," Fred said quietly, wrapping a protective arm around Ell's shoulders. "He's been good to me."

"Hmmm, has he?" Loch grinned slyly at Fred. "By the looks of things, I'd say you figured out the problem with your penis."

"Loch!" Sloane hissed, smiling apologetically as Ell turned a very bright shade of red. "I'm sorry, he's a spoiled god with absolutely no filter."

"It's okay." Ell laughed and offered a gloved hand to shake Sloane's. "It's kind of charming."

"See?" Loch puffed up his chest. "I'm charming!"

"Aren't you supposed to be waiting for me somewhere else?" Sloane scolded affectionately. "Isn't it bad luck for us to see each other?"

"That's just Lucian nonsense." Loch hugged Sloane's waist and kissed him. "Mmm, you look amazing. Why wouldn't I want to see you?"

"I love you." Sloane rolled his eyes and grinned. "I can't believe I'm marrying you."

"I know," Loch agreed. "You really are quite lucky." He leaned in for another kiss. "And so am I."

"Mmm, very lucky." Sloane glanced around to some of the unfamiliar faces of their guests. "So, who is everybody else? I don't think I know everyone here!"

"Ah, yes! Come!" Loch took Sloane's arm and led him over to a small girl with curly pigtails.

"Hello," the girl said with a small, reserved smile.

"Sloane, I'd like you to meet my great-grand-uncle, Babbeth." Loch was absolutely beaming.

"God of Death," Sloane breathed in awe. He shook Babbeth's little hand, gushing, "Wow! It is such an honor! Thank you for coming!"

"A pleasure." Babbeth yawned. "Mmm, my apologies. Still waking up."

"Nearly took blowing up an entire planet to wake him," a new voice teased. It belonged to a husky balding man. He immediately pulled Sloane into a big hug. "Oh! It's so nice to meet you! I can't believe our little Azaethoth is finally being mated!"

"Ugh! Hey!" Sloane gasped as all the air was pushed right out of his lungs.

"Ah, well." Loch ducked his head. "It was worth the wait, Uncle Yeris."

"Yeris," Sloane squeaked, still trapped in the man's tight embrace. "God of the Ocean, Yeris?"

"That's me!" Yeris laughed. "God of anything wet with shit swimmin' in it!"

"Charming as always, Yeris," drawled a young man with long hair and tattooed hands. He made a face as Yeris came over to grab him with another giant hug, clearing his throat as he protested, "Ugh, that's enough! You're getting my vessel all dirty!"

"Ah!" Loch swept an arm back around Sloane's waist, waiting for the young man to be free of Yeris before he said, "Sloane, this is my Aunt Shartorath."

"Hi!" Sloane exclaimed, reaching out to shake her hand. His mind was buzzing with how surreal it was to currently be surrounded by a host of immortals. He didn't know what to say, and he blurted out, "My mother was a huge fan of yours."

"Thank you," Shartorath said, smiling kindly. "It's lovely to meet you, Sloane. Welcome to our family."

"Where's Grandpa Baub?" Loch pouted.

"We couldn't wake him," Shartorath explained. "I'm so sorry, darling. We tried."

"These are all seriously gods?" Milo hissed in Sloane's ear as he snuck up beside him, gawking openly. "Whoa."

"Yes," Sloane whispered back, glancing away from Loch chatting with his family to address Milo. "In human bodies, but yes, they're all gods."

"Who's Bob?"

"Not Bob, it's *Baub*," Sloane corrected. "He's a God of War and Loch's grandfather."

"Oh, got it. I knew that."

"And Uncle Gordoth?" Loch was asking hopefully as Sloane tuned back into their conversation. "Were you able to wake him?"

Yeris and Shartorath exchanged a worried look, and Yeris said, "Well, not exactly. Urilith told us how much you wanted him to come, but... eh...."

"We couldn't find him," Shartorath explained with a strained smile. "He may have woken up on his own—"

"Come along, children," Urilith urged, clapping. "Galgareth is waiting!"

"Ah! Let's go!" Loch winked and suddenly vanished from sight.

Sloane laughed, trying to search through the crowd to figure out where he'd gone. He thought he heard Loch's snickering and followed the sound toward one of the garden's courtyards. "Over here?"

"Here!" Loch called back. "Keep going!"

Sloane stepped through the shrubbery, and he gasped at the sight before him. There was a giant archway right in the middle that was made of black branches with glowing lights hovering all around it. There was a whole pathway of them suspended in the air that led from the courtyard entrance right up to the arch.

Sloane thought they might be lanterns, but closer inspection made him realize they were tiny stars hung right there in the air over their heads.

Loch was waiting for him with Galgareth at the arch, and the smile on his face took Sloane's breath away. He had never looked so gorgeous, and his eyes were glittering with stars of their own as he gazed adoringly at Sloane.

Sloane started walking to him, but Loch couldn't wait. He sprinted over at an impossible speed, whisking Sloane up into his arms, and carried him back to the archway.

"Loch!" Sloane laughed, flushing as he gently swatted at his shoulder. "Put me down!"

"I can't marry you like this?" Loch grinned and smooched his cheek.

"No!"

Pouting playfully, Loch set Sloane back down on his feet. "Fine, if you insist."

"Are we ready?" Galgareth asked, trying to bite back a giggle. "Not that I'm in a rush or anything. I've got Toby here until at least the end of summer."

"Almost." Sloane reached out to take Loch's hands. He turned his head to see their guests filing in to join them. He waited for everyone to find a spot to sit down in the lush grass and get settled before confirming, "Ready."

"Welcome to all of our friends, our family, and our loved ones," Galgareth announced happily. "We are here today to witness the union of these two bright souls being joined together as one.

"We gather to celebrate the bonding of Azaethoth the Lesser and Sloane Daniel Beaumont because love is truly the most powerful magic of all, a unique and special phenomenon, a gift bestowed upon us directly from Great Azaethoth himself."

Sloane listened intently to every word, but his eyes never left Loch's. He could feel tentacles weaving around their wrists and pulling him in closer. Sloane's heart was pounding so fast, and he could hardly believe this was happening.

"Marriage is a sacred bond, not to be taken lightly," Galgareth said as she wrapped a long ribbon around Sloane's wrist and wound it over Loch's since he didn't have a tentacle to share. "It is a commitment for life and into eternity. You will be bound to each other forever."

"Forever," Loch and Sloane repeated together.

Galgareth laid her hands over theirs, reciting, "I call on the blessings of earth to give your marriage strength. I call on air to grant you joy. I call on water to bring you clarity. I call on fire to bless you with passion."

Above their heads there was a bright shower of glittering lights, raining down upon them like a storm of falling stars.

"And I call on the stars," Galgareth said with a blissful smile, "to always light your path, even in your darkest hours." She held up their joined hands and declared, "What has been joined today, may no mortal or god ever tear asunder! Congratulations to the happy couple!"

Loch swept Sloane up in a passionate kiss as their friends and family burst into a roar of applause and excited cheering. Sloane kissed him back eagerly, laughing as Loch spun him around.

The sky was lit up with a cascade of falling stars, and Loch lifted them both up into the air. The stars created a smooth platform over the archway, and Loch rocked Sloane back and forth with a happy smile.

"A floor made of fallen stars," Sloane recalled Loch's promise with a grin. He took Loch's hand, letting him lead as they danced in lazy circles. "This is pretty amazing."

"Hope no one looks up," Loch said cheerfully. "I'm not wearing anything under my kilt."

"Oh my gods!"

"I love you." Loch gave Sloane a slow spin before bringing him back into his arms.

"I love you too," Sloane said, hugging Loch's neck and kissing him sweetly. "This is the happiest day of my life, Azaethoth." He barely noticed that Loch was taking them higher and higher into the sky, so caught up in their dance.

"I bet I can make it even happier."

"If you put your tentacles up my kilt, I will smack you."

"Later," Loch said, smirking smugly. "Close your eyes, Sloane."

Sloane did so, unable to resist a grin. He still half expected to feel a tickle between his legs and was surprised when a faint rush of air blew over his whole body. "Can I open them now?"

"Yes… go ahead."

Sloane gasped, staring all around at the endless void of space surrounding them. They were in Zebulon, the home of the gods, and a swarm of glowing green orbs swirled around them. It was warm, peaceful, and Sloane couldn't look away.

Off in the distance, he could see the familiar blocks that made up the palace Sloane had visited before. Right now they didn't appear to be standing on anything, and Sloane clung a little tighter.

"Here." Loch reached out to the swirling green wind. Two of the emerald lights rested in his hand, and he offered them to Sloane. "Listen…."

Sloane hesitantly accepted, trying to focus on the bright little lights. It took a moment, but then he heard it:

"We love you so much, we're so proud of you…."

"We love you, Sloane…."

"My parents?" Sloane asked, tears instantly filling his eyes. He clutched the lights to his chest, but they grew too hot and he had to let them go. He smiled, trying to hold back tears and failing as the lights rejoined the others in the wind.

"Sloane?" Loch asked worriedly. "Was that not a good gift?"

"No, it was wonderful," Sloane promised. "I could hear them. How much they love me, I could... I could feel it. I just miss them so much."

"We can visit whenever you'd like," Loch said, kissing Sloane's cheek. "I always know where to find them, even if more than seeing and hearing their lights is impossible while you're a living mortal."

"Thank you." Sloane wiped away his tears and smiled. "Now! We have a wedding feast to get to, don't we, husband?"

"Yes, my darling," Loch agreed. His arms tightened around Sloane as he prepared to whisk them away, but something happened to make him pause.

"What is it?"

"Look," Loch whispered.

Sparkles of starlight were beginning to fall all around them. They fell as softly as fresh snow and twinkled with a stunning violet radiance that took Sloane's breath away. He could feel immense power in every glowing fragment, watching them all cling to their hair and clothes.

"What... what is this?" Sloane was stunned by the magnificent display.

"Great Azaethoth," Loch murmured, closing his eyes and smiling.

"Wow," Sloane whispered.

Great Azaethoth, Creator of All, was with them. Sloane could feel tears stinging his eyes from the intense sensation, his mortal body nearly overwhelmed to be in the presence of such power. He knew this was but a small fragment of the mighty god, and Great Azaethoth was visiting them this way for his sake.

His full godly glory would have probably crushed him, but this—a piece—was more than enough.

Sloane could hardly breathe, and he was surrounded by an enveloping warmth that resonated in every pore of his being. He had never felt anything like this before, and although not a single word had been spoken, he knew exactly what message Great Azaethoth was sending them:

Love.

The starlight swarmed around them for a brief moment, almost like a hug, before finally vanishing away.

"Holy shit," Sloane gasped, grabbing on to Loch to steady himself. "That…. That was amazing. That was, that…. That was Great Azaethoth. That was really him!"

"Yup!" Loch was positively smug. "Told you I was his favorite."

"Obviously!" Sloane laughed.

"Mmm. Are you ready to go back, my love?"

"Yes," Sloane breathed out. "I'm ready."

"Let's go." Loch held Sloane close and took them back to the garden in a blink.

Sloane found himself seated next to Loch at the head of a long table piled with all sorts of food. There were roasts and cakes and pies, and Sloane didn't even know where to begin. All of their friends and family were already seated and waiting for them, cheering joyfully upon their arrival.

Of course, there was a very large bonfire.

"Now," Loch boldly proclaimed, "the ritual is complete, my mate is mine, and we shall feast!"

"He's only yours after you've consummated!" Yeris jeered.

"No need to worry about that, Uncle!" Loch cackled while Sloane bashfully hid his face in his hands. "We will be consummating until my husband's mortal body is completely exhausted! For hours and hours until he is damp with perspiration from my persistent pounding and dripping with my—"

"Okay, okay, okay! They get it!" Sloane moaned, laughing as he bumped his shoulder against Loch's. "You're so gross."

"Hmmph. I thought 'perspiration from my persistent pounding' was rather poetic."

"It's beautiful. Now, isn't it time for cake? Presents?"

"I know you're just trying to distract me," Loch accused, "but it's working." He kissed Sloane. "Mmm, yes. Presents and cake, please."

"Don't we need to eat first and then do presents?"

"No, I am a *god*, and the god wants to eat cake while he opens presents!"

"Whatever you want, my loving husband."

"My gift is also the cake, so I'll be going first!" Urilith presented them with a towering layered sponge cake soaked in lavender milk that made Sloane's mouth absolutely water. She kissed them both and embraced them together with a wave of tentacles. "I wish you both an eternity of happiness together."

"Thank you, Mother," Loch said, a few of his own tentacles slithering out to hug her back.

"Thank you so much!" Sloane gushed as he watched Loch cut them each a gigantic piece. He eagerly dug in, moaning out loud as the moist cake melted in his mouth. It was the most delicious thing he'd ever tasted, sweet and fragrant, and he felt Loch staring at him. "Wuh?"

"I've never heard you moan like that from eating food before!" Loch huffed.

"You're jealous of a cake?"

"Yes."

"Mmm, well, you watch all those cooking shows." Sloane chuckled. "Maybe you should actually try, I dunno… cooking?"

Loch perked up at the thought, musing, "If I provide you with mortal sustenance that pleases you, perhaps it will put you in the mood for mating more often…."

"Only one way to find out!"

"Hey!" Milo exclaimed, Lynnette at his side as he approached. "Congratulations, guys!"

"Thanks, man!" Sloane stood back up to hug Milo, and he grunted from the force of their embrace. "Ugh, I love you."

"I love you too! And hey! I love you too, your godliness!"

"Of course you do," Loch said proudly. "I am absolutely worthy of all mortals' love."

"Congrats, sweeties!" Lynnette presented Loch and Sloane with a small envelope. "We tried to think of something to give you, and really nothing felt like it was enough." She hugged Sloane and then Loch, a quiver in her voice as she said, "You gave me my brother back. He gets to be an uncle now, and… and…."

Milo squeezed Lynnette's shoulder when she began to cry. "Look, we love you both, but it's, like, pretty much impossible to get a proper gift for a god and his Starkiller hubby, okay? We are mere mortals, you know. But we thought you would like this."

Sloane didn't want to be tacky, but he had to peek inside the envelope. "Oh… oh! Wow! Thanks, guys! It's uh… uhm…."

It was a generous gift certificate to a custom sex toy company.

"What is it?" Loch asked, trying to see.

"We'll look later!"

Thankfully, Galgareth was already bustling through to give them her gift, a lusciously soft blanket she'd made for them out of starlight that promised a lifetime of good luck. Yeris was right after her, offering amber bracelets that glittered like the sun and would save whoever wore them from drowning. Shartorath gave them a glowing bag of incense to bless their new married home, and Babbeth gave them an old gold coin.

He pressed it into Sloane's hand with a sly little smile and no other explanation.

On the youthful visage of his current vessel, it was a bit disconcerting.

Before Sloane could question the unusual present, Robert and Lochlain were coming to present their gift and exchange hugs. It was another envelope, and Sloane repressed a groan when he saw what was inside. It was also a gift certificate to the same custom sex toy company Lynnette and Milo had given them.

"I don't understand why you won't let me see," Loch loudly complained.

"It's rude to look in front of our guests."

"But you're looking!"

"Oh, hey! Fred! Ell!" Sloane greeted their final gift givers, ignoring Loch's pouting as he got swept up into a rib-shattering hug. "Ugh, hey, Fred. Thanks again for coming."

"Congrats," Fred rumbled, releasing Sloane to shake Loch's hand.

"If you ever need help with your sexual performance, I am at your disposal," Loch said solemnly. "Mating is very important to every relationship."

"It's totally fine, thanks." Ell smiled bashfully and shoved a big box into Sloane's hands. "Here, this is for you guys."

Sloane's fingers touched Ell's, and even through the glove, he felt... *something*.

A spark of power, like a crack of lightning.

Sloane froze, and he stared at Ell with a new level of scrutiny. He didn't know the young man very well, though what little he'd heard from Lochlain or Lynnette had always been good. They all trusted him with the truth about Loch's identity, and Sloane shouldn't have felt so suspicious.

And yet, he wanted to raise his hand for a perception spell because there was no way that Ell was human—

"Oh! Look!" Loch exclaimed as he brandished two pairs of black silk boxers. "They match!"

Loch had already opened the box, and Sloane saw it was full of several little gifts. The first was a matching set of boxers with "Groom" emblazoned over the butt. He was already pulling them on and shamelessly flashing his ass to their guests as he showed off his new underwear.

"Oh, maybe you should open the rest later!" Ell had turned away, giggling into Fred's shoulder while Fred shook his head.

"But why?" Loch continued to paw the bundles of tissue paper. "Ohhh! Lubricant! Look, my love! It's strawberry flavored!"

"It's pretty good stuff," Fred mumbled encouragingly, and Sloane swore he was blushing.

"By all the gods," Sloane moaned and started laughing as he tried to wrestle the box away from Loch. "I think these are gifts meant for the wedding night—"

"So why can't we look at them now?" Loch fussed.

"Because people don't need to know what we're going to be doing later!"

"I think they already know," Loch said, smooching Sloane's neck noisily.

"At the bottom, there is something safe, I swear," Ell piped up.

Sloane found a hard edge, a book, pulling it out and tearing away the paper. He gasped when he saw what it was, murmuring in awe, "It's *Starlight Bright*."

"What's that?" Loch ceased his assault on Sloane's throat long enough to look at the book.

"It's a children's book," Sloane explained. "It's a book about the gods for kids. I used to have a copy when I was little. My parents read it to me." He smiled at Ell, surprised by such an unusually touching gift. "Thank you."

"You probably don't remember, but, uh, you read me one of the poems in there," Ell said with a shy shrug. "I would have loved to have a book like that growing up."

"Wait, when?" Sloane blinked. He didn't remember meeting Ell until Robert and Lochlain got married and certainly didn't recall reciting any poetry.

"Lynnette's Galmethas party," Fred reminded them with a smirk. "You were both trashed."

"Oh gods," Sloane groaned as a recollection of fractured memories came rushing back to him. "It was right after we came back from the temple with all the erotic murals...."

"That was such a fun party, glorious and wonderful." Loch paused to reflect, as his own memory was apparently lacking. "I think."

"I didn't wanna say anything and embarrass you guys," Ell said earnestly, fidgeting, "but that poem… it just meant a lot to me. I was raised Lucian, you see, so I never had that growing up. And, uh, well, Fred told me that you and Loch are planning on spawning a lot—"

Sloane cut his eyes at a very guilty Loch.

"—and I thought it would be nice for your kids," Ell went on. "I'm really glad you like it."

"I love it," Sloane promised, reverently placing the book back in the box. "Thank you, guys!"

"I helped pick out the other stuff," Fred said quietly.

"You did well, my mortal child." Loch clapped a tentacle on Fred's shoulder. "When I'm feasting on Sloane's body later, wet with artificially flavored strawberry glycerin, I will think of you."

"Ugh." Sloane set the box aside with the rest of their gifts. "You're terrible."

"You married me," Loch said proudly.

"What was I thinking?"

"That you love me and adore me and the thought of being apart from me for even a mere moment is complete and absolute torture?" Loch suggested.

"Yeah," Sloane said with a warm smile. "I think that was it."

"Come on, my love!" Loch purred, pulling Sloane into his lap and putting a glass in his hand. "Now it's time to feast!"

Wine flowed, the feast was devoured, and Sloane was having the most fantastic time. He forgot all about the strange moment with Ell, reveling in his wedding celebration.

The gods were especially happy, twirling around the fire in wide circles and dancing to music that only seemed to play when they moved. Glowing stars kept descending upon them all like magical fireworks, and Sloane was completely entranced.

So captivated by the divine beauty and relaxed by several glasses of wine, he was only mildly alarmed when Yeris tried to make out with Shartorath and was promptly slapped.

Loch was eager to get Sloane up for a dance, grabbing him by his waist and stumbling as he carried him toward the bonfire. "Come along, my husband! It's time for a dance!"

"Loch! Ah! Be careful!" Sloane laughed, definitely fearful that Loch might drop him for a moment. He was relieved when his feet touched the ground again and laughed again as Loch swung him around. He'd definitely had more than a modest amount of wine, swaying as he wrapped his arms around Loch's neck as they danced.

"You look so beautiful," Loch gushed, nuzzling their noses together.

"Mmm, so do you," Sloane replied. "My very own beautiful god…. This is seriously the best day of my entire life." His attention was drawn to the fire as the flames grew, the fuel provided by Yeris chucking portions of the table into it. "Oh… hmm. So that's happening."

"Now this… this is how you have a wedding!" Loch beamed.

"No offense to Robert and Lochlain?" Sloane chuckled and planted a firm kiss to his lips.

"All the offense. It was terrible, boring, and there was no fire."

"Mmm, but ours is okay?"

"This is perfect," Loch promised.

"I'm so happy." Sloane reached up to pet Loch's curls and cup his cheek. "Seriously, I can't wait to spend the rest of my damn life with you. I'm so thankful for everything that's ever happened in my entire freakin' life right now."

"Even the bad stuff?" Loch's brow furrowed.

"Yes! Even the bad stuff!" Sloane smiled. "Because everything that's happened, good or bad, has brought me right here to this moment with you. I wouldn't change a single thing. I'm married to the god I love, to you, and now we have an eternity together."

"Oh, Sloane." Loch's eyes were dark and starry as he gazed at Sloane. "I love you, my dear husband."

"And I love you," Sloane replied earnestly. "My mate."

"My mate," Loch repeated, sighing adoringly as he leaned in to start sucking and kissing at Sloane's neck. "My beautiful, *beautiful* mate...."

"Mmm, Loch.... Wait, Loch!" Sloane gasped when a tentacle slid up his kilt. "Loch! Stop! Everyone is watching!"

"I know." Loch hiccupped. "You just taste so good...."

"Wait, Loch, are you drunk?" Sloane eyed Loch's flushed cheeks. "By all the gods, including you. You're drunk, aren't you?"

"My sister may have brought some godsmead that is much more potent than mortal libations, and I'm a tad intoxi, *intocica*... yes, I'm drunk."

"Me too," Sloane confessed. "Better be careful or we're gonna have a repeat of Lynnette's party."

"Would that be so terrible?" Loch nipped at Sloane's ear. "I'm sure we had a lovely time."

"I wanna make sure we remember every second of this," Sloane insisted, swatting at Loch's invading tentacles.

"Very well," Loch groaned dramatically. "I shall cease my alcohol intake at once."

"Mmm, let's get some more of that cake your mother made," Sloane suggested. "It's so good! I think it's some kind of love cake, because I'm actually getting kind of...." He dropped his voice. "Ahem, like, *really* in the mood for mating."

Loch studied Sloane's face before very loudly announcing, "I wanted to thank you all for coming, it's been lovely, but now I'm going to mate with my new husband."

"Wait! You mean right now? Like right this second?"

"Right this very second," Loch confirmed. He waved to all of their guests, calling out, "The consummation will begin shortly! I hope you all have a lovely night!"

"Oh, come on—"

"You boys have fun!" Galgareth cheered over Sloane's protests. "We'll make sure everyone gets home safely!"

Loch picked Sloane up into his arms and marched through the garden toward the lush clearing with the giant bed. The hedges and trees rose up around them to give them privacy, and Sloane laughed as Loch clumsily dropped him on the sheets.

"Sorry," Loch said, melting their clothes away with a thought. "Mmm, perhaps I drank a little too much...."

"It's okay." Sloane scrambled back to rest his head on the pillows. He grinned as Loch crawled over him, claiming his lips in a deep kiss. "I'm sure it won't affect your performance."

"Very unlikely." Loch chuckled, one of his slitted tentacles slithering down between them to start sucking Sloane's cock.

Sloane's hips twitched, and he moaned softly at the brilliant suction wrapping around him. His cock flexed, hard and throbbing, and he gasped as Loch increased the pressure. He could feel warmth resonating throughout his entire body and grabbed Loch's hips to brace himself.

"Oh, my love." Loch nuzzled the side of Sloane's neck. He wrapped his arms around him, his other slitted tentacle sliding up between Sloane's legs.

Feeling himself getting wet and gently stretched open was so familiar now, and Sloane savored the sensations. He kissed and hungrily mouthed along Loch's shoulder, spreading his legs wide to receive him. "Oh, Loch. I love you so much."

"I love you, my darling husband," Loch replied, sharing a breathy groan as his tentacle began to slowly dip inside. "Mmm, you always feel so perfect...."

"So do you." Sloane gasped again as Loch's tentacle lazily thrusted. It was slow but deep, and the sweet friction on his cock was leaving him panting.

"Feel good, my love?"

"So good...." Sloane surrendered himself completely, the muscles of his legs and stomach tensing. He could feel the heat building inside of him, and he was desperate to come.

He couldn't remember the last time he'd been this turned on, and he was absolutely aching for relief. Sex with Loch was always spectacular, but there was a new level of passion he'd never experienced before. Loch was his husband now, his mate among the stars, and they were truly going to be together forever.

"Loch!" Sloane cried, his hips stuttering as he climaxed, the tentacle sucking his cock and eagerly drinking down every drop. The one inside him curled at an angle that made him moan, his orgasm going on for so long that Sloane was left shaking.

Sloane felt the rush of Loch's come deep within, whimpering softly as the tentacle on his cock took its place to fill him again. He was so full, his cock limp but still drooling a slow pulse of come across his stomach. It was almost too much, and Sloane whimpered brokenly, "Holy fffuck!"

"Mmm, that was amazing." Loch pressed warm kisses all over Sloane's face, asking breathlessly, "Ready for more, my love?"

"Mmmph, hold on…."

"Take all the time you need. We have all of eternity."

"Ha! I don't plan on taking that long." Sloane hooked his ankles, the tips of his fingers dragging up Loch's spine. He held him close, petting the base of Loch's tentacles with slow, gentle strokes. He had learned that this was a particularly sensitive area for Loch, humming in satisfaction as he heard him begin to purr.

"Sloane," Loch moaned, his thick tentacock moving to start pushing its way inside Sloane's slick hole. He slid in deeper, his entire body moving like a wave, rolling slowly, and each crest was the swell of his hips, thrusting into Sloane's tight body until he was fully seated, knot and all.

Sloane's back rose off the bed, his hips pushing down to further deepen the connection, groaning in delight, "Oh, Loch… fuck, yes…." He hung on for the ride, taking every thrust with a loud cry, his legs shaking and soon falling off to the sides from the force of Loch's thrusting.

Loch's tentacles came to Sloane's aid, curling around his calves and ankles, holding them up to maintain a pleasurable angle. Loch was getting close, his movements more erratic, his grunts louder.

Sloane knew this wasn't a conclusion, only the first act of what would be an entire symphony of ecstasy. He submitted himself to it, screaming Loch's name as they climaxed together again, loving the feeling of their bodies shuddering as one. He whimpered when some of Loch's massive load leaked out from his hole, and rubbed his hand across his stomach with a pleased smile.

"Good?" Loch nosed against Sloane's cheek. He had let Sloane's legs slip down to stretch out, but hadn't let go. He remained coiled all around him, purring and kissing him.

"Uh-huh," Sloane sighed contently. "Fuck, feels very good. I love feeling this full…. Mmmph. You spoil me, you know, beautiful husband of mine."

"I believe that's always been my intention." Loch chuckled, his thick tentacock still rigid and pushing back inside Sloane.

Sloane's eyes fluttered closed, and he moaned quietly. "Again?"

"Mmhmm…."

"I always want it to be like this," Sloane panted, mewling as Loch thrusted a little harder. "This passion, this love… fuck, you mean everything to me."

"It will, my love," Loch promised.

"Oh, Azaethoth," Sloane murmured, wrapping his arms around Loch's neck as they made love. "Mm, I just wanna stay here with you for the whole damn honeymoon and never leave this bed!"

"My beautiful Starkiller," Loch moaned, immediately locking their lips together in a fierce kiss, his cock pounding away passionately. "I love you so much."

Sloane had to choke back a scream, gritting his teeth as Loch ravaged him. There were moments when he could almost forget that Loch was a god, despite the unique way they made love.

But then there were times like this, when Loch gave him a taste of his full strength, and he didn't know how his mortal body didn't break from such potent passions. The strain was intense, pushing the boundary of pain, but the ecstasy was practically spiritual.

He couldn't even count how many times he found climax, Loch taking him to the very height of physical pleasure again and again. He didn't stop until they were both sticky, hot, and their bodies were gliding against one another.

Sloane was impossibly full, his stomach aching and warm, laughing against Loch's lips as he groaned, "Fuck, baby…. That was fucking incredible. You've never come in me that much before…. God, it feels amazing."

Loch had the queerest look on his face, confused and a little sheepish. He pressed his hand against Sloane's stomach, glancing up to him with a very concerned grimace.

Sloane couldn't shake the funny warm feeling he had now, his hand moving to rest over the top of Loch's. "What is it? You look like you're about to throw up."

"Sloane," Loch said slowly, his voice strained, "I have to tell you something, and there is a good chance that you'll be very angry with me."

"What are you talking about?" Sloane blinked, apprehension stealing his smile.

"Do you remember what I told you about spawning?" Loch asked with a visible cringe.

"That we never had to worry about it?" Sloane started to feel nauseous. "Because you could stop yourself? Godly birth control?"

"Except…."

"Except *what*, Loch?"

"Except we just got married, and I couldn't stop thinking about when you said you wanted to spawn with me…."

"Loch…?" Sloane's eyes widened.

"And you were so beautiful and so open for me," Loch went on, groaning irritably, "and I was thinking about that book and how lovely it would be for you to carry my child. Our child."

"No."

"Yes."

"You didn't."

"Oh, but I did."

"Please tell me I'm not freakin' pregnant right now," Sloane pleaded.

"I would, but then I might be lying," Loch replied miserably.

"But… it's… it can't be!"

"It is."

"Oh, you've gotta be freakin' kidding me!" Sloane snapped, wiggling away from Loch and trying to sit up. Pregnant. He was pregnant by a god. "I am so freakin' mad at you right now!"

"But you love me." Loch followed Sloane with his tentacles and dragged him back into his arms.

"Right now, I kinda hate you!" Sloane slapped at his firm grip.

Loch took Sloane's hand, pressing it against Sloane's stomach and resting his own over the top of it.

Sloane tried to pull away. "Ugh! What are you doing?"

"Sloane, please," Loch said earnestly, closing his eyes. He tilted their palms until Sloane suddenly felt a little heartbeat. It was faster than both of theirs, rapid and frantic.

"How is that… how is that possible?" Sloane gasped, his eyes flooding with tears. "It's only been, like, five seconds!"

"I'm a god," Loch replied quietly, cradling Sloane close as the little heartbeat continued to flutter beneath their hands. "A very irresponsible god who is very sorry."

Sloane clutched his stomach, completely overwhelmed. This shouldn't be possible, but there it was: a little flicker of life burning away inside him. The warmth he felt was sweet and comforting, and he was amazed knowing there was a new little person now growing within his belly.

Sloane tried to speak, his voice cracking as he began, "Loch… it's…."

"Stupid, I know," Loch mumbled. "I'm sorry—"

"No…. It's beautiful," Sloane whispered, taking a big breath and swallowing back tears. "Okay, yes, I'm still a tiny bit mad at you… but I love you. And yes, I wanted to wait, but this is… this is incredible."

"Really?" Loch checked over Sloane's face, as if to gauge his sincerity. Finding it satisfactory, he suddenly grinned and kissed Sloane, laughing, "I love you too."

"Holy crap." Sloane's thoughts were still careening all over the place. "I can't believe this. I'm pregnant. With a baby. With a god's baby. A baby god."

"We're going to be a family," Loch purred, embracing him tenderly. "Oh, my love. I'm so happy."

"Crap, we have so much to do! How, how are we even going to explain this? I mean, am I gonna start showing soon? How do I even freakin' give birth! What do…." Sloane clung to Loch's shoulders. "What do I do?"

"I don't know," Loch replied honestly, kissing Sloane's hair. "But we're going to figure it out. We'll do it together."

"Together?" Sloane asked breathlessly.

"Yes," Loch promised. "You're my husband, Sloane. My mate. I will always be here to take care of you, and I will always love you." There was a hint of mischief as he added casually, "And when your hormones start to fluctuate, I will gladly help with any additional mating needs that you might have…."

Sloane rolled his eyes. "Mating is what got us into this mess!"

"But it was very fun," Loch said gleefully.

Sloane groaned. "This is going to be insane. I mean, raising a child… I don't even know where to begin."

"My darling Starkiller," Loch soothed, "you've saved the world and killed two gods. Certainly you don't think raising a child could be that hard?"

"Guess we're gonna find out." Sloane laughed, kissing Loch's lips with a sweet smile.

"Mmmm," Loch purred, "yes, we will."

K.L. "KAT" HIERS is an embalmer, restorative artist, and queer writer. Licensed in both funeral directing and funeral service, she's been working in the death industry for nearly a decade. Her first love was always telling stories, and she has been writing for over twenty years, penning her very first book at just eight years old. Publishers generally do not accept manuscripts in Hello Kitty notebooks, however, but she never gave up.

Following the success of her first novel, *Cold Hard Cash*, she now enjoys writing professionally, focusing on spinning tales of sultry passion, exotic worlds, and emotional journeys. She loves attending horror movie conventions and indulging in cosplay of her favorite characters. She lives in Zebulon, NC, with her husband and their children, some of whom have paws and a few who only pretend to because they think it's cute.

Website: www.klhiers.com

A SUCKER FOR LOVE MYSTERY

ACSQUIDENTALLY
IN LOVE

K.L. HIERS

"A breezy and sensual LGBTQ paranormal romance."
—*Library Journal*

A Sucker For Love Mystery

Nothing brings two men—or one man and an ancient god—together like revenge.

Private investigator Sloane sacrificed his career in law enforcement in pursuit of his parents' murderer. Like them, he is a follower of long-forgotten gods, practicing their magic and offering them his prayers… not that he's ever gotten a response.

Until now.

Azaethoth the Lesser might be the patron of thieves and tricksters, but he takes care of his followers. He's come to earth to avenge the killing of one of his favorites, and maybe charm the pants off the cute detective Fate has placed in his path. If he has his way, they'll do much more than bring a killer to justice. In fact, he's sure he's found the man he'll spend his immortal life with.

Sloane's resolve is crumbling under Azaethoth's surprising sweetness, and the tentacles he sometimes glimpses escaping the god's mortal form set his imagination alight. But their investigation gets stranger and deadlier with every turn. To survive, they'll need a little faith… and a lot of mystical firepower.

www.dreamspinnerpress.com

A SUCKER FOR LOVE MYSTERY

Kraken My
Heart

K.L. HIERS

"A breezy and sensual LGBTQ paranormal romance."
—Library Journal, "Acsquidentally in Love"

A Sucker For Love Mystery

It's just Ted's luck that he meets the love of his life while covered in the blood of a murder victim.

Funeral worker Ted Sturm has a foul mouth, a big heart, and a knack for communicating with the dead. Unfortunately the dead don't make very good friends, and Ted's only living pal, his roommate, just rescued a strange cat who's determined to make his life even more miserable. This cat is more than he seems, and soon Ted finds himself in an alternate dimension… and on top of a dead body.

When Ted is accused of murder, his only ally in a strange world full of powerful magical beings calling for his head is King Grell, a sarcastic, randy, catlike immortal with impressive abilities… and anatomy. The two soon find themselves at the center of a cosmic conspiracy and surrounded by dangerous enemies. But with Ted's special skills and Grell's magic, they have a chance to get to the bottom of the mystery and save Ted. There's just one problem: Ted's got to resist Grell's aggressive advances… and he isn't sure he wants to.

www.dreamspinnerpress.com

Also from Dreamspinner Press

www.dreamspinnerpress.com

Also from Dreamspinner Press

FATE'S ATTRACTION

DIRK GREYSON

www.dreamspinnerpress.com

Also from Dreamspinner Press

www.dreamspinnerpress.com

THEIR DARK
Reflections

AMANDA
MEUWISSEN

www.ingramcontent.com/pod-product-compliance
Lightning Source LLC
Chambersburg PA
CBHW051647260626
47170CB00004B/1374